VARSITY
Captain

by USA TODAY bestselling author
GINGER SCOTT

VARSITY CAPTAIN

VARSITY SERIES BOOK 4

GINGER SCOTT

Cover Design by Ginger Scott, Little Miss Write LLC

PRINT ISBN: 978-1-952778-13-1

For Team Lucas.

CHAPTER ONE

Lucas Fuller

I t's hard not having anything to say to the man I've idolized half my life. That's what our rides home from practice have become, though—disciplined silence with momentary flashes of politeness between father and son.

"Is the air on high enough for you?" *There's his contribution.*

"I'm good." *My polite response is now in the can.*

I'm still months away from getting my license. I can't wait until I'm able to drive myself to football workouts. There's already a brand new Nissan pickup truck in the driveway, and it's hard not to think of it as a bribe. I'll take it, though. That's the least I can squeeze out of the shitty situation I fell into simply by being Todd Fuller's kid.

I still can't see how we got to this point. It just seems so . . . I don't know, impossible? I guess that's what every kid thinks before their parents' marriage falls apart. Mine are clinging to the scraps, and Dad seems desperate to repair those tattered threads. Mom, she just seems angry. Maybe a little unwell too. And her rage seems dialed in on the one person I need to talk to—June Mabee.

My best friend and neighbor is the only person who has ever gotten me. She's the only person I can vent to when I'm sick of the pressure from football. Sometimes it feels as though my dad is shaping me into his trophy just so he can brag about me to his friends and colleagues, and June is the only person who doesn't make me feel like a whiny privileged asshole for feeling crushed by it all.

I guess I can understand my mom's fury and wanting to keep "our business in our house," as she frequently says, but June isn't a threat. She's as much an innocent bystander as I am.

Dad pulls into our driveway and I chance a quick glance to June's house. Our driveways nearly connect, and when I stand in just the right place I can see life inside her house— she and her mom moving around the kitchen, or June running up the stairs, the shadow of her passing across the curtains in her room. I wish I could run into that house, into her room, lock myself inside and avoid everything else for a little while. *Forever.*

"Get cleaned up for dinner. Mom made a roast. She'd like us to eat at the table." Dad kills the engine on his truck and climbs out, but I give myself a tiny moment inside alone.

We started eating dinner together as a family when it all unraveled. It's part of my mom's need to hold on. My dad says it's important to her. I don't know. I think they're focusing on a lot of the wrong things to call important. But what do I know: I'm a fifteen-year-old kid.

Dad pauses at the garage door leading into the laundry room, waiting for me. I relent and climb out after him, and the second my feet step over the threshold, my stomach tightens into the impossible knot that seems to live there when I'm in this house.

Dad heads to the right, toward the kitchen, and I veer left, to the stairs. I take them two at a time. I open the door and drop my bag just inside, then close it with a gentle click. My back falls against the woodgrain and I breathe out, my tight shoulders relaxing a tick as I rub my hand over my face.

It doesn't take long for the shouting to start. The rounds of arguing have gotten shorter over the last few days, but they still happen regularly. Dinner seems to be a trigger. Probably because my dad always missed dinner . . . *before*. Now, his mere presence at the meal is an opportunity to remind him of the ones he missed, and the lies he used as excuses.

At least Mom is sober. Still, I'm always on guard, watching over her and looking for signs that she's slipping. I've started a daily practice of sifting through the backs of our cabinets, behind the dry goods and the rarely used cleaning products—her common hiding spots. They've been clear for weeks. Dad cleared out his office liquor cabinet when she came home, but I'm sure that's only temporary. I tell myself I'd be able to tell, that there would be obvious signs she's drinking or taking pills. Would there, though? I missed them the first time. Of course, I wasn't really looking. I was too absorbed in my own shit to notice. Not that it's my job, but if not me, then who?

My pocket buzzes with a message to my phone and I lift my head to stare out my window. I already know who it's from. Summer has always been June and my time. She's been helping me find a part-time job that might work around my football practices. I haven't responded to the last job posting she sent. It's getting harder to be two people—the person I am in this house, and the one I am with her. It feels like a betrayal both ways no matter what I do. But June doesn't need to feel like I do. She has enough happening in her life. Her dad moved out weeks ago. I watched him pack up and go. As bad as things are in this house, my dad stayed.

She must be somewhere else because I don't see her light on in her room, and downstairs seems quiet. I hope she's made a new group of friends. I hope she is out enjoying her summer. I hope she doesn't depend on me to be her person, because I don't know if I can.

Curious, I pull my phone out to read her text.

JUNE: *Hey! Everything ok? Haven't heard from you for a few days, but I know practice already started for summer. Did you check out the job I sent? It's for ice cream. Ice! Cream! Lucas—free ice cream. That's all I'm saying. OK, well, enough of that. I also wanted to see if you wanted to get dive-in movie passes for the pool this year. They're half off if I get them now. Let me know! Ahh! Summer!*

I'm smiling by the time I'm done reading. Spending time with June does that to me, even if it's only time with her words. Tory keeps nudging me to ask her out, like *out* out, as in a date, but it seems wrong. She's like my sister, only . . . very much *not* my sister. I think if I asked, she'd say yes. And that makes it scarier. Things with us would change, and as much as I've thought about the *what ifs*, there's a whole lot of risk involved. I open her message to reply and hover my thumbs over the keyboard, dying to type YES to all of it. Then the yelling grows louder.

"I'm sorry but I don't feel bad about her divorce. That's what that woman gets!"

"Shannon, you're getting carried away . . ."

I wince. My dad always stokes the fire. It's as if he wants her to go back to rehab.

"You are done helping her, you hear me? She can get a new lawyer, Todd. She has a job. No more charity from you.

No more *anything* from you or I swear to God, I'm gone! I'm gone and I will make sure everyone knows exactly what that house is all about."

I slip my phone back into my pocket at the sound of someone's heavy feet stomping up the stairs. I'm not sure who I want it to be more—*or less.*

The soft knock on my door spikes up my pulse. I hold my breath and twist where I stand, cracking open the door . My mom's eyes are wild, but I can tell she's trying to calm down. She shuts them and draws in a deep breath through her nose, huffing out once and letting her shoulders drop as I open my door wide and move to my bed.

"I'm sorry," she says, coming in and taking a seat next to me. "I know you can hear that, and that's not right. Not fair to you."

"It's fine." More blanket lies from my mouth. I'm never fine or good, but that's all I can seem to tell people.

"We're gonna be okay, Lucas." My mom's tone is oddly assured. I lift my head and meet her gaze, feeling as if I have to play along. I'm also hopeful, but along with that feeling comes a sense of falling, like walking along a very thin edge.

"Okay," I croak out.

I hate this.

"I bet the Mabees will move. So even that won't be weird after a while. And we'll just go on with our lives, and be stronger as a family. Hey, why don't you invite the D'Angelo boys over, have a sleepover?"

She's excited by the idea, and even though it's the last thing I'm in the mood for, I smile and nod.

"Sure. Sounds fun," I lie.

She gets up from the bed and runs her palms down the front of her slacks, straightening out the wrinkles. She's flaw-less somehow, even after coming home from work and stepping right into the kitchen. My mom works so hard at holding the façade together. I hope she doesn't do it for me. I'd just as soon deal with crumbles.

"Hey, and Lucas? I know that you and June are close, but maybe . . . maybe give each other some space for a while. She's been told a lot of lies, and I'm not sure she's ready to deal with the truth yet. It seems maybe it's easier if you sort of drift apart. You're getting older anyhow. It happens. And besides that, I'm sure they'll move."

She presses her lips into a forced smile so I do the same.

"Yeah."

She nods at my response, pleased. My phone buzzes in my pocket just before she leaves, though, and her eyes twitch. I know she wants to stick around to see who my message is from. I'm sure she already knows.

"I'll call Tory now, see if they want to come over."

She fixates on my slight grin, studying my face for a full breath. My need to swallow consumes me, but I don't—that would reek of guilt. And I am guilty. June is in my pocket. My mom is in my room. My family is broken.

One more nod, this one tinged with a sour bitterness that injects me with guilt, is all I get before she shuts my door and leaves me alone with my dilemma. I glance at my phone again.

JUNE: ?

It's clear that June doesn't know what's going on. She's in blissful ignorance, and honestly, I hope she stays there. Unfortunately, I can't go back.

We can't go back.

As painful as it is, I let my thumb continue its destructive movement over my phone screen, sliding June's name to the side, revealing the option to block her texts, her calls—her everything. It won't be forever. It's just for now, until things get figured out, until my parents work through their issues and her mom finds them a new place. I'll call her as soon as it's over and explain everything, and maybe we'll still get to have our summer. Maybe she'll understand.

The lies. They just keep on coming.

CHAPTER TWO

Two years later, the night before senior year

"You know those D1 offers can be rescinded."

I wonder how many times this year my dad is going to rattle off that line. I bombed one test last year—*one*—and I didn't even truly bomb it. I got a C. But it was enough to get the *you know those D1 offers* comment from my old man.

Tonight's offense? Acting like a typical eighteen-year-old boy.

It's not that my dad has a thing against me going to parties. It's that he has a thing about me going to parties at the D'Angelo house. Tory and Hayden aren't trouble really, but they do throw big parties that sometimes get out of hand. Their parents are gone a lot, and there's not much to do around here, so when the twins host a party, everyone we know shows up.

Almost everyone.

"I'll probably be home early. Relax," I shout as the door

shuts behind me, cutting my dad off from throwing in one more empty warning. I couldn't give a shit about my D1 offers, which, of course, I can never say out loud. I'm pretty sure my dad's head would actually blow off of his neck if I told him that. Me playing ball for a big school has been on his dream list for me since I was born. Making up for his short-comings, I guess. My old man only got a year in before his arm gave out.

Sometimes, I wonder if mine will, too. A part of me wishes for it.

Tory's waiting in the passenger seat, and the fucker scares the shit out of me when I climb in my truck. I punch his bicep. *Hard.*

"Damn, Fuller!" He rubs the sore spot. I hope it bruises.

"Don't sneak up on me like that. I thought I was picking you up. What'd you do, walk here?" I glance around and check my mirrors, looking for a car that dropped him off.

"Just back out. I'll tell you when we start rolling."

Despite his request, I leave my tires parked right where they are and glare at him. It takes about two seconds for him to break.

"Fine. I had Hayden drop me off. While you were changing and talking to your dad, I snagged some top-shelf shit from his cabinet. We're seniors now. Time to graduate from beer, get a little more *fucked up.*"

I roll my eyes and crank the engine.

"I'll stick with the beer, thanks." I sigh.

My friend shakes his head while I reverse. He can peer pressure me all he wants, it's futile. I do what I want, and I'm impervious to the power of adolescent suggestion. I refuse to be a lemming.

"I heard Abby say she's bringing June tonight," Tory

pipes in, nodding toward the dark house next door as I shift and race down my street.

"Like Abby would actually talk to you."

"Fuck off. She did. So what if when I asked if she was coming she said 'Yeah, and I'm bringing June so we can both shoot you down at once.'"

I can't help but snort out a massive laugh.

"*Pshh*, whatever. You're gonna have to deal with June is all."

I let my laughter linger, but it quit being real seconds ago. As much as I want to pretend June isn't a problem for me, she very much is. I have forbidden myself from even thinking about her, which came easily when she switched schools for our junior year. I guess she's back now. Her mom lost her job or some shit, so private school was a no-go. She probably deserved it. I'm sure her boss found out about her side gigs. I just don't know how June hasn't figured it out yet. Whatever, though. Not my problem.

"I mean, it's not like you're really *with* Ava anymore, so I don't see why talking to June is such a big deal," Tory continues.

"My issues with June have nothing to do with Ava. Drop it, Tor."

He mocks me, repeating my words in a whiny voice that sounds nothing like me, then turns the stereo up and quits provoking me. Tory knows my story, mostly. He was around when the Mabees drove my mom over the edge. It's hard to hide your mom's alcohol and pill addiction, especially when it ends with her being hauled off to rehab. I needed someone to talk to about it, and Tory is my best friend. He was my support system. And yeah, he's right about Ava, my ex. She hates June more than anyone I've met, besides my mom. If I spend even a second talking to June in front of Ava, she'll probably punch a hole through Tory's wall. I can't do anything to send Mom on another spiral like the one my dad did a couple years ago. No girl is worth doing that.

June was a childhood friend. A crush. People grow apart. It happens, like my mom said.

Cars are already piled up on the street surrounding Tory's house, so I find the closest spot I can. Tory's twin, Hayden, is shooting hoops in the driveway when we show up, and a few girls are outside drinking. I back away to give my friend room to take a pass from his brother and dunk the ball so he can get the applause that follows. He eats it up.

Tory's ten times the athlete I am. He'll be in the NBA one day. No doubt. But I don't think anything gets him going quite like the adoration of females watching him put on a show.

"Come on, Lucas. One quick game. What do you say?" He's taunting me, his shirt already off as he spins the ball on his fingertip. Two of the girls sitting on the back of the twins' car giggle at the sight.

"I'm good. Not much in the mood to get my ass kicked, but thanks." I carry the bottles of liquor he swiped from my dad into the garage and then the house. I think my dad kept booze out of our house for a full month before he quit caring about the temptation it was to my mom. I often wonder if he was trying to lure her off her path again so he could look righteous while she looked weak. At the same time, part of me thinks she refuses to take his bait just to spite him. Maybe I'm giving their mental warfare too much credit. I don't know.

The music is already up to an obscene volume. I don't mind it because it makes it hard to talk to people, and I'm not much in the mood to talk. I nod hello to a few people I recognize on my way in, then bury myself in the kitchen, tucking the whiskey and vodka into a corner before getting myself a cup and filling it with beer from the keg.

I'm mid-sip when the last voice I'm in the mood for crawls around my neck and into my ear.

"I brought your jersey. If you want it."

Why I ever gave Ava my old jersey to wear is beyond me. I was probably drunk, angry, and horny. Three toxic ingredients to combine. It was summer, and I'd just gotten my first D1 offer. My dad was already planning how to turn one offer into a dozen. Most of the guys on our team loved that the school let us keep old jerseys when the program got new ones. I couldn't wait to get rid of it.

I couldn't wait to get inside Ava.

Problem met solution, and I got my dick wet as a result. Seemed like a win-win at the time.

I was desperate to be someone else. *Anyone.* As long as I didn't have to hear about all the ways I was failing to be the man my dad never was. Hearing his bullshit gets harder and harder, especially given his massive flaws. I don't call him on it, though. I play the part of a good son—the Fuller's *perfect* son. I do it for my mom. If I seem happy, she can be happy, or at least continue to pretend she is. Our lives are a fragile house of cards simply waiting for the fan to blow them over.

Downing a third of my beer, I turn slowly, the feel of Ava's long fingernails dragging along my skin from neck to shoulder, then chest as I meet her gaze.

"You have it with you?"

A coy smile plays at her bright red lips. I kinda figured.

"It's in my car. We could go get it now, if you want." She drags her long-ass nail down the center of my chest and tugs on the waist of my jeans. My dick swells, because it's desperate. The rest of me knows better, and I'm not drinking more than the contents of this cup tonight.

I wrap my hand around her wrist and pull it away from my pants. Her lips puff up into her signature pouty face, but that look doesn't work on me sober, and I'm, well, done with the games.

"You keep it. Think of it as a souvenir."

I meet Ava's eyes long enough to see the flinch followed by the simmer of anger. I walk away, leaving her to seethe and plot methods to strike back at me. I'm sure she will. It's what she lives for. She isn't a nice person, not really. She's hot, and for a while, that's what I was into. Or maybe that's what I told myself I needed. Now? I just want to do my own thing. When my dad finds out that thing isn't football? I can kiss my college fund good-bye.

"Hey, why so mopey?" Tory slings his sweaty arm around my neck and pulls me toward him. I shrug it off, feeling trapped. His breath already reeks of tequila, and I've only been away from him for five minutes.

"I'm not mopey, I . . . I don't know. I'm gonna just reset my head. Give me a few, okay?" I tilt my head toward the garage door, thinking maybe I can sit in one of the D'Angelo cars for a while and play some music while Tory's brother plays basketball.

"You mean, you're gonna go mope in the garage alone," he says, a brow quirked.

It's accurate, fine. But it's still irritating.

"Dude, whatever. Go drink some of the top shelf shit you stole from my dad so the ass-beating I'm going to get will be worth it."

My friend winks and tells me he's on top of it, and the moment his back is turned, I duck into the garage. I guess the pickup basketball is done. The garage is closed, leaving me alone under the buzz of fluorescent lights. I maneuver my way through the space. The sedan is parked inside, leaving a gaping hole where their dad usually parks his truck. I head to the far corner and pull one of the folding chairs out from the stack leaning on the wall, flipping it open and straddling the seat. I amuse myself with the non-stop stream of puckered lips on social media. Why every girl in this town has to make the same duck-face in her selfie, I have no clue. I make a game of counting each one, and eventually chuckle out loud at the massive number of images that look exactly the same. Even Tory makes that face in a few. Then one of them stops my laughter. This shot, it's different.

I pause on Abby Cortez's account. It's not her I'm staring at. Abby doesn't post many pics of herself. Probably because her face is already all over the magazine stands and social ads. She's the most famous person in this town, having been in a GAP ad twice. I'm paused on an entirely different person, one with long dark hair wrapped around a heart-shaped face, cheeks speckled with stardust-like freckles, and wide green eyes. June looks as though she's about to swear in the photo, and her hand is half raised in protest, her smile caught somewhere between surprised and irritated.

I've seen her make that face a million times. It's the version of her being playfully teased. I smile without realizing it at first and instantly force it away when I do. I'm not supposed to feel things when I see pictures of June. But for some reason, seeing that picture just now makes me feel lonely. It makes me miss her. Even if we never became something, we would have been friends. She'd know exactly what to tell me about college and football. She'd tell me to talk to my dad.

I laugh softly and close the image app, switching to my email. The admissions portal is still highlighted with my last offer from Northwest State. My dad doesn't even know about this one. He wouldn't want me to go there anyhow. It's too small. Funny, that's the only school that really appeals for football. I like the academics. But I might come out of there with a degree and nothing else, and that's not good enough for Todd Fuller. What would he tell his friends?

The voices pick up on the other side of the door, and the music is thumping more than before. I could probably head inside and get lost in the crowd, maybe even slip away after an hour to go home and just sleep. I'd give anything for a restful night. All I do is toss and turn and think about what I want but can't have. Lately, I've gotten an average of four hours of sleep a night, and those hours are broken up by long rounds of self-doubt and internal debate. My conclusion is always the same: I'll play college football to make my dad happy. What's four years, really? I can handle four years of college football. I'll get a degree out of it. Sure, it will be business and not engineering, but I can turn that into something. Maybe grad school on my own if my grades hold up. I'll do dad's dream to pay for mine.

A squealing laugh draws my eyes up to the garage door and out of my endless mental loop. It's Lola, one of Ava's friends. I recognize the timbre of her exaggerated laugh. She's trying to impress Ava by laughing at one of her jokes, I'm sure. I've seen her do it for the last two years just to keep her coveted place in the Ava Pryor social circle. It must be exhausting.

I'm about to go back to surfing my phone when the garage door pops open and a body thrusts through, almost as if it's being pushed. Long, wild hair tangles over her face, but she pushes the strands from her eyes in time for us to make eye contact.

The lights go out.

The door clicks locked behind her.

"Oh, fuck me." I realize as it's happening that I say those words out loud. I probably sound like a dick. But seriously, locked in a dark garage with June Mabee is the last position I want to be in. What kind of night is this? First Ava, now June. I'm not in the mood for layers of family drama, and June is basically one big family drama bomb. Staring at her face in a social media post is one thing, but being stuck with her in a small space? No. I can't do this. I didn't even want to come to this party. I just didn't want to be at home. And since everyone I know is here, that left few options.

I should have gone bowling by myself.

"Shit!" June's hands are rubbing along the wall near the door. I'm sure she cut herself on one of the broken nail heads while searching for a garage door opener. One hasn't hung there for years. But when it did, it hung on that nail head. She's probably bleeding. I've cut myself on it before. It fucking hurts.

A slight gasp slips from her mouth, followed by the clonking of her phone as it tumbles along the ground. It glows for a second, but shuts off mid-crash. I'm pretty sure she busted the screen.

It's damn near impossible to see in here, but I can make out enough of her profile to tell she's squatting and patting along the concrete, feeling for her phone. I should help instead of just sitting here. Solidifying my reputation as a massive prick, I guess. It's better that way. She'll have less interest in talking to me. With a little luck, we won't have any classes together and life can go on, business as usual, as if she never came back to Public at all.

Guilt grips at my chest, though, the longer she crawls on her hands and knees, probably bleeding from that damn exposed nail. *Tory should hammer that shit. Seriously.*

I flip my phone around and shine the flashlight on her, illuminating the ground.

"Thanks," she says.

My lips part to say "you're welcome," but nothing comes out. I don't remember how to talk to her like a human.

She sits back when she reaches her phone, and I peer over her shoulder long enough to catch a glimpse of the busted-up screen. Giggling echoes from the opposite side of the door, and Ava's devious laugh lingers a little longer than the others. June's in here because of her. One big two-for-one prank, it seems. Ava found a way to get back at both of us, not that June deserves any of her shit. It's my fault June is even on Ava's radar and for that, I have major regrets. I said things to Ava when I was at my lowest, things I didn't fully understand, and I let my anger rule. I let secrets slip.

I step away from the chair, the metal legs screeching along the floor. The racket draws June's attention and she turns her phone brightness in my direction. My eyes dart to the ceiling and I stretch my arms up in order to avoid making eye contact with her again. It's suffocating in here, being alone with her in such a confined space. My belly itches with this need to scream. I don't know what words would come out, though. They probably wouldn't be nice, and that's not fair to her. It's just the way I've trained myself to react. Why couldn't her mom have moved? Why did they have to stay? They flaunt their smiles and carefree attitudes in front of my mom, rubbing what happened in her face. Their presence is a constant reminder, and I'm worried that one small thing will send my mom back down the spiral that almost killed her the first time.

If Ava's going to play games, I'm going to end them. I step around June and tug open the driver's side door, leaning in enough to press the garage door button clipped to the visor. I pull the opener out with me to hand it to June and let her decide her own fate. My breath catches, though, when I find her rising to her feet. The ends of her hair brush against my chest as she flips her head up. I don't think she noticed, but the feather-light tickle brought about a million memories from our past scorching to the front of my mind. Her damn hair was always getting in the way. She somehow hooked it on my braces once in the pool, and the first major haircut she had to get came after my gum got tangled in her ponytail.

My jaw flexes as I stare down at her. I've always been taller, but I swear she fits beneath me now, a perfect fit. Green eyes like emeralds, wide and frantic.

"I didn't know you were in here." The words spill from her lips in a desperate excuse, and there's a sharp pinch at my insides. The epiphany fills my chest all at once—while I've been avoiding June Mabee, she's been avoiding me right back. I drew boundaries, and she respected them. I want to ask her what she knows, to see if she's embarrassed about her mom's behavior, angry about things the way I am. But that would only rekindle our connection, and we're better off severed.

My mom is better off.

I hold the opener up for her to take, and she hesitates at first, eventually uncurling her shaking palm below my hand. I drop the device in, avoiding skin-to-skin contact as if one touch would burn me.

Our eyes meet one last time, hers still wide and uncertain. Her lips part, and I'm terrified she's going to speak again. I don't want to hear apologies on her mom's behalf, and I don't want to explain why I've been distant. I don't want to do any of this in Tory's garage, or anywhere . . . *ever.*

"Tell Ava she's a dick," I say, settling on the one true thing that June and I can agree on. I won't make this moment about us, but instead about the person who used our circumstances for her own amusement.

I leave June with the key to leave when she wants and head down the D'Angelo driveway and to the dark street toward my truck. I never look back, and when I get home, I go right to bed where I don't sleep a damn wink.

CHAPTER THREE

First day, senior year

I always thought I would feel like a king pulling into the school parking lot on the first day of my senior year. The reality is far less gratifying. Everyone is the same. Everything looks the same. Even *I* look the same—the same letterman jacket, my name stitched on the right side, my number on the left.

It's all so typical.

Tory slaps his palm into mine for a shake as I get out of my truck.

"Yo, Lucas! You hear about your girl June last night?"

I bristle.

"Why would I hear about June? And she's not my girl." I look around to make sure nobody is listening. I don't want people starting rumors that aren't rooted in anything other than Tory's big mouth.

"Yeah, whatever you say, man. Anyway, she called out

your ex, told her she was a dick then stomped off into the sunset. Fucking epic, yo! It's all everyone's talking about."

I lift my brow and nod, feigning mild interest, but as I lean against the front of my truck and glance out toward the road leading to our school, I full-on grin. June called someone a dick. That's so completely out of her comfort zone, and I'm almost proud of her; maybe more proud of me for giving her the tools to use. I wipe the grin away before turning back to my friends.

For a few minutes, I let myself indulge in the attention. Letter jackets and workout shirts tend to catch girls' eyes. So does a six-foot-plus frame. Other than the twins, I'm probably the tallest guy on campus. And what they have on me in height I make up for in muscle mass. I get a lot of looks, and it doesn't hurt when half the cheer squad insists on giving me welcome hugs on their way from the parking lot into the school. Ava doesn't bother, and I'm relieved that I don't have to replay the scene from last night with her. I've already decided I'm dropping any class I have with her. I don't care if I have to take pottery to make up the credit hours.

That thought reminds me that I haven't picked up my unofficial transcripts from the front office. I'm sending them off to MIT, without my dad's blessing. I have to know whether I'm good enough, and if I manage to get myself in, I'll worry about the next part.

"Hey, I'll catch you at lunch. I've gotta check in with admin." I grip Tory's hand as I peel away and leave them to gossip about who's already hooking up this year.

I push through the glass doors into the office, and three guys are already sitting in a line outside the dean's office, blood on one of their shirts.

"Fighting already on the first day?" I say to Maggie, the front office secretary.

"Oh, my God, right? Freshmen," she jokes, shaking her head. She holds up a finger as she takes a call on her headset. Maggie runs just about everything up here—attendance, records, lost items, delinquents. If you're on her good side, she also takes care of you with special treats, like the Snickers bar she tosses me from the top drawer in her desk.

I unwrap the bite-sized snack and pop it in my mouth whole, spending the next minute amusing myself with the three terrified fourteen-year-olds slowly dragging their feet into the dean's office.

"You here for this?" Maggie says, drawing my attention back to her. She hands me the sealed envelope and I tap it against the counter, feeling the weight of it. It's like gold.

"Thanks," I say, smiling and winking. I can't help but ooze charm when I'm talking to Maggie. She's easy, and the fact she babies me as if I were her own kid doesn't hurt. I crave that kind of parenting, and I'm sure it would break my mom to see me eat it up. I also know the days of getting this kind of attention at home are over.

Maggie reaches forward and pats my cheek and I smile as I back away as she takes another call. I'm riding the high of a good mood as I push into the glass door to head out into the halls. I'm met with resistance—and bright green eyes. The universe has it out for me. After two years of barely catching a glance of June, I'm literally running into her everywhere.

I step to the side, waving a hand to usher her through. She does the exact same thing, then mouths a quick "sorry" when our eyes meet, and for some reason, I'm so fucking entertained a smile takes over my mouth. I correct it, but I can't erase it completely. She's still June.

It's okay to smile. It's not as if I can't be cordial, right? That's how I'll get through senior year. I'll make June an acquaintance; be polite in passing. But no talking.

She takes me up on the invitation and pushes through the door. It's heavy, and if she lets it go it's going to clang loud enough to turn everyone's heads our way, so I reach to grab the edge. Timing is everything, though, and my fingertips pass over her knuckles on the exchange. My hand curls on reflex and I abandon the door, pulling my fist back to my chest as if I've been scorched. My initial worry is that someone saw us touch—*that someone saw the way my eyes dipped and my lips parted*. In that slight millisecond, though, I also catch the blush that colors June's neck and cheeks. As far down as I have buried my instincts to care about this girl, I can't seem to keep them from showing when I least expect it.

"June!" Thank God for Maggie's enthusiasm. She rushes around the counter to hug June and hand her a packet, probably her registration papers. I take advantage of the distraction and duck out, but before the door closes behind me, Maggie calls my name.

I should keep walking. Get out of the situation—free. My feet betray me, though, as do my deeply entrenched manners when it comes to adults. My fingers find their way to the door's gap, slipping in to hold it open, and my eyes flit from June to Maggie in a flash.

"Can you take June here to your first hour? She's in your class."

Fuck.

I think I just blacked out a little. I definitely took too long to respond because Maggie is shaking the papers in her hand at me, as if rousing my attention back to the present. June grabs the papers, her cheeks once again red, probably from being embarrassed.

"Sure," I say, forcing my tight-lipped smile to make an appearance. It keeps me from talking, and I'm not sure what would come out of my mouth right now. I'd either apologize and become too friendly or vomit out the impossible position June is putting me in just by being here.

I turn, assuming June will follow me, and I'm steaming, lost in my mind, and unable to hear whatever Maggie tells her on our way out the door.

Of course June is in my first hour. And of course it's on the opposite end of campus. It's about half a mile from here. I know it is because we run the length of campus during spring football workouts. I'm tempted to start jogging now, to get this little jaunt over without us feeling the need to make small talk.

"I'll be sweaty and breathless by the time my ass finds a seat in there."

Too late. I roll my eyes at first, but I slow a step because I might be speeding a bit. Okay, a lot.

"Not my problem," I level back at her.

My throat tightens and my chest feels heavy. That was a shitty way to react, but seriously, this isn't fun for me either. She has to get it on some level, doesn't she? She should be just as mad at me. Not that what her mom did isn't worse than my father's indiscretion. I'm not even sure how many lives that woman destroyed, all for cash. June doesn't know that part, though, and as angry as I might get, I'm not cold enough to hurt her with it. It would crumble her small life. Her dad's already gone, and her grandma died while she was caring for her. No, June doesn't need a ruined relationship with her mom on top of everything else. She has enough to work through, including finding a new way to pay for college now that her mom's money stream has stopped.

I barrel through the double doors of the A building, pushing them extra wide so June has enough time to slip through. Her body bangs against one of the doors, and I wince at the thought of what that probably looked like. I'm so mad, and I need to calm down. I drill back to what the therapist told me to do when I first saw her two years ago. I close my eyes while I walk because I know the route by heart, and I draw in a deep breath, holding my lungs full for four steps before letting the air slowly stream out through my lips. My pulse doesn't seem to be slowing, so I draw in a breath again, this time opening my eyes.

"You know, it's like eighty, and humid."

June's remark fucks up my mobile meditation session. I do my best to reset but all I hear is her voice, repeating that dumb sentence over and over. I get the subtle dig. I'm wearing my letterman jacket, and she's taking a pot shot at my ego. What's funny, though, is she knows I'm not about ego. Or at least, she did. She hasn't really *known* me in a while, which means I can be whatever guy I need to in order to keep our relationship basically non-existent.

I stop in the middle of the walkway, and a small part of me hopes June is close enough behind that she'll run into my back. I'm not sure whether I want to do it to rattle her or physically touch her, though, and that tangled debate continues to mess with my head. I'm resolved to draw a firm line, regardless. If I don't, we are going to keep going on like this—swiping at each other, glaring, and then wondering what it all means.

I'm going to define it now. It means she and I can't be anything. If I rebuilt the bridge between us, it would kill my mom, maybe even literally.

"We don't have to do this, you know." I point at her, then to my chest. Her eyes draw in, that little wrinkle denting her forehead. God help me if she cries. I could never handle seeing her cry. I press on. "Pretend we have some bond or shit. You have your life, I have mine that I've built here. Just go to class, hang out with your friend, get your straight A's or whatever."

"Friends," she fires back.

Shit. Yeah, I did go there.

I shrug her response off, pretending I have no clue what she's getting at.

"You said I should hang out with my *friend*, but I have *friends*, Lucas."

I used to be one of them.

"Sure. Just . . ." I draw in a sharp breath and press my molars together. I can feel my jaw popping. I forgot how much June could frustrate me, even when we were close. I glance up and remind myself how easy life was when I could pretend she didn't exist, that she wasn't just next door. I drop my chin when I feel strong enough to push on, and I fight through the resistance to say these terrible things when our eyes meet.

"I'm just saying, it's not like we really know each other now. That's all."

I turn and head toward our class building, not bothering to stick around to hear—*or see*—her reaction. I get the gist when her shoes are no longer trotting on the pavement behind me, trying to keep up.

There are a few seats left when I file in, so I take the one in the second row, gambling that June won't want to be in the front row on her first day back. But fate has other ideas, and as the remaining students slip through the door and take up the open spots, I'm left with one empty, the one in front of me. All hopes that June changed her mind and decided to drop out—*like that would ever happen*—fizzle the moment she barrels through the door. She tries to cool her entry by catching the handle before the door slams into the wall, but it's too late. We're all looking at her.

"I'm sorry. I'm new, and I had to stop at the office." She gives her excuse, and her papers, to our teacher and I slink down in my seat and try to become invisible. It's not that June has any other choice but to sit here, but I don't have to react to it. The class giggles when our teacher calls her *Miss Mabee,* and I sneak in a raised lip on the opposite side of my face. Alliteration is funny.

"I hope you're all right with a front-row seat," the teacher says.

I glance her way briefly and avoid making eye contact as she works her way to the desk, sliding in from the side. She's trying to make herself small. I can tell, but in her efforts to wrangle her hair into a twist at her shoulder, she manages to snag her mechanical pencil, flinging it around like a yo-yo. It drops to the floor, right by my shoe.

"Oh, my God," June mutters.

Her chin is tucked into the crook of her shoulder. I'm about to put her out of her misery and bend to get her pencil when I overhear one of the girls in our class behind me.

"They totally hooked up freshman year."

That's a rumor I haven't heard in a while. People around here like to make that claim about a lot of pairings, and the only reason someone is uttering it now is because June is back, and yeah, she and I used to spend a lot of time together when we were freshmen. But it's a lie. And it's a lie I can't have making its way around town and social circles and hitting my mom's ears.

June has contorted herself in her chair, her head practically resting on my desktop at this point, her hair swimming all over the place, sticking to my jeans and my hands. I pull my palms from my desktop as she waves her arm around the floor, fingers stretching to reach her pencil. The giggling picks up steam behind me, so to end it all I tap June on the head.

"Sit up," I bark in a whisper. She does, and I feel a bit like I scolded her. I kind of did. I grab her pencil easily and hold it out for her to take. Both of our hands grip an end as I prep myself to respond with *you're welcome*, but she doesn't say *thank you*, instead hitting me with, "You could have picked it up sooner."

My mouth hangs open and a breathy laugh puffs out my chest as stifled laughter builds behind me. She's turned in her seat enough to meet my gaze, and I lock on this time, glaring at her hard. I tug the eraser from her pencil tip and toss it on the floor to punish her. *There. Take that.*

God, I'm a child.

She shakes her head at me, admonishing me with a quick roll of the eyes as she shifts back to face the front. "Good thing I don't make mistakes," she spits over her shoulder.

I feel the stares from everyone around us, and even if nobody's whispering yet, they will be. I'm irrationally mad now. More than that, I'm embarrassed. I haven't felt this ugliness since people started to talk about my dad having an affair. I tap my own pencil on the cover of my notepad, biding my time and waging war with my own thoughts, hoping I'll make a smart decision.

Be the bigger man, Lucas.

Maybe June was right about my ego. Maybe it has grown, and maybe I like it that way. How dare she take shots at it. I lean forward before I realize, my mouth hovering inches from her neck, which is now exposed thanks to her finally getting her long hair under control. I breathe, just a little, and tiny bumps form on her skin. I like the power I have over her, even when she pretends to hate me.

"June. You are so far from perfect, you have no clue."

29

I hang where I am for just a breath, leaving her on edge, waiting for me to say more. I won't, though. I don't need to. It's true; she doesn't have a clue. That's what this has always been about. I know our families' snarled, sordid secrets, and June doesn't. Maybe I am being cruel, but I could be so much crueler. All I have to do is let her in on the hard, cold truth.

CHAPTER FOUR

Two days later

"Are you trying to hype me up or melt me down?" I ask Tory as he stares down at me while hanging from the rim in his driveway.

It's not like guys can just go play quick games of pick-up football, and since my best friend is destined to play pro basketball one day, I'm relegated to being embarrassed on the court anytime we play pick-up.

"We can switch to HORSE if you want," he teases, dropping to the ground with the grace of an insect-bitten super hero.

I grimace and march over to the ball that now rests in the gutter of his driveway. It rolled there after he slammed it so hard it literally bounced back high enough to go through the hoop again.

"I should probably just get this over with. Quick and painless, like you said." I toss him the ball and he tucks it against his side, checking something on his phone.

"You know who you really should get advice from?" He flips his phone screen around to flash a photo from social media of him and June, from the class they both assist in, and I tilt my head up and fall back a few steps in sync with my eyeroll.

"Have I told you how awesome it is that you and June are instant friends again for some reason? Because if I haven't, let me now. It's so fucking awesome. Not annoying at all." I pick up my gray T-shirt and slip it on before running my hand through my sweaty hair. I swear I work five times as hard to keep up with him out here in the driveway than I do out on the football field on Friday nights.

"I do believe you're jealous," Tory says. This is not the first time he's made that remark. And *that* is *also* annoying.

"Yes. So jealous," I deadpan.

The tightness in my chest and stomach pisses me off, but I chalk it up to Tory's constant needling.

He follows me to my truck, and we slap hands before I get in.

"In all seriousness, dude, you need to have this conversation with your dad. If you want to go to MIT, then that's what you should do."

I hold his stare for a beat, trying to see myself in his eyes. I bet if Tory were dealing with this dilemma, he would take his own advice. He would do what he wanted, follow his heart. I'm so used to making sure both of my parents are happy with my decisions, though, and for my dad, me playing D1 ball has always been the dream. There are thousands of hours of Pee Wee football, youth leagues, private lessons, and trainers wrapped up in that dream. And he'll fund the incidentals for anywhere I get an offer. MIT, though? That dream is one I have to fund. Not that I don't expect to get a pretty sweet offer. Schools like that don't invite you to apply for special programs if they don't think you can hack it, and they're not willing to cover a chunk of the cost.

"I'll let you know how it goes," I say.

Before I can shut the truck door, Tory gets in one more round of advice. There's something about his expression this time that's more serious. He isn't snickering, or wiggling his eyebrows. His gaze is set and his mouth is a straight line.

"Talk to her. It will help. I know it will."

I let his suggestion fall flat, shutting my door and staring at him through the glass of the closed window. I don't know why he thinks talking to June is so important all of a sudden. I keep kicking around the idea that June secretly *wants* to talk to me, that she's planting the idea of mending bridges in Tory's head during their class. That's the guilt eating at me, though. I recognize it, from those first few weeks two years ago when I stopped taking her calls and quit looking in her direction. I knew it wasn't nice then. It still isn't. But it's necessary, and the separation has kept my mom sober and happy.

Tory isn't wrong about one thing, though. June does give great advice. Even now, with our relationship as fucked up as ever, I truly think she would want the best for me. She would support me. She always had a way of making me feel strong when I felt weak.

The glow from her kitchen window as I pull into my driveway is just another beacon calling out to me. My parents aren't home. They're at a fundraiser for one of the charities my mom volunteers for. It's in the city, so they'll be spending the night. If ever there was a time for me to break the pact I made with my mom, it would be now.

I have a built-in excuse. June's my partner for the physics

project, and I would venture to guess she's working on it right now. I can stop by, chalk it up to us needing to act like adults and do a class project together. Small talk can lead to questions about our future, where she's going, and where I am. And if the mood fits, maybe, for a tiny splice in time, I can get my best friend back.

I check the garage to make sure my parents are gone, and double check the house with a quick shout inside to make sure one of them didn't stay behind. Satisfied that the coast is clear, I cross that forbidden line onto the Mabee property, not stopping until I get to the side door that leads into their kitchen. June's back is to me as I peer through the window, and the toy car tracks for our physics project are set up on her dining table. My fist forms and my arm primes to knock, despite the hot lava making its way up my throat thanks to nerves. A fraction before I connect with the door, though, her mom steps into the frame from across the room. Our eyes lock. There's no way she doesn't see me.

Before she can alert June, I turn and sprint. I don't register the distance I cover from their driveway to mine. I don't bother to rush through the garage or the front door, opting instead for the darkness of the back yard. My parents almost always leave the sliding glass door unlocked, and I'm relieved their habits haven't changed as I slide it open barely enough to fit my body through, heaving it shut behind me.

I'm breathing hard, and it's not because I ran. Maybe June's mom didn't notice. *That's absurd. We made eye contact.*

I pace, first around the table and into the kitchen then back to the glass door, my eyes scanning my back yard with a suspicion that I've been followed. I go through the same motions a few more times, my pulse finally calming when enough time has passed to assure me that June, or worse, her mom, isn't marching over to find out what I was doing.

What I was doing was indulging in what felt good. I was remembering home, simpler times when I could talk to June the same way Tory seems able to all of a sudden. It was a dumb idea. What would I have even said? It's good June's mom caught me. She stopped me from making a huge mistake.

My palms are still sweaty so I tug open the fridge door and grab two beer bottles. I plan on drinking them both. I sync my phone to the speakers outside and put on my favorite Kanye album. I slip back through the glass door and kick my feet up in one of the loungers, popping the cap from the first beer and taking a long sip. It numbs my nerves enough to let me take a full breath.

I pull my phone out to check my messages, finding one from Ava. I stare at it, leaving it unread, as I finish the first beer.

She's bored. We broke up. Well, *I* broke us up. But we've broken up before. I'm not sure we were ever really a thing. It would be so easy to fall into old habits. Ava would listen to me. She just doesn't take in my words. And I won't get any good advice from her about how to deal with my dad. I can't bring up what happened at June's just now either. She'd lose her shit.

Ava has held a grudge against June since her eighth grade birthday party. All her friends bullied her into admitting she was in love with me. I was shocked to hear those words—terrified, actually. I knew Ava wasn't in love with me. We were barely in our teens, and the only thing she knew about me was that I played football and she liked my hair. Rather than laugh at her, I told her I was sorry but I was in love with someone else. When she pressed, I said it was June.

I don't know why I said that. It wasn't a crush I'd been harboring. It's just that when the subject of love came up, June was the only person I could think of.

I thought of June.

I set the empty bottle on a nearby table and pull the cap off number two. I'm rattled at my own thoughts. I've never self-analyzed this before, but now that I am, there has to be more to it. My stomach feels heavy, maybe a little sick, and I know it's not the beer. I can hold my beer. I've had plenty of practice. This uneasiness is something else entirely.

Instead of opening Ava's message, I find myself skimming through my list of contacts, pausing over the one name that is grayed out.

JUNE MABEE

I blocked her to protect us both. I did it to keep me from slipping, to make sure I didn't expose my mom to a message she wouldn't want to see or think I was hiding something behind her back. I knew I would be weak when it came to June.

I hover my thumb over her name, taking one more swig of liquid courage before giving in and unblocking her number. I slide across her name, pausing one more time before selecting *unblock*. The minute I do, her image populates her contact file. It's an old photo, one I took three years ago. It's a portal to our past, and I find myself studying the odd details, like her braces and the small cut on her right cheek where I hit her with a Frisbee. She wasn't looking when I threw it, sure, but June could never catch very well.

Our old messages read like a frozen moment in time, a blip before the world ended. Her question mark, waiting for my response that never came, punches me in the gut. I wonder how many messages she sent that went nowhere. I built a wall that kept it all out, but I never once considered she kept trying to get through. Or worse, *she didn't.*

I lay my phone flat on my chest and nestle into the lounger, rolling my head to the side where all I can see are the overgrown shrubs and tall grass poorly hiding the old Buick in June's yard. Her dad had plans for that thing. June always hoped he would give it to her when she turned sixteen, but that wish was a pipedream. Her mom ruined that. I bet her dad couldn't stand the thought of working on that car anymore after they split. It's probably why he left it here, abandoned.

It's easier to slip into anger. The other option is to miss June. I've been good about keeping those feelings at bay, but fucking Tory had to get all friendly with her. I hate him a little for it. A beer and a half in, I'm willing to admit I'm a tad jealous too. June's off limits, and he should respect that. If I have this massive crush he likes to tell me I do, then he should know better. I down the rest of beer number two and toss my phone on the side table then head into the kitchen to grab myself two more. I come back to a new message notification, and the fact my heart skips with hope pisses me off. As if unblocking June automatically made her text me. She's probably texting Tory.

I open to see it's Ava, and I read her message thread now that she's pinged me again. Her first message was a simple 'what's up' kinda thing, but this new one has my bad instincts tingling.

AVA: *On my way. Friend dropping me off.*

I stare at her last words and calculate the time as I crack open beer number three. I know what her message means. Ava's coming over here to fuck. That's what we do. It's not a relationship, it's an on-again-off-again itch we scratch. It isn't right, and it's not healthy for either of us, but I'm not telling her no.

Raising the music's volume on my phone, I leave it on the lounger and move to the trampoline, taking my beer with me. I kick off my shoes and throw my sweatshirt out toward the patio table then climb up to the center of the trampoline where I bounce on my toes to the rhythm of Kanye. It takes Ava two songs to show up, and by the time she reaches the trampoline, I'm so gone in my head with jealousy, resentment, and a cruel need to smudge out any pure thoughts I've had for June in the last hour.

"How was practice?" She crawls up on the trampoline, her legs parted as she sits on her knees. She couldn't give two shits about my practice. She's already unbuttoning the flannel shirt she's wearing.

I polish off my beer and toss the bottle into the grass, sinking to my knees and moving toward her. I tug on the front of her jeans as soon as they're within reach, and when they open, she gasps.

"Come here," I order.

Her mouth curls on one side and she bats her oversized lashes. Once she's close enough, I sweep my arm under her back and legs and lay her on the center of the trampoline. My mind plays evil tricks, though, and for a flash, I look down and expect to meet green eyes. I'm searching for dark hair, but instead it's waves of blonde around her face.

Ava. This is Ava.

Attempting to drown out this sudden craving for June, I kiss Ava hard, my teeth grazing her lips and neck as I nip and taste her skin. She grabs fistfuls of my gray T-shirt, and usually by this point I'm hard as fuck. Tonight, though? Yeah, I'm aroused, but it's as though my dick is waiting for something else. *Someone else.*

"Fuck," I growl. Ava assumes it's dirty talk for her, but really, I'm angry. I'm confused.

I kiss my way down her shoulder, a curve I've been on before, one I swore I'd give up. I'm so weak. I wish this was June.

What the fuck?

Squeezing my eyes shut, I press my forehead against hers as I lift myself over her body. Holding my weight up with one arm, I trace the curve of her breast down to her stomach with my fingertips. She arches against my soft touch, and I flatten my palm on her stomach.

June. Fucking June.

I bite at her bra strap, gripping it with my teeth and tugging it over the bend of her shoulder. My mouth covers her breast and the hard peak pushes through the lace against my tongue. My teeth act as a vice, clamping down on the raw tip as Ava writhes under me, her hips bucking, wanting my hand to travel lower. Something seems to be stopping me, though, and as much as I'd love to give myself credit for having self-restraint, that's not the case.

My cock is harder now, and I could lose myself if I wanted. My body doesn't care if this is Ava or June or my goddamned pillow. I need release. But it's my head holding me back. Someone *in* my head.

My fingertips push under the band of Ava's panties, and she moans into my mouth. This should be enough. I should take this all the way right now. Why the fuck can't I?

And then she's here. June is fucking here, not in my mind, not in some delusion, but actually fucking here.

Goddamn her mom for telling her I came by. That's why she's here. She's a dozen yards away, and I'm fucking grinding on Ava. I glance across the patio as June steps closer. My chin rubs against Ava's nipple and she whimpers, and the kind part of me wants to tell her to be quiet. I want to hide this from June.

Then there's the evil prick side of me that wants her to witness it. I want her to call Tory and cry about it. I want her to hate me a little more, to tell her mom they have to move. I want her out of my school, out of my fucking head.

My hand slides into Ava's panties, and she's wet and so fucking ready for me. My finger dips inside her and she moves with me. My cock flexes in my joggers. Ava pushes up into me, my hand covering her, and the momentary relief of feeling her hips roll into me draws a growling moan from somewhere deep inside my body.

Ava does the work, lifting her hips again and pushes her jeans over her curves, down her thighs. I pull them all the way from her legs, and as she kicks them away, metal scrapes along the patio about a dozen feet away.

Reality comes crashing in.

Fuck.

Fuck. Fuck. Fuck.

I run my forearm over my brow, trying to work feeling back into my face. Guilt has me in its grip. That was cruel. What I just did? I tried to hurt June, and that makes me no better than her mom and my dad and the damage they did. Squeezing my eyes shut, I lay down at Ava's side, my finger still inside her. Her leg lifts, her knee moving over my thigh, and if I let this go on, I'll be buried inside her in seconds. I won't care what it says about me. I might even pretend it's June the entire time. Ava won't care, and that part . . . that's not okay either. She should care.

"No," I grunt, pushing her leg back down and urging her to lay flat.

"Just you," I say, my eyes meeting hers briefly. She bites her lip, melting into pleasure as I tease her with my thumb and dust her mouth with a feather-light kiss. I force a smile on my face, a heavy one, full of unrelenting physical need and twisted with self-hate. I fight my thoughts, my inner voice on constant replay, calling me out for the piece of shit I am for doing this to both girls. I please Ava, because that's the least I can do. And I hold her against my chest when she's done, tickling her back with my fingertips, pretending it's June the entire fucking time.

CHAPTER FIVE

My head is killing me. I went through five beers last night. Ava had one. I let her sleep on the couch, and I must have fallen asleep in the chair playing that stupid rock crushing game on my phone. I don't remember nodding off, but I do remember everything else. I have to quit making bad decisions. I feel like a massive asshole. Ava's making it even worse, sitting next to me in my truck, trying to hold my hand. I keep flinching and pulling my hand away.

"You're fucking moody." She shuts the passenger door with a little extra zip and leaves me with my thoughts, heading toward her friends.

She's not wrong. I *am* fucking moody.

Tory and Hayden are sitting on the curb near their car with Cannon, the new guy. *Maybe he'd like Ava?* For a few seconds, I consider hooking him up with an intro while my eyes scan the rest of the parking lot. It doesn't take long for my gaze to meet June's. She's leaning against the front of her friend Abby's car with her arms crossed. I get the sense she's been watching me for a while, which means she saw Ava get out of my truck a few seconds ago.

I drop my focus to my door handle and swear off all things June and Ava for the next twenty-four hours as I exit my truck. My plan is foiled the second I join my friends, thanks to Tory and his nosey ass.

"You talk to June?"

I groan at his question, leaning my head back and pushing both fists into my seriously tired eyes.

"No, but I drank a six-pack of Miller and apparently invited Ava over." Tory was bound to find out anyhow. He starts laughing, covering his mouth with one hand and slapping my chest with the other. I flick it away.

"Dude, just . . . *stop*," I say.

The bell rings, so we all head toward the main doors. Cannon peels off first, and Hayden ditches us about midway through our walk. I'm acutely aware of how close June is behind me. Tory must be, too, because he keeps insisting on talking about her in his roundabout way.

"You need to quit Ava, dude. She's bad for you. And frankly, you're bad for her," he says.

"Thanks." My answer is gruff and clipped.

"I just mean—"

"You mean I should say fuck it all and get with June," I cut in.

Tory spits out a hard laugh.

"That's the *last* thing I think." He's still chuckling as I turn and glare at him. I've got a dozen more steps before he leaves me for his weightlifting class. When it becomes clear he doesn't plan on elaborating, I hold out my palms.

"What the fuck does that mean?"

He turns to head toward the weight room, spinning on his heels to walk backward. "It means I'm starting to think she's too good for you." He winks and turns to jog the rest of the way.

I can't tell whether he's joking or being serious. Whatever his intent, it pushes my buttons. I'm hungover, my head's a mess, and I still have the whole MIT conversation hanging in the balance. I practically fall into my seat for physics, and I pull out my notebook and pen so I look prepared. I'm staring at the white board at the front of the class, letting the scribbled notes blur together as my eyes relax when June literally sucks up all air within a five-foot radius. My eyes dash to her, ignoring my mental plea to not engage.

I keep spinning the pen in my hand and ready myself for her inevitable questions. *Why did I come to her house? What's my deal with Ava? Did I see her? Did I know she was there? Was I trying to hurt her?*

Mental screams echo between my ears, my answers all muddled and confused and desperate for her to tell me that none of it matters and I'll be okay. I can't believe I'm sitting here in the same clothes I wore yesterday, my breath a toxic mix of fermented wheat and grain and the milk I chugged this morning straight from the carton. The longer June stands there, just . . . just . . . smirking, the louder my inner debate grows. The bigger the threat of nausea building in my gut and throat. The more I start to see the ways Tory was not joking. Not even a little.

"What?" I finally spit out.

She reaches into her backpack and pulls out a pair of panties then tosses them on my desk.

Fucking hell. Those are Ava's.

"Pretty sure these are yours," she says. Her voice is smug. *Why isn't she hurt by this?* Clearly, Ava did this to mess with her. It's mean. It's *more* than mean. It's female psychological warfare. And yet here she stands, unscathed. Unaffected. Not a speck of jealousy.

I waited too long. June has moved on.

I puff out a laugh to mask my pain and she takes her seat. Leaning to her side, she reaches into her bag again, and I prepare to have one of Ava's bras thrown in my face. Instead, she pulls out the project she spent the night working on alone. Her mom had to have told her. She knows I tried to come by. As seconds turn into minutes, though, I realize she's done. Throwing my dirty deeds, so to speak, in my face was her big finale.

"Hey, June," I find myself saying.

She turns her head, just enough to let me get a good view of the curl of her lashes and her soft jawline marking the space between her ear and lips—perfect lips. Pouty, but not pretend. Soft. *Kissable.* Her hair is in a braid today, one that zigzags from the right side of her head to her left, loosely gathered at the nape of her neck. I lean forward enough to gently tug on it. Her lips part.

Bingo.

"Thanks," I say, letting my hand slowly cover the lacy, heart-patterned panties. Her eyes shift in rapid movements, letting me know she saw it in her periphery. I tuck the garment into my pocket and hold her stare. This time, I'm the one wearing the smug smile on my face.

"You're welcome," she says, her voice a fraction of the confident one she used before. "Don't mention it," she adds, trying to really sell how little she cares.

I know better, though. As much as she and I both have tried to erase old bonds and feelings, there's history there. And it tells me that she's as mixed up and confused about us as I am.

CHAPTER SIX

F riday could not come fast enough. As little as my heart
beats for the game, the routine of it is comforting. And
it doesn't hurt to lose myself for a little while and play the
part of varsity captain. Applying to MIT? That was hard.
The inevitable argument coming my way over going there
instead of one of the dozen schools offering me starting roster
spots will be hard. Running through a paper banner held by
cheerleaders and shouting at the people in the bleachers to
get up and show their support for this meaningless game is
easy. It's a role I play. I'm good at it. *Maybe I should just give
in to my fate.*

The emotions come easy. I lead the pack of grunting
teenage boys through a guttural countdown until we all shout
"Public" and I rush at the banner, breaking through, flag pole
clutched in my fists, the red, white, and blue fabric waving
over my shoulder as I blaze onto the field. Coach jogs toward
us and I hand him my flag before I peel off with the other
seniors to gather the team and lead our prayer.

I volunteered for this. It felt like my duty as quarterback.

Honestly, the prayer before every game stresses me out more than getting into the end zone. I'm definitely unqualified—a sinner born from the king of sinners. But for some reason I was born with this innate ability to lead, or at least fake it really well.

The weight is heavy on my chest as I stretch my arms out and cup my hands, urging my boys in close. Our collective hot breath mingles with sweet smell of wet grass and the stench of body wrap spray, sweat and unwashed pads.

"Alright, boys. Let's do this," I begin.

Eyes closed and heads bowed, but I keep mine open for a few extra seconds, scanning my teammates for signs that one of them isn't buying into my words. I kept expecting it last season, but nobody ever caved and called me out on my bullshit. So here it goes, recycled words from the year before, rearranged a little so they sound brand new. I shut my eyes.

"Lord, we ask you to give us the strength to perform at our best tonight, to make our parents, our siblings, our fellow students and teachers proud with our actions. Let us have each other's backs, even when it's hard. Let us find the strength to carry one another one more yard when our legs are tired and heavy. Keep us safe so our mothers don't worry. Bless us with good health so we can be our best. And let us play with the same respect and sportsmanship we ask of the men on the other side of the field. In your name, Amen."

"Amen."

"Alright, let's bring it in!" Tory takes over and I finally exhale and open my eyes. I clap loud, contributing to the thunder we create as a unit with our hands while Tory yells so loudly his voice cracks. We grunt and repeat random, violent words—*hit them hard, take them out, they ain't nothin'!* It's all such a contrast to the words I just said, yet the hype easily spills from our mouths.

We break with a final clap and everyone dashes to the sideline but me. I need time alone to fully transform into the man I need to be for the next three hours. I'm going to get knocked around, flattened on my back, and I have to be in the mental state to take it, to *live* for it. Every time I lose my wind tonight, I must fill my lungs up fuller. I will find a way to score. I will be flawless on my feet. I will hit my spots, take care of my receivers and never—ever—drop the ball.

I breathe in one last draw through my nose and lift my gaze, my eyes zeroing in on my dad in the stands. He's just off the fifty, already on his feet with his arms crossed over his chest, evaluating. I don't need to be close enough to detect the details. I have them memorized—the divot in his forehead, the way he gnaws at the inside of his mouth as he formulates his evaluation of everything. No matter how perfect I am, there will be flaws for us to discuss.

This is how he loves me.

I'm realizing this is really more about how he loves himself.

My mind switches off, and for the next two hours, my body carries me through. Easy. Mindless. A golden boy. Beloved. And when the game is over, they're all cheering my name. Everyone but the guy still standing in the cleared-out bleachers, arms crossed over his chest.

I'm not much in the mood to party tonight, but the other option is going home and being held prisoner by my father's mental notes and desire to watch game film just hours after the game finished. Lucky me, my father gets the film link sent to him from the drop box, a request the coaching staff grants because they love how invested he is in the team's success.

It's a nightmare.

Pretty much everyone is going to be blitzed by the end of the night, so I offer to pile most of the offense into my truck, leaving their vehicles at school. It's not that I'm being responsible; the pressure of having to drive people out of here will keep me from getting totally shitfaced, and after drinking *way* too much the other night with Ava, I'm not interested in a repeat.

Shit. *Ava.*

I've been avoiding her the last few days. Nothing too obvious, but making myself busier than necessary to avoid having to talk about what we are and aren't. I've already heard her opinions through the not-so-quiet rumor mill. She's claiming us "back together" and is already plotting how we'll be crowned homecoming king and queen. Maybe it would be easier to go along with her plans. It would definitely keep June away.

My truck weighed down with five linemen in the back, I make one last stop to pick up a few of the cheerleaders. Two of the guys leap from the back to help Katy, the cheer captain, roll a keg down her driveway and hoist it into my truck. Her mom is either the coolest or worst on the planet, depending on perspective. She always supplies us with kegs on game nights. She's single, and behaves a lot like a teenager herself. She's shown up to a few of our parties in the woods, and I'm pretty sure she's hooked up with a senior or two. I'd rather not know the truth, so I don't ask for details when the whispering starts. The gossip doesn't seem to embarrass Katy, and maybe that's because her mom sleeping with a few eighteen-year-olds is nothing compared to what went down between June's mom and my dad, and a whole lot of other men around Allensville.

I'm sure Ava's told Katy about my dad's affair. I'm sure she's told *lots* of people. I managed to keep the truth about what went down to a small circle for two years. Originally, it was out of respect for June and my mom. Now? I just want to graduate and get out of this place without having to rehash my shitty family life. And if June doesn't know the part her mom played by now, that's on her mom. I'm sick of managing the collateral damage, and I'm even more tired of Ava holding my secret over my head as a way to pretend we're close. She doesn't overtly threaten to spill it, but the suggestion is always there. Even the other morning, after I fucked up and spent the night with her, she dropped little hints about how she's always there when I need to deal with my "trauma," and how she'd make sure June left me alone if her presence at school ever became too much for me to handle. Her hate for June has nothing to do with me and I know it. Those emotions are born of petty jealousy.

With everyone piled back into the truck, I peel down the street and out of town. One of the girls passes around an open can of beer while someone blows weed into my fucking face. My jaw is locked tight and I'm half tempted to pull over in the middle of the forest and kick every damn person out of my truck, leaving their asses to walk the rest of the way in for the party. I hold it together, though, because the other option is home, and as fucking annoying as being the bus driver for these idiots is, it still beats game film with Pops.

I press the gas when my tires hit the dirt road and a few bottles clank in the truck bed as I wind through the thick trees toward the clearing. The glow of parked cars, head-lights, and the bonfire motivates me to drive faster, and when

I see the front of the twins' dad's truck, a sense of relief washes over me. Their car would never make it out here.

Slamming the truck into park, I kill the engine and flop back into my seat while everyone tumbles out. They're already lit. An hour from now, most of them will either be barfing in a ditch or passed out.

When the last passenger slams the door shut, I indulge in a heavy exhale. My truck stinks. I roll down my window so maybe it will air out before I head home then hop out and scan the crowd for Tory. He's not in the mix. Instead, he's right next to me, sitting in the back of his dad's truck, holding June's hand. *What the fuck?*

I force my gaze up to my friend, but I'm not fast enough to not get caught looking. He's doing this to be a dick. It isn't cool, leading June on just to get under my skin.

"Hey, man. Can you help me with this keg?" Even with my inner voice commanding me to keep my focus on my friend's face, my eyes disobey and zero in on the place where Tory's hand is wrapped around June's. *What is she even doing here?* She hates parties. This makes two in a row. Goddamn, do I have anywhere left to hide?

"Yeah, bro. Where we takin' it?" Tory answers, his thumb stroking June's knuckles, a move he makes because he *knows* I'm looking.

Asshole.

June's had enough, thank God, and pulls her hand away, shoving her fists into the front pocket of her hoodie. I turn my attention to the keg and my tailgate.

"Uh, Jake's truck, I guess. Isn't that where the rest of the shit is?" I glance toward June without thinking and she's sucking in her lips. I can't tell whether she's embarrassed I caught her holding Tory's hand or simply uncomfortable around me. I pull my hat off and twist it around backward, studying June the entire time. Her eyes flip up nervously, and I have to admit the power I have over her makes me feel a bit smug.

Tory finally hops down but leans close to June, whispering something. I turn away before he gets the satisfaction of knowing I saw him, and a second later he's helping me hoist the keg out of the back of my truck.

"Hey, Hayden! Come give us a hand!" I shout when I spot the other D'Angelo twin. The three of us carry it over to Jake's truck where nearly everyone is gathered, including June's friend, Abby. *Why the hell was June hanging out away from everyone, alone . . . with Tory?*

Tory pats his hands together when we get the keg situated just right and I pull a cup from the stack nearby and hand it to him. He shakes his head and glances over his shoulder, smirking.

"Nah, I'm good with the shit I brought."

I hold steady until he turns back to face me and our eyes meet.

"You're good, huh?" My mouth in a hard line, I challenge him with my stare. He's fucking with me, and I'm so not in the mood to engage. If he thinks hanging out with June tonight is going to bother me, fine. Let him waste his entire night on that shit.

"Yep. I'm gonna grab a Coke for June." He reaches across my body, pulling a soda from the cooler along with a bottle of Miller, his smile growing into that aching grin of his, the one he gets when he dunks on me. *Fucking show off.*

"How nice of you," I say, rolling my eyes and turning my attention to the keg to fill a cup for myself. By the time I turn back, Tory's already jogged halfway across the clearing toward June. I drink more than I intend to on the first sip while I catch what I'm pretty sure is a genuine smile on her face, and that's the last bit of attention I plan on giving those two for the rest of the night.

"How cute. Tory's showing her pity attention. Or maybe . . . maybe he's into her." Ava's voice snakes over my shoulder just before her hands creep around my sides and slide under my T-shirt, nails clawing at my chest. I tip my cup back and swallow more beer. I should be into this. Any other guy here would kill to be in this position.

"Whatever," I mutter, turning my head and dropping my chin enough to meet her mouth. I kiss her, a move I'll regret but one that temporarily drowns out the noise in my head.

"I heard Katy brought some of the good shit. Wanna smoke?" She lifts up on her toes, bouncing.

I don't want to smoke. I hate the way that shit smells; even the pen crap meant to smell like candy smells like chemical ass. Ava knows I don't do that shit. She caught me looking at June, and she aims to keep close tabs on me.

"Yeah, I'll hang with you. But don't get stupid. I'm not in the mood to play babysitter to your high ass." I shrug her grip from my waist then down the rest of my beer before tossing the cup toward Jake's truck. I walk backward and hold on to Ava's hungry gaze, willing my mind to play along.

Quit thinking about June. Quit thinking about June . . . and Tory.

Ava pulls her mouth into a tight smile, her eyes flirting with me as she folds her hands together and holds her knuckles to her lips.

"Be right there," I say, scolding myself internally for the direction I'm headed.

"Hey, bro!" Tory slaps my back before I spin around. I twist and meet his palm mid-air with my own and we shake.

"I hear Katy brought a blunt!" He points over his shoulder to the thick forest Ava slipped into when I walked away. I nod and my friend shoots me a crooked smile. He doesn't smoke often, but the few times he has have made him a nightmare to deal with. He gets paranoid, and childish— somehow more immature than he is normally. He's left June to sit alone in the back of the truck, and I feel a little twinge in my gut. I'm worried he's going to abandon her there. She'll sit there waiting for him to come back, because that's how she is—trusting. *Gah! Why do I care?*

"You comin'?" He cocks a brow.

I nod.

"Yeah, give me a minute."

His gaze darts over my shoulder, toward June, and an arrogant chuckle escapes his mouth.

"I'm just checking my truck. Relax," I lie.

"Uh huh," he says through a growing smirk. He holds up his empty beer bottle and spins around, so damn sure he caught me.

I keep my eyes on the ground most of the way to my truck, taking a wide route so June can't see me walk up. I left my phone in the center console, so I pop into the driver's side unnoticed and grab my cell before moving toward the back of the truck to lift the tailgate. The latch has been giving me trouble lately, and naturally, it's in rare form tonight. It takes me three tries to get it to catch, and I feel June's eyes boring into me without even looking to confirm she's staring.

I should just walk away. The smart move would be to head in the other direction, to follow the same path I took here. *Do not engage, Lucas Fuller. She and Tory and whatever the hell bond they're forming is none of your business.*

Against my best judgement, I look up. Her eyes are wait-ing. My chest burns. I look back down and press my molars together, my jaw popping. I breathe out through my nose and shake my head.

"Be smart with that," I say, nodding toward Tory. He's chugging a beer now, and he's about to take a hit. He's going to act like a real asshole soon. June twists to look in his direction and I adjust my hat, spinning it so my brim hides my view of her.

"You jealous or something?"

I can't believe she said that. I chuckle quietly, my eyes on the ground. *Yeah. I am. I'm fucking jealous, and I hate it because I don't want to care about you.* Those feelings? They stop right now.

I pop my head up and give her a crooked smile.

"Sure, June." I force my eyes to remain indifferent, my stare blank. I've got a slight buzz forming from the beer, so I give in to it and let it wash away the tightness in my belly. I can tell it's working by the way her cheeks flush and her eyes shift from side to side. I made her feel uncomfortable, and I feel both guilty and satisfied.

I leave before I say anything else—*before she responds*—and make my way toward Ava and the others who are getting drunk and high by the riverbed. I take a seat on one of the flat rocks near the small trickle of water and Ava plops herself onto my lap, her laughter loud and obnoxious. I'm not sure how many minutes pass before I snap out of my head—an hour perhaps? But after tuning out everyone around me, I'm abruptly brought back to the present as Ava leaps from my thighs, her sudden ire focused on a now-full truck bed. Tory made his way back to June, and half of Ava's old friend circle is sitting with them, laughing.

"I wonder if they know what a social pariah she is." Her words come out in a slur, but she's coherent enough that I sense the dangerous anger in her tone. She's going to make a scene.

"Just leave her alone. Come back. We were having a nice

time," I say, reaching my hand out to her and curling my fingers. Her eyes dip to my hand and for a moment, I think she might be giving in. Then another round of laughter echoes across the way, drawing both of our stares in their direction.

Ava punches out a laugh and tosses her hair over her shoulder as she looks me in the eyes.

"Your mind has not left her all night. Don't you fucking lie to me, Lucas Fuller," she seethes.

I sigh, because that's what I'm supposed to do. She isn't wrong, though, and I'm pretty certain she sees through my sad attempt.

"No, she needs to go. She's not welcome here," Ava mutters, her hands forming fists as if she knows how to use them. I don't doubt that drunk and angry, Ava could be a scrappy handful. But she's never really thrown a punch, and she sure as shit isn't athletic. June outweighs her by twenty pounds. Not that June's a fighter either, but I think she'd defend herself if she had to. Ava wouldn't stand a chance.

"Ava, stop," I call after her, pushing myself up from the rock. Nobody around us seems to be paying attention, thank God. But she catches enough eyes during her march across the clearing toward June and the others to make this scene worthwhile.

"Fuck," I breathe out, dropping my hands into my pockets and feeling for my keys. I need to get her out of here.

I'm not sure what Ava said to make June leap from the back of the truck, but the fact she just did has me doubling my strides toward them. And when June hauls off and slaps her, I break into a jog. I reach the two of them just as Ava regains her balance and lunges at June. I thrust an open palm against Ava's clavicle and manage to catch June's oncoming fist in my other hand. June's eyes are red and wild. I'm not sure what Ava said, but I have a feeling it was personal and cruel.

"You!" I stare into Ava's eyes, willing her to peel her crazed gaze from June and onto me. There goes any hope of keeping this incident low-key. Everyone, and I mean *everyone,* has gathered around us to watch.

"Lucas—"

"Get your ass in there. That's enough!" I push her toward my truck, and she pouts but jerks her body away from me, thank God in the right direction.

Behind me, June begins to laugh. This is a game to her. Being at this party, in my business, next to my house—in my life. A fucking game! *Doesn't she get it?*

"Just . . . fucking stop, June," I plead, rolling my head until my eyes land on her. She freezes under my stare, her eyes wide with shock as her shoulders drop and her muscles relax. I let go of my hold on her wrist and shake my head.

"Your mom's a fucking whore, you know!" Ava shouts from behind me.

I spin around and point at her.

"I said get your ass in my truck!" She's drunk. That's what I'll tell June. High and drunk and . . . mean. Everyone knows she's mean.

I turn my attention back to June, and while I figure she'll be hurt, the pure devastation that seems to have colored her cheeks and sunk in her eyes catches me off guard. Ava's a bully. This can't be the first time she's said something like this to June, can it? Or maybe it is. Maybe June doesn't even know how close to the truth Ava's insult is.

Now is not the time to sort this out. I'm not her therapist. I'm nobody's therapist. June's lips part with a hopeless breath, and before she can speak, I shake my head, backing away from the girl I used to run to when I felt the way her eyes tell me she feels right now.

"Is she your girlfriend? That?" June grunts out a laugh and points to the passenger side of my truck. Thank God the door is shut, otherwise I'm sure Ava would come out with her claws ready. *Don't do this, June. Don't make this worse.*

"Or is she just some girl you fuck? No matter what, you know she's part of your story now. That . . . that is what you are."

We are surrounded by silence. I don't even think the people staring at us are bothering to breathe, too afraid they'll miss some of the drama. My teeth clench and I meet June's stare, her eyes glossed with tears she wants to shed but is too angry or stubborn to.

No, June, she is not my girlfriend. And yes, June, she's some girl I fuck. And it's none of your business. See, I'm a piece of shit just like my dad, but at least I don't make promises to people only to break them. I don't wreck marriages and bust up families.

I hold those thoughts in, despite the fire raging in my chest. They aren't the right words to say; they're fueled by hate and anger—reactionary. I would only make things worse, pour gas on smoldering embers. In less than a year, I'll be out of here. Out of June's life and away from my parents. I can keep my mouth shut until then.

I lean forward a tick, eyes still squared with hers, and I spit on the ground, turning my glare toward Tory. I swear he's smirking as he holds up his open palms and plays innocent. Fucking pot-stirrer, that's what he is.

I turn my back to June and climb in my truck, firing it up and pulling away from this nightmare with enough zip that my back tires kick dirt up at the lingering onlookers. That's what they get, nosy fuckers.

Thankfully, Ava doesn't pick a fight with me until we're well on our way toward home. I'd love to lay on the gas and speed our asses home, but my breath is still fresh from that beer and the last thing I need to deal with is getting pulled over and hauled in for my dad to come pick up.

"She started it, you know. She *always* starts it." I figured Ava wouldn't be silent the entire way home.

"She didn't start anything." I sigh.

"You always defend her!"

I glance to my right in time to see her huff in her seat and cross her arms over her chest like a petulant child. I chuckle at it, which pisses her off even more.

"You do!" Ava retorts.

"Sure, whatever," I mutter, rolling my gaze away from her and back to the road. We're back in town, minutes from her house.

Even Ava's silence is obnoxious. She fidgets for attention, sighing and shifting her legs, tucking one leg under the other only to switch them seconds later. She wants me to console her, or to pull over and have it out so we can end up making out. I'm not in the mood. Honestly, all I want in the world is to be alone.

I pull to a hard stop in front of Ava's house and her hands fly forward, slapping against the dashboard.

"Jesus, Lucas!"

I breathe out heavily and tighten my grip on the wheel, preparing myself. *Please, just get out of my truck. Get out of my truck. Get out of my truck. Get out—*

"Are you in love with her?"

Fuck.

Ava grips my arm, tugging it from the steering wheel and toward her chest so she can hold on to it. It's a power play move she does, clinging to me physically to express some weird desperation.

"Tell me, Lucas. Is that why you let her get away with so much? Because you love her?" Ava has been jealous of June since junior high. Back then, yeah, I had a crush on June, and we were close. Ava always had a thing for me; therefore, June was the enemy. It's been literal years now, and Ava is fully aware of the bad blood between my family and June's. She's looking for attention.

"No, Ava. I'm not in love with her." I shrug the rest of her tirade off as I sink into my seat while she continues to hang on to me. I want her to get out of my truck, to go inside and not call me the second I drive away. I want to take back that night on my patio that should never have happened. Hell, the entire year of off-and-on hookups between us—take those back too!

I run my palms over my face as I groan.

"All I want, Ava. No . . . all I *need,* is for there to be nothing linking me with June Mabee other than our goddamn property line. And when you start shit with her, all you do is force me to acknowledge her, talk to her. I don't want to do any of that. Do you understand?"

"I'm sorry." She hums two words she doesn't mean. She wants me to console her and tell her it's okay, but I'm not that guy. I don't know why she thinks I would be. I've never been that way with her. I'm not sure I'm capable of being conciliatory. Loving. Fuck, I'm barely amicable.

"You drank a lot tonight. Go inside and get some rest. We'll talk tomorrow, when we both have clear heads."

I'm pinching the bridge of my nose so hard I may actually crack the bone. Ava sidles closer to me and raises herself enough to press her lips to my cheek. I shift my eyes as she does, glaring at her. I'm not doing this.

"You're right. I don't know what came over me. I just get so angry at her, seeing her, knowing what she did—"

"What her mom did," I correct. That's the one line I won't let Ava cross. She's intent on ascribing June's mother's misdeeds to June herself, and that's not fair. She can resent June for plenty of other reasons she's cooked up in her head, but that one isn't going to fly, not ever.

"Whatever." She shrugs my response off and pops open the door, slipping out of the seat, her balance a little off. She's playing it up some. She's drunk, but I've seen her knock back several shots of tequila and walk just fine. This little show is for affect.

"Call me," she says, hazing her eyes and blinking slowly as she tugs at the frayed bottom of her cropped T-shirt. A month or two ago and I would say fuck it and tell her to climb back in here with me. Something's changed. *I've* changed. I'm not sure why, but I feel it.

Ava shuts the door, her eyes flaring when I let it latch, and before she can grip the handle and jerk it back open, I drive away. I crank the music up and smack my palms against the steering wheel, keeping time with this new rapper Tory's got me listening to. I like the guy's lyrics, but they hit a little close to home when he repeats the phrase *girls from your past show up like ghosts*. I flip the stereo off and drive the rest of the way home in silence.

I sit in my driveway for several minutes, the motor off and lights out. It's peaceful in this small space. Nobody yelling, zero passive-aggressive digs about fidelity, no game film and coaching tips from a forty-five-year-old has-been. I'm tempted to spend the night in my driver's seat, but when my cab lights up with the glow from a pair of headlights pulling into June's driveway, I slink down and curse myself for not going inside sooner.

June drove her mom's van. I can barely see the top of her head as she climbs out of the driver's seat. I hold my breath, listening for the sound of another door or the sliding one on the side. After a few seconds of silence, I exhale, glad June's come home alone. For some reason, I feel that if Abby were with her she'd be braver, more likely to march over to my truck to inspect the insides or pound on my front door and demand to see me. She's alone, though, so I sit up and spy as she hovers at the edge of her driveway and stares up at the sky. Eventually, she runs the back of her palm over her eyes and slumps her shoulders, heading inside. She leaves her back door slightly ajar, and I'm both curious and cautious. The longer she's inside and the door remains open, the more jacked up my nerves become. I can't let her go to bed with her door beckoning some intruder. I'll have to close it, which puts me way too close to that house. Again.

I'm reaching for my door handle when June suddenly appears from the house. I sink lower in my seat but look on as she shuffles toward the thick weeds and tall grass near the back of her driveway. That brush obscures her dad's old Buick. That relic is the only thing he left behind when he moved out.

The familiar creak of the car's door cuts through the quiet air, penetrating its way into the cab of my truck. The *clunk* of the door closing comes next. It's been awhile since I've seen June wander out there. She and I used that car like a play-house, and as we got older, we hid in there and watched scary movies on my phone. For a while after her dad left, she would sit in that car late at night. I caught her looking up at my window once, and I'm not sure whether that's why she quit hiding in there or the car just lost its luster. Tonight, though? The Buick called to her.

I pull one leg up and rest my arm on my knee, staring into

the darkness for any sign of movement. There's no glow from a phone, so she isn't in there texting Abby or reliving the night on social media. That sort of stuff isn't really June's style anyway. Not that I know *what* her style is anymore. My gut tells me some things haven't changed. She's still the type of girl who would rather spend the night on the fringe of a party than in the mix of things. But I never pegged her as one to drop the kind of words she did tonight. Maybe the June I remember has blurred into something else entirely. It would make sense, given what she's been through. I know how the last few years have changed me—how what our parents did changed me.

I feel trapped in this truck, and part of me wonders if she's sitting in the Buick staring right at me, waiting for me to make a move so she can rush out and pounce, blasting me with more insults. What was that bullshit about my story? *Pffft.* I've never been in control of my narrative. She knows that. Every line of my life is written by my dad's wishes. Any freedom I had was dashed by his mistakes. I'm the way I am because cold and callous doesn't require feeling. I wrote June out of my story because I wanted to keep my mom in it. And if she thinks that makes me an asshole, fine. I'm an asshole. She's an asshole, too.

After twenty minutes of stewing, I decide to put an end to this charade. I thought I'd been distant enough, unfriendly and unwelcoming. Now, I'm going to be mean and direct. I hop out of my truck and ease the door closed. She doesn't need to know I've been watching her this whole time. I cut my way through the brush, and by the time I'm four or five yards away, our eyes meet. My hand knows what to do, operating on memory as it tugs open the piece of shit passenger door, popping loudly when the spring catches. I get in, my weight kicking up a cloud of dust from the old seat.

"You didn't have to come check on me. I'll survive."
June's tone is coated with contempt. Unlike Ava, June doesn't
fish for affection. She lashes out. She and I are more alike
than she realizes.

I sigh as I slap my hands on my knees and curl my fingers,
clawing against the denim.

"I'm not here for you, June. I'm here to tell you—no, to
beg you—to please keep your nosy ass out of my life." There, I
did it. No mystery to solve with my request. There is no
secret, hidden message, no undercurrent that contradicts
what I'm asking.

I glance at June as her mouth falls open, and I can feel it
in my bones that she's going to argue with me. I can practically hear her response formulating in her head—*I didn't do
anything, Lucas. It was all Ava.* Still, she was there, at a party
I damn well *know* she didn't want to be at. She's inserting
herself into my life just to needle me with her presence. I
don't know whether she thinks it will wear me down or that
I'll suddenly cave and decide being friends with her is worth
sending my mom down a spiral again right before I leave for
college. But it needs to stop. This game between us . . . it's
done.

I shake my head, twisting in the seat, taking up space to
command this exchange. My palm covers the dash, more dirt
and debris puffing into the air.

"You judge—" I begin.

"No, I don't."

I groan inwardly as my eyes flutter shut in frustration. So
damn quick to argue with me. I pat down on the dash again,
laughing out hard.

"You do, and it's so . . . hypocritical. What I do with Ava,
whether she's my girlfriend, whether we break up, whomever

I decide to be with and however far that goes? None. Of. Your. Business."

I lean back and level her with an angry stare. My pulse is drumming, and I'm tempted to scream I'm so frustrated that I have to have this conversation right now. I hope like hell my mom isn't seeing this.

"You missed most of everything I said, Lucas. I wasn't talking about you. That rant—it was about me."

Bullshit. I hold her gaze hostage, unwilling to blink.

"I heard you. And you're right, every person you *fuck* becomes a part of your story."

June swallows hard as I throw her words back at her.

"But people write themselves into our stories lots of ways, June." I shake my head and look down at my lap. My fingertips draw lines in the dust as my hand falls from the dash. My throat burns. As hard as I try to close this door, it's still painful being this close to her. Memories of *us*—of my friend and the girl who made me laugh and do stupid things like make snow angels in the winter—break into my armor. I can't let them.

I push the door open, stopping just outside to lean down and level her with one final glare.

"We've never fucked, but you sure are part of my story. I can't delete you, but I sure don't need you taking up any more chapters. Stay the fuck out of my business, and go find yourself a boyfriend who can be all of these things you think are real."

I force out a quick laugh as my mouth ticks up on one side, then slam the door behind me. The urge to turn around and apologize is instant. That was easily the cruelest I've ever been, and I'm ashamed. I told myself it was necessary, but now that I'm on the other side of it all . . . I'm not so certain. Those are the worst words I have ever uttered, and I said them to the one person I used to consider the most important person in my life.

One foot in front of the other, that's my mantra all the way back to my house. One step after the other, until I'm upstairs. I drop the shade because if I don't, I'll spend the rest of the night trying to catch a glimpse of the girl I just broke into a thousand pieces inside a Buick. And then my heart will beg me to put her back together.

CHAPTER SEVEN

My mom is dragging my dad to church. She does this every few months, and he goes because he knows it makes her happy. I think she likes that everyone there doesn't know the history of their marriage over the last few years. They're this perfect couple, and she can play the professional married to a lawyer who is so busy—too busy to join her every Sunday.

I opt out every time. It's a few hours to myself at home, and it's blissful. Today's stint stretched into the evening, though. My parents were invited out to dinner, and they went. I spent the entire day going through old things in my closet and filling two trash bags with crap that doesn't fit. My dad probably wants to hang on to my old jerseys so he can make a shrine or some shit, but I'm not going to give him the chance. I might regret it, but for now it feels right to shed this old stuff, so I go with it.

My phone buzzes as I drop the stuffed bags into the back of my truck. I pull it out and answer without looking. It's Ava.

"Hey, I'm hungry and the girls are at Two-fers. Come pick me up?"

I stop at my door with one foot inside and pinch the bridge of my nose. My stomach rumbles.

"Yeah, I guess I'm hungry." *You should make a sandwich at home, Lucas. You know you're giving in to her trick. She wants to spend time with you, and you're weak. You feel guilty because you were mean to June. Now you want to cover it up with an Ava-shaped Band-Aid, you fucking loser.*

"Awesome. See you in five." She hangs up before I can back out, not that I would. My conscience puts up a pathetic fight. Besides, it would be nice to be gone by the time my parents do get home, stretch this day of bliss out as long as I can.

I hop in my truck and peel down our street, slowing when I see the twins' car heading my direction. It's Tory, probably on his way to my place. We stop next to each other and roll down our windows.

"Hey, Tor. What's up?" My body is jumpy. I'm literally sneaking out to see a girl I don't want to and if Tory asks, he'll give me shit about it.

"Just . . . out." He shrugs and puckers his lips into his signature smirk. He's up to something.

"I'm headed to Goodwill, dropping off some donations." I tilt my head toward the back, as if I need to show him visual proof. He glances toward the bed of the truck and nods.

"Ah." His smirk lingers.

"You need something?" My eyes squint in consideration, part of my top-notch acting job.

"Nah. I'm good." His answer is quick, and it digs at me a little, my face morphing into a questioning expression with an eyebrow up, head cocked.

"Thought I'd see what June's up to. Maybe ask about working at the bowling alley with her." *And there it is.*

"Oh, yeah? That's a good idea." I force a tight-lipped smile on my face in follow-up, and Tory does the same. Eventually, a laugh slips out his mouth.

"You going out with Ava?" He lifts a brow, so damn proud he caught me.

I shrug.

"I dunno. Maybe. She mentioned something about grabbing dinner at Two-fers with some of her friends. I'm pretty hungry." *Or I was hungry until I ran into Tory and he dropped June's name.*

"Oh, yeah? Maybe I'll swing by. You know . . . after." He looks toward the Mabee house, and I know that mind of his is scheming. I wish he'd drop this fascination with me and June. If he's truly into her, then he should ask her out and they can date. It's fine. Whatever.

"Yeah, well, I should get going." I give him a nod and he reciprocates as we pull away from each other. I leave my window down so the rush of air can hit my face in an attempt to wash away the deep wrinkle I feel between my eyes. I get that line when I'm pissed or anxious. The last thing I need is Ava asking about it, offering to give me a head rub.

My pulse feels less like a death metal drummer living in my chest by the time I pull up to the Goodwill. I toss my bags into the donation bin and head to Ava's house. She's on her phone when I pull up to the curb and she keeps talking to whomever is on the other line as she gets into the truck. I do my best to ignore her conversation, something about dress shopping for the winter formal that's not for a few weeks. She ends her call just as we pull into Two-fers and unbuckles her belt so she can slide closer to me. My arms stiffen, and she huffs audibly.

"This place is really going downhill," she announces, crossing her arms over her chest.

At first, I assume it's some petty reaction to my cold shoulder, but I get what she means the second I look to my left and see Tory's car pulling through the end of the drive-thru lane, June in the passenger seat. *That motherfucker.*

I park near Ava's friends, and thankfully, she gets out of the truck and starts gabbing before she realizes Tory and June stuck around. I'm sure it's no coincidence that he's here with her, after I dropped the info about where I was going. I'm also certain he parked where he did—fifty feet away and staring right at us—on purpose.

I slip out of the truck and glance their direction, glad they aren't looking my way. I stop at the bumper and pat my hand on the hood, getting Ava's attention.

"What do you want?"

She bunches her face as if she's going to get anything other than a chicken wrap and a water. It takes her about five seconds to answer—"chicken wrap and a water."

"Right," I say, turning and laughing quietly at the predictability.

I dash to the walk-up window and place our order, leaning against the wall while I wait. I pull my phone out and drop a text to Tory.

ME: *Classy move, bro.*

I wait a few seconds for him to write back, but he doesn't. He probably won't in front of June. I push my phone into my back pocket when my name is called and grab our bag of food before jogging back to my truck.

I hand Ava her food and she sets it on the passenger seat so she can keep talking about whatever the latest rumor is to travel through her circle of friends. I'm not fully engaged, but I hear someone cheated on someone else, and it sounds as if they're blaming it on the new guy, Cannon. I lean toward the window to get Ava's attention.

"Hey, don't do that." I shake my head, chastising her.

She holds up two open palms.

"What?"

"You know what." My chest deflates. This is the reason I could never fall for her. She's too focused on drama—making it, spreading it, turning it into a forest fire of bullying. "Cannon's a good guy. He just got here, and he's here for baseball and that's it. Don't rope him into your web of immature bullshit." I circle my finger in the air for affect, which earns me a harsh glare.

"You're in a mood," she huffs back, glancing down at her food and drink. She grabs it and makes brief eye contact with me before turning her attention back to her friends. If she wasn't here, they'd be talking about her right now, because that's the sad reality of it. That's who they are.

She's part of your story now. That . . . that is what you are.

June's words haven't left my mind for two days. She was trying to hurt me back, and I know that, but she was also on point. *Who am I? Am I the guy who sits in this parking lot talking shit about people who aren't here to defend themselves?* I glance around, pods of people all doing the same thing Ava and her friends are. Then I shift my gaze back to Tory's car, where he and June are laughing. She punches his arm lightly, which she used to do to me. I rub my bicep instinctually just before catching Tory leaning toward her with what looks like a packet of ketchup.

"You don't put ketchup on hot dogs, you asshole," I mutter to myself. My lip curls into a familiar grin on one side the moment June pushes his hand—and the offending ketchup—away. She and I once spent an entire summer watching Dirty Harry movies, and our big takeaway was that

Clint Eastwood hates ketchup on hot dogs. It was our inside joke every time we went to Two-fers.

Laughter booms from outside my side window, catching my attention. Ava and her friends have noticed June, a few of them craning their necks, no doubt making up stories about her hooking up with Tory. She wouldn't give him the time of day like that. And he wouldn't cross that line. At least, I don't think.

I look back to the car, to the lightness in their movements, the way June picks up her soda and sucks at the straw through a smile. I'm a voyeur, and my stomach twists inside itself. I shouldn't care about any of this, but I can't stop indulging in looks inside that car. I want to know what they're saying. I want to know how Tory got her to come here, whether he said I would be here or if he tricked her, as I assume he did.

I pick at my fries, watching the scene before me like a guy alone at a drive-in movie, munching on my snacks and watching the slow, unwinding plot that's narrated by thoughts in my head. *Would I be okay if Tory dated June?* I said I would be—to him, to myself. I really don't think I would.

I'm caught in this inner debate when movement catches my eyes and breaks my stare into nothingness. I'm instantly drawn inside Tory's moving car as he slowly pulls out, and June glances up from her lap in time for our eyes meet. It's brief. No light glares glinting off the windshield or cars driving between us to break the connection or distract us. Everything gets undeniably slow, but it's only that way for the two of us. Her lips part, and even though there's no way I possibly can hear her, I swear I do. There's a gasp. It's painful, filled with our youth, our past, our friendship, and that constant *what if* that was there between us. It's changed. It's become a *why*.

Why are we so broken?

I follow her profile when she turns away, and I watch Tory's taillights fade in the distance. Fighting the urge to dump the rest of my food and ditch Ava so I can follow them home, I pull out my phone to see if my friend has texted me back. His answer is short, and the last thing I need to consider.

TORY: *Jealous?*

CHAPTER EIGHT

I rolled up to school late this morning, leaving myself barely enough time to slip into class. I'm sure Tory spent the morning congratulating himself on making me jealous or admit to feelings for June, thinking that's why I was late. I wish it was. As loathe as I am to deal with that emotional baggage, it would be a million times easier than the shit pile my dad threw on my lap this morning.

"This is Jon Foster, from Tennessee."

I was barely awake when I ambled down the stairs into our kitchen. Apparently, Jon Foster met my dad during their dinner. He's friends of a friend from the church my dad has no honest interest in attending. Never one to miss a chance to network, Todd Fuller was at his very best last night and managed to lure the new head of recruiting for his alma mater over to our house for breakfast. My dad wasn't a stud in his day, which is half the reason he put the effort into making me good. But he was good enough to get a back-up gig at Tennessee, and still be a name people recognize, though they aren't totally sure why.

"Now, this isn't an official visit, you understand, Lucas?" Jon Foster winked as he shook my hand and spoke those words. Of course I understand. This is how my dad has brokered half of these meetings. They've all turned into offers, so it's not that he doesn't know the game. It's that I don't want to participate. He's bringing these people to our home under false pretenses. They're getting sold a bill of goods—*me*. I will never be the player they think they'll get if I commit to their school. My heart isn't in it.

I sat through breakfast and nodded when it seemed I should. My dad did most of the talking, as is the norm, and I managed to skip out of there with mere minutes left to get to school. Dad was ready to call me in sick. Mom ignored the entire situation, gathering her things to head out for work, a scowl on her face because my father was gushing over some stranger he just met more than he ever has for her.

I guess if there's a bonus to any of this, it is that my rushed morning left me zero time to interact with June. Other than the staring contest in the Two-fers parking lot, we haven't made eye contact once since I said those things to her in the Buick. As soon as the guilt begins to ebb, something happens and it comes roaring back to my belly. It creeps up in the weirdest ways, too. Like when I spotted the bottle of ketchup in our refrigerator this morning during breakfast.

"Lucas, I need to see you after class for some recommendations I was asked to submit," our teacher says as I take my seat.

"Sure. Thanks," I answer. My eyes train on June's neck and the small swirls of hair that curl at the base. She doesn't flinch at my voice and I fight the urge to taunt her.

Jealous?

Tory's text hit me square in the face again this morning. I was flipping through my phone, trying to stem my anxiety while my dad talked me up to the rep from one of the country's top colleges. I'm man enough to admit to myself that I am jealous of Tory and June's relationship. I envy him for being able to talk to her so easily, to laugh with her. I bet she gives him great advice. I'm sure she's making him a better person—*not hard, since he's a total douchebag.* Jealous romantically? I didn't think so, yet here I am, wanting to pull her braids and doodle a smiley face on her neck, like a fourth grader with a stupid crush.

I slouch into my seat and set my focus on the front of the classroom. I'm not really listening, but I manage to copy down the notes on the screen. I pick up the sealed envelope from my teacher when she dismisses us. It's not until I'm out the door that I read it and realize it's made out to MIT with room for me to fill in the admissions address.

I stop mid-stride and peel off to the quad, taking a seat atop one of the picnic tables. Holding the envelope up, I study it closely to see what words I can make out. At least four of my teachers had to fill out this form, answering questions about my academic record and character. *My character.* They hold my future in their hands—in this envelope. I could rip it open and read what they wrote, beg Maggie for a new stamped envelope with the school logo and type up the address at home. But what would that say about my character?

My character.

That temptation is quickly dashed as I glance over my shoulder and catch a glimpse of June opening the door to the media center. That's fate telling me to put the envelope away and let it be whatever it will. I've already used up my questionable character free pass with this girl.

I zip my personal Hail Mary for my future into my backpack and sling the strap over my shoulder. That's when my gaze comes square with my father's. He's here. On campus. With his new friend.

I breathe in deeply and try not to let my true feelings make their way into my expression as I stride across the quad toward him.

"Hey, pal." My father reaches out a hand to shake and then pats me on the back with the other. He has never done this. *We* have never done this. It's a performance, and I'm going along with it. I hate myself a little.

"Jon wanted to check out the school, talk with Coach. Ya know." Dad nods and winks, his signal that another offer—his favorite yet—is in the bag.

"Great!" I beam, my smile aching where it presses into my cheeks. I reach an arm around to press my palm on my dad's back. If I look as though I'm playing the part, he's less likely to rope me into lunch or something. "I'm sorry I have to run. I have a lab to finish for chemistry. I look forward to seeing you out there today."

I point toward my dad's new temporary best friend and smile as I skip backward. When I turn my back, I hear my dad mention something about my academic work ethic. I should feel proud, but honestly? I hate that the only reason he brags about my brains is because he thinks it will give me an edge in football recruiting.

I lied about the lab. I finished my work last week, which *thank God!* I spend the rest of the hour sitting on my stool by my clean work station while I research various techniques for seeing through envelopes on my phone. To keep myself from dwelling on the envelope for the rest of the day—and from doing something stupid with it—I jet home during lunch and fill out the address, pop on a stamp from my mom's desk drawer, and drop the documents in the postal box on my way back to school.

The act takes away my temptation, but it does little to stop me from thinking about my future and MIT. In fact, the second I mail that last piece of admissions content off, my brain goes into overdrive with panic. I'm not sure which has me freaked out more—failing and not getting into the special program or getting the call that I'm in and having to make a choice.

I obsess over that quandary through my last two hours of the day. Usually, in a situation like this, I would race to practice, ready to take snaps and sweat out half my body weight. The one thing practice is good for is letting me clear my mind. But my dad made sure that wasn't possible today. Coach Loma is in his office with Jon Foster as I walk into the locker room. A few of the guys recognize him. He's wearing a subtle Tennessee polo shirt, and that name carries serious weight in this room.

"Dude, you see that?" Tory elbows me while he stands on the other side of the bench, bare-ass naked.

"I'd rather not," I joke.

"Ha! Funny," he deadpans.

He steps over the bench, pulling his practice gear out to get dressed. He doesn't press me again about the meeting happening a dozen feet away until Jon Foster leaves Coach's office.

"Are you seriously going to pretend you know nothing about that?" Tory's sitting now, straddling the bench and facing me while I suit up.

I drop my arms as soon as my pads are on and let my eyes stare at the back of my locker. I blink a few times and chew at the inside of my mouth.

"You know I wish I could be like you, right?" I say, turning to face my friend, whose face is screwed up and confused.

"You mean *so good looking?*"

I snort out a laugh. I needed that.

"No, man. I mean . . . I wish I wanted this. Like you with basketball. That's your passion." I glance toward Coach's office. He's on the phone with someone, but our eyes meet and he shoots me a crooked grin. I know he's excited about this visit.

"I knew what you meant. But seriously? You are like me, only in your way," Tory says, standing and slamming his locker door shut. He backs up a few steps, giving me room to lace my cleats.

"I am?" I'm not so sure about that. It would be so much easier to take what's being offered.

"Dude, you want to use your brain the way I want to break ankles on the hardwood and dunk on power forwards who are too slow. You have the same level of passion. You just happen to be good at two things. Guess I'm lucky I'm only good at one. Oh, I mean, I'm also an amazing lover, so there's that."

"*Pshhh*, fuck off!" I smack his chest as I stand.

Tory's words do their job somehow, and I jog out to the field with a clearer head. I guess it doesn't hurt to entertain these football scouts as a backup, in the event those forms I mailed today have nothing good to say about my character. If my dream comes in, though, I'm going to need another pep talk. I'll need to grow some balls for when Brainy Lucas lets down everyone rooting for Football Lucas.

CHAPTER NINE

I f I didn't see her every morning in our shared class, I would start to wonder if June transferred out. Other than our forced contact, she's nonexistent in my world. It's exactly what I wanted—for her to leave me alone.

I hate it.

It's sick, but I think I miss the push and pull. I fought against myself all week to not do *something* in class. I flirted with the fantasy of attaching a paperclip to the end of her braid just so she'd get pissed at me. I also thought about showing off my test grade, since I aced it and saw over her shoulder that she got a B. And when I passed her in the office after school yesterday, I noticed that her shoe was untied. I was going to offer to tie it for her and then leave it in knots. Why I have to be such a childish bully in every scenario, I haven't a clue. But I know it has to do with missing that feeling I get when she and I are arguing, even if it's only giving each other a heated glare.

Everything about this week has me feeling off. My dad and Jon Foster, the mountain of offers I don't want, the pending deadline for hearing back on next steps for MIT. It's all too much, and I can tell it showed in the first half of tonight's game. We're up fourteen to seven at the half, but it should be double that. We're the better team.

"Coach is going to unload. Brace yourself," Tory jokes, spraying water from the sport bottle into his mouth as he sits next to me on the bench, the rest of the team filing into the locker room behind him.

"I'm playing like shit," I admit.

"*Pfff*, whatever. I'm the one who dropped your pass in the end zone."

"'Cause I threw it too high."

Tory's letting me off the hook, but I don't need him taking the fall for me. I'm letting our team down because my head is a mess. It's not fair. This game means something to a lot of the guys in this room. For them, their performance is the ticket to their dream. I can't half-ass things because I'm not feeling inspired or whatever. I'm letting the team down.

Coach storms through the door last, his assistants all lined up at the front of the room, their heads down as they wait for his volume. I tether my hands and press my thumbs together, ready to get reamed.

"D'Angelo!"

"Yes, Coach." Tory is the pillar of respect next to me.

"Check your hands, son. That was some sloppy-ass work out there. You need to wash the butter off?"

"No, sir." His response is quick, emotionless, exactly as it should be.

Coach grunts and turns his posture to face me directly. I look up to meet his hard stare.

"Fuller, nice work out there. Let's see if this O-line can get you more than a second to get a pass off next half."

And that's it. That's my ass-chewing. Tory got blamed for

my shitty pass and he took it. The offensive line gets ripped apart for my lazy footwork. Meanwhile, I get an *atta boy*.

Coach spends five minutes yelling platitudes about how we "just don't seem to want it bad enough" and "we're the better team, and now's the time to prove it." It's all meaningless bullshit, but everyone around me seems oddly inspired. Coach leaves the locker room, and me and the rest of the seniors start to shout, hyping everyone to their feet as we stomp and clap and grunt until we're transformed into wild, rabid beasts. We fly out of the locker room and tear up the field with our aggression for another twenty-four minutes of play.

The third and fourth quarters pass like a dream, my body working on rote, my passes meeting hands in the right places while I somehow manage not to get flattened into the sod more than once. My head rings from the hit, but nothing I haven't handled before. That bullshit and hype session did its job on me too, even though the entire time, the voice in the back of my head is telling me I'm weak and not good enough.

The buzzer sounds, and it's maybe the best game of my life, but I feel like a total failure. It's because despite being great for my team, I'm letting myself down every day I don't tell my dad the truth about what I want. I'm a faker. A scared little boy.

"Yo, you may not like this game, but it fucking loves you, Fuller!" Tory leaps on my back and slaps my shoulder while I carry him across the field for our celebration. I clutch his knees and jog, trying to find my spirit. If I let myself, I'll break into tears right now. The feeling is that heavy, like a wet blanket over my shoulders and head. I can't give in to this sense of doom. I have to fight it until I can be brave enough to do what I want.

"Yeah!" I shout, forcing my body's chemistry to shift. My

face contorts and I pound my chest as my friend slides from my back. I let myself go complete Neanderthal, my nostrils flaring as I pace the forty-yard line and bump chests with my teammates. The knot in my stomach eases, replaced by the familiar ease of competition and victory. I allow myself to eat up the compliments, to accept the "good games" and praise. I shake Jon Foster's hand as he steps to the sideline, and I smile when he tells me he'll "be in touch." I smile, though his offer is not the one I'm waiting for. I smile so my father sees it on my face, and I leave it there until I believe it to be true.

Families spill onto the field, dads high-fiving their sons, moms hugging them with pride. I blink around the scene and my focus goes to the one place I know I'll find my dad. Still standing, still analyzing, he's perched in the center of the stands, about a dozen rows up, his view unobstructed. The world around him is abuzz in celebration over this game that I play to make him happy, so he'll keep making Mom happy, and he's still disappointed. I see it on his face, in his mannerisms. His body is closed off, brow heavy and lost in thought. He's replaying that first half and wondering how he can rid me of bad performances like that in the future. He's rehearsing what he'll say about my game play to anyone who asks. He's making excuses that he will drill into my head until I believe them to be true. My mom is sitting, clutching her purse, ready to go home and pretend their marriage is good.

Rather than put myself through anything else tonight, I turn and throw an arm over Tory as we make our way to the locker room. They drove themselves here. They can drive home without talking to me first.

The buzz of pretending manages to last until almost everyone's cleared out, but by the time it's only Tory and me, my body can't fake it anymore. I drop my bag at my feet and fling my locker door shut so hard it bounces back open.

"Whoa, hostile much?" Tory chuckles as he reaches over and gently shuts the door. I flop down on the bench, elbows on my knees and head in my hands.

"I don't know, man. I'm sorry. I'm just so . . . so sick of it."

Tory props a foot on the bench next to me and places his hand on my back.

"I hear ya. This winning shit is so not my style." He doesn't laugh at his own joke, but I shake once under his touch to let him know I was amused. He didn't say it to be funny. He said it to point out how dramatic I'm being.

"Talk to your dad."

I shake with another laugh.

"I'm serious. Can I be real with you?"

I lift my eyes, not sure what expression I'll see on my friend's face. I'm not sure I'm relieved to see his mouth set in the hard line and his eyes serious, almost heavy. I breathe in through my nose and turn to face him as he straddles the bench about a foot away.

"You spend a lot of time making sure your parents are happy, and I know—" He holds up his hand before I can protest. He knows me so well he senses my knee-jerk need to defend my mom and keep her life intact. "I get it with your mom. I do, and I think you're a pretty awesome person for putting her first. But maybe, Lucas . . . she would love to see you put yourself first. Your dad might not get it right away, but your mom will. MIT? That shit's for *real!* Like, she would get to tell her friends her son's a rocket scientist and shit."

"I'd be on the engineering side, actually, focusing more on—"

He waves both hands in front of me, stopping me cold.

"I won't know half the shit you're about to say, and frankly, I don't care. You're smart. You'll do smart shit. Cool. I'm just saying your mom will be proud, and your dad will get over it. Think about it, at least. Because you cannot keep beating yourself up like this, and if you give in and do what your dad expects, you're going to resent the hell out of him—and maybe yourself a bit too."

I blink, stunned at the wisdom that just spilled from the mouth of this guy I've seen drink beer out of an actual bullet hole.

He leans forward and ruffles my hair like I'm a kid then stands and tugs his bag up his shoulder.

"And for fuck's sake, call June."

I grimace and he laughs, sticking out his tongue and pointing at me. He had to add that last little bit in there. We haven't talked about the whole drive-in debacle at Two-fers and the fact he drove her there just to goad me into feeling something.

"Party's on at our house, by the way. See you there?"

I nod, but I'm not sure I'm in the mood to party. I don't want to rush home either, so I end up gathering my things and climbing in my truck, listening to the low hum of the motor while I replay Tory's speech over and over in my head.

I'm putting off the inevitable. I'm going to get in to MIT. It's my destiny. I want it, too, so badly. Leaning forward, I turn on my stereo, tuning in the local pop station. It sounds like every high school dance I've been to, so I flip stations until I land on the local sports show. High school football is big out here, and in the case of Allensville and the dozen other county schools that make up our region, it's the second most popular talk sports topic, just behind Pacers basketball.

"Now, what did you think about the way Lucas Fuller lead his Fighting Eagles into that second half tonight?"

I lower the volume down before I can hear the response. My phone has already buzzed with a stream of messages from my dad. I haven't bothered to open them because the preview on my screen was enough to ward me off. It's his notes from the game. The radio guys are probably praising me while my dad's stream of text messages is ripping me apart. In reality, my performance was probably somewhere right in the middle of their assessments—perfectly average. I did the job.

I lean forward, feeling the weight cascade over my shoulders again, the claws of anxiety gripping my neck, squeezing. I draw in a breath just as my forehead hits the steering wheel. Right now, I would give anything to be able to talk to June. But she's leaving me alone, just as I asked her to.

CHAPTER TEN

I knew there was a chance June would be working. I told Tory I'd join him and the guys for bowling anyway, and so far, he has loved every minute of it.

"She's right there," he says, leaning into me while we lace up our shoes.

"Yep." I don't bother to look up. I won't give him the satisfaction of seeing me react. Besides, I spotted her as soon as she ducked into the back side of the lanes. She's probably back there hiding from me, and I'm fine with that.

"You really are something. Like a rock. Stoic." He chuckles as he slides his regular shoes under the seat and gets up to search for a ball.

Yeah, that's me. One big stoic rock.

I draw in a breath and let my hands fall to my knees before getting up and searching for a heavy ball. I don't bowl very well, so I like to sling the added weight in hopes the increased velocity helps the ball take out a few extra pins.

"You wanna go first?" Tory asks me as he drops his ball on the return and slides into one of the seats by the scoring computer. I nod *sure* and grab the only fourteen-pound ball I can find. I allow myself a quick glance toward the pins on my way to the return, and catch June's reflection in the ceiling mirror. She isn't working back there. She isn't doing *anything*, besides hiding.

"So are you depressed or just trying out the grunge look?" Tory pulls on one of the strings of my hoodie, cinching up the hole around my face.

"Ass hat," I say, stretching the hood back out. "I'm cold. And my hair's nuts this morning. I kind of rushed out of the house to avoid a session of football 101 with my dad."

Tory grimaces and drops his jokes about my lazy attire. I'm definitely not feeling myself lately. And maybe he's not wrong to mention depression. I wouldn't say I'm feeling low the way my mom does sometimes, but I'm definitely not feeling *up*. I'm sorting out a lot in my head lately, and my body is finally feeling the repercussions.

"Hey, Lucas. Great game last night. On the house." Morty, June's boss, slides a hot pizza on a nearby table, along with a stack of cups and a pitcher of beer.

"Thanks, Mort," I say, holding up a hand in appreciation.

"I sure do love how the people around here idolize you," Tory teases as he pats my shoulder and stands to pour himself a beer. I laugh along with him, but that adoration is part of the problem. If I don't go on and do something big in football, I won't only let my dad down, but I'll be disappointing people like Morty, too. That guilt doesn't stop me from snagging a slice of pizza, though.

Tory and I finish setting up the scoring system while Tory's twin, Hayden, and our friend Kade dig in and pour beers of their own. I opt for water.

"You think she knows we can all see her?"

Tory's asking about June. I shrug.

"I'm gonna tell her." He pulls out his phone and on instinct I reach out to stop him. The second my hand touches his wrist he freezes, and that know-it-all smirk rears its ugly head.

"Oh ho ho!" He leans back, pulling his phone close to his chest as if he needs to protect it from me. "Someone doesn't want me to get June Mabee's attention."

"That's not it at all, Tor. She's back there because she's trying to avoid us."

"You. She's trying to avoid *you*. June and *me*? We're tight. You're the one she has a problem with."

"*Pshh.*" I roll my eyes. "Whatever. Fine, tell her we can see her. Have at it."

"I will," he says, defiant, like he's ten and about to win a game of Sorry.

I do my best to ignore his back-and-forth texting, but when he howls in laughter I glare at him and he nods his head toward June, urging all of us to look. I stand when my friend does, and my eyes find June's panicked face on the other end of the lane. *Poor thing was just trying to get through her shift. Nice, Tory. Real nice.*

"I'm inviting her over. This is ridiculous," he says.

I wave a hand, knowing he's going to do whatever he wants anyhow, which he does.

I hover around the ball return, holding my open palm over the fan while Tory stands on one of the seats and cups his mouth, as if he needs any assistance in being loud.

"Maybe Mabee would like to come say hi to her friends?"

I cringe and glance with side eyes, almost certain I see June's shoulders scrunch up with embarrassment. My eyes fall back to the ball return, and I push my ball around a little to find the thumb hole.

"Oh, shit!" Tory's unnerved tone spikes my adrenaline,

and I look up in time to see June's legs fly out from under her body, which cascades through the air, her head on a perfect path for impact with the corner of the gutter.

Fuck, she's hurt!

"June!" Her name flies from my lips out of habit and need. She hit her head—hard—and my heart thunders in response.

I sprint down the lane, my feet sliding along the slick floor the entire way until I'm at June's side. Her eyes are rolling, her pupils wide. This isn't good.

She's gasping for air. She probably got the wind knocked out of her on impact. I push her disheveled hair from her face and brace her head between my hands. She's squirming.

"June, careful. Don't move."

Her eyes search wildly and I hold her still, forcing her to focus on me. Her pupils have shrunk, which is a relief, but she's hell bent on moving. She starts to roll to her side and I decide I need to get her off this floor.

"You can't carry her on that. You'll slip, too!" Morty's worried about a lawsuit, so I shoot him a glare and do as I damn well please.

I scoop June into my arms, her body rolling into my chest as I lift her and fight to steady my feet. She wraps her arm around my shoulder, her fingers gripping my hoodie. I'm glad she has the strength and coordination to do that. It's a good sign. Her eyes flutter closed as she tucks her face against me, so I adjust my hold to grip her tighter against me. This floor is no joke. How I sprinted across it a second ago beats me.

"I can walk," she croaks.

"*Shhh*," I hush, laughing slightly. Still stubborn June, after all this time.

My right foot slides out about a foot so I bend my knees and stop. June clutches me.

"This shit is slippery," I say to my friends. They're about a dozen steps away, all standing with their legs spread, knees bent and arms out as if they are in any position to catch me or June if I tumble.

I cut my step length in half, sliding my feet as if I'm on ice. I've got this. I'm decent on a hockey rink.

"Almost there," I say, tucking my chin.

I take a gamble and lunge forward when I see unwaxed floor ahead. June flinches in my arms, and I check her face the second my legs are steady. Our eyes lock, and my insides rush with this overwhelming sense that I need to take care of this girl. My arms feel numb, and it's not because June is heavy. Hell, I lift things twice her size for a workout. No, this is more like a morphine drip. I'm a little sick from the feeling, but it lingers in my body, slapping me around on the insides.

"Tory, someone needs to drive her home, man. Get your car."

I kneel and set June on one of the nearby seats. I try to stand but June's hand grasps at my sweatshirt and her eyes flash wide. I'm not sure if she's feeling sick or uneasy or what, but I react with the same instincts I have for the last two minutes—as if she is mine, and I'm the only one in the world who can take care of her.

I crouch again and leave a hand on her shoulder, near the base of her neck. She clutches my arm as if she's holding on to find her center. She's definitely concussed.

"She's your neighbor, Lucas. Get over yourself and drive her home," Tory says.

I jerk my head in his direction and meet his stare. Driving June home is a bad idea. My mom should be home soon, and the odds of her seeing me with June in my truck are pretty high. The thought of putting her in a car with Tory, though, who has already finished his beer, or Hayden or Kade, who frankly aren't that far behind him on finishing theirs, feels daftly irresponsible.

My attention slips, as does my hold on June, and she drops to the floor, palms spread wide. She pukes a little on her shirt on her way down. Tory's right—I need to take her home. I toss Tory my keys and he takes off for the door to bring my truck around. Some dude who works with June, meanwhile, starts mopping up her mess right next to us. I grunt at him and he pauses while I scoop June up and hoist her against my chest. The smell of Pine Sol is potent, and I'm half tempted to vomit from it. I can't imagine it's helping June in her state.

I push through the doors and Tory pulls my truck along the curb, shifting in park and racing around to the passenger side to help me load June inside. She grabs at the metal parts of the seat belt the moment I set her down, banging the pieces together as if they're magnets. I cover her hands with mine and her head pops up, eyes wide.

"You're not even close."

She lets go of the buckles and I finish the job, securing her in her seat. I shut the door and race to the driver's side.

"Text me and let me know how she is," Tory says as I pass him.

"Will do," I respond.

I pull away the moment my door is shut, buckling on our way out of the parking lot. June moans at my side, her body weight resting on the door and her head braced between the seat and the window. She's going to bump her head more if she stays like that. I keep one eye on her and one on the road, slowing when I notice potholes or dips. The railroad crossing is coming up, though, and there's not much I can do to avoid those.

"Hey, the tracks are coming up. I'll try to take them slow, but you might wanna pull your head from the window."

She straightens her body and I drop my speed to a crawl, doing my best to avoid any jerks or jolts. The rocking motion seems to make her sick again, though, because she moans and brings her forearm to her mouth as if that will hold everything in.

"I think we need to get you looked at."

I reach for her shoulder to help her sit upright as she falls toward the window again. Her head wobbles and rolls to the side and she blinks at me with sleepy eyes. I stop at the intersection closest to where we live and I meet her gaze. She looks high, and terrified. I can't leave her like this.

"You wait in the truck. I'll run in and get your mom," I say, slowly pulling through the intersection. Her hands peel away from her thighs and flatten against her forehead.

"She's not home," she says.

Fuck.

"Okay, well, I need your phone, then, so I can call her."

She reaches around her body, feeling for her phone. Her dexterity is a mess and she ends up flinging it to the floor.

"I'm so sorry," she croaks. Her voice teeters on a sob, and she leans forward to retrieve her phone. I touch her shoulder, stopping her as I pull to the side of the road. I scoot to the middle of the seat and bend down until I'm practically laying in her lap as I feel for the phone. Grasping it, I sit up and move back to my seat. I tap the screen to bring up her keypad and type in her birthday and her mom's—04080901. The device comes to life and I press her mom's contact info. June is staring at me with her mouth wide open and I realize that I basically just hacked her phone, like I'm a Jedi. Or a former best friend. *Her person.*

"Your birthday and your mom's, same as the

garage." I blink once as if it isn't a big deal that I remember any of that. She hangs on, though, her stare lingering, and eventually I drop my focus to my lap because the discomfort in my chest is becoming unbearable.

Her mom answers after three rings.

"Mrs. Mabee, it's Lucas. Fuller."

"Lucas . . . *Lucas!* Oh, my God, is everything okay? Is the house on fire?"

"It's all right, but June slipped at work. I was there with some of the guys, and I didn't want her driving." She gasps, and I sense it's part worry and a dash of relief.

"Thank you."

"Yeah, of course." I lean forward and sort through my thoughts, my head falling to my fist, which is wedged against my steering wheel. I know what I *should* do. I also know what I *want* to do, and that's help June. I want to be that guy who has character. I want to be her friend, and do the right thing. But my mom is going to make this into something it isn't, and then it's going to stir up old memories and rip open closed subjects.

"I can maybe get home in an hour. I'm pretty far, at the market on the north side, and I'm not sure how traffic is right now, but . . . would you mind waiting with her?"

June groans, and her head falls forward a little. She's nodding off.

"Sure, I can wait here. I kinda think she needs to go to the ER though?" *Shit, I'm really doing this.*

I roll my head to the side and eye June. I think she's trying to smile at me, but she also looks as if she's about to be sick.

"Did she vomit?"

"Yeah, she threw up once," I answer. I study her, looking for more signs of trauma. Her symptoms seem like a typical concussion, but I'm basing that off of shit I learned at football camp.

"Do you think you could take her? I can call in the insurance and maybe get there to relieve you if it takes too long?"

I blink a few times, anticipating that sinking feeling that's plagued my chest ever since June showed back up at our school. It doesn't come.

"I can do that. Yes."

"You're sure? It's not too much?" Her mom's voice is shaky, apologetic and vibrating with nerves.

"No, not a problem."

I shift the truck into drive and check the rearview mirror.

"Thank you, Lucas. We're both so grateful."

I swallow hard because her tone is earnest. She's not lying, and I wonder how someone could appreciate someone else on the other end of what our families have gone through.

"I will call you the second we're there," I say.

I end the call and slip June's phone into the nook near my stereo. I make a wide U-turn and check June as soon as I straighten the truck out.

"Your mom said she's at the market or something? Is she like a cashier?" I didn't realize she was working at a grocery store. I wonder if she has multiple jobs or maybe they're in debt.

"What? No, umm," June stammers. She brings a hand to her face, her fingertips on a hunt for an injury or swelling. The bruising is starting to make itself known. *I've been there, June.*

"She sells her photography. She's shooting on her own now, and it's a farmer's market up north. Good for business."

I nod, my gut tensing again with those pesky guilt pangs. Of course her mom is capable of running her own business. She's always been an incredible photographer. Before things turned sour between our families, she was going to take our family portrait when I turned sixteen, and I always kind of thought she'd do my senior photos.

"Am I going to die?"

June's question, uttered in the most pathetically frail voice, comes out of left field. I can't help the laugh that flies from my body. I flash my gaze to her, expecting to see her face break character. She has to be joking. I see quickly, thanks to the small worry line between her brows, that she is not.

"No, June," I assure her. I turn my attention back to the road, but give in to the need to care for her as I reach over and pat her knee.

Her phone rings and we both reach for it, our hands brushing. She slaps mine away.

"You're driving," she scolds.

I recoil and chuckle.

"Yeah, well, you thought you were dying so I thought I should maybe answer."

She grimaces at me, and normally she would follow that up with a playful punch in the arm. I don't get one, and I'm not sure whether it's because her head is jacked up or because I don't rate play-punch level anymore.

Her hands cradle her phone as she answers and puts her mom on speaker.

"Mom?"

"June? It's gonna be fine. We just want to make sure it's only a concussion, okay? Lucas? Are you there?"

I clear my throat and correct my posture, making sure my hands are at ten and two on the wheel, as if she can see me.

"Yes, ma'am."

"I called the advanced urgent care on Seventy-Fifth. She's on the waiting list so hopefully you can walk right in and get through. They have my card and insurance on file. If you don't mind taking her home after? I would never make it there in time."

Home. I mean, I figured I would need to bring us both home . . . together. My mom will be home by then. My chest tightens.

"Got it. I'll make sure I call you when we get out of the doc," I say, switching lanes to turn on Seventy-Fifth.

"Thanks," June's mom says.

I smile, something deep in my soul soothed by her gratitude. What a simple thing I'm doing. Anyone would do this. But *I'm* the one doing it, and it feels . . . nice.

"I'm a little freaked out," June says in a soft voice.

I start to answer, but when I glance her way I realize she's taken her mom off speaker and is talking to her one-on-one. Her eyes are drawn in, brows wrinkled, knee bobbing up and down. She shouldn't be fidgeting. Without pause, I reach toward her and take her hand in mine. I hold on tight.

The urgent care wait is, as predicted, a nightmare. Even with the call-ahead reservation, June and I are stuck in the waiting room for forty minutes. She's tired, and the last thing I can let her do is give in and doze off. That's dangerous for concussed people, masking signs of more serious injuries . . . like hemorrhaging.

I swallow and nudge June with my elbow, a move I've perfected over the last hour. She grumbles and tells me she's not sleeping, but she's tired. I don't mention the word *hemorrhage*. That will only freak her out more.

We finally get called back and I call her mom to keep her on the phone through the exam. It's a standard concussion, as expected, and I see the relief in June's relaxing muscles, her shoulders dropping from her ears, and her breathing slowing from the shallow, rapid pace she had going throughout the exam.

She lets me guide her back to the truck and I adjust the air vents to make sure she isn't getting blasted in the face. I'm keeping it cool to keep her awake. I get in and give her a reassuring smile, knowing deep down that in a few minutes I'm going to have to figure out a way to hide her from my mother. I know she's home. With a little luck, she's inside the house and maybe I can slip into the driveway without making a scene.

That hope is dashed when I turn down our road. I see my mom's SUV, the taillights glowing as she parks in the center of the driveway. She's wondering where I am, probably. Or she's wondering where my dad is, which . . . I have no idea. If I pull up with June right now, it is going to set off a domino effect of emotional baggage toppling around my life.

I stop my truck and kill the lights without thinking this through.

"Get out."

My mouth is so dry, and I feel like such an asshole, but the massive chaos in my chest is guiding me. I have to get out of this situation. I need to spare my mom the visual.

June jerks in her seat, clutching the fabric.

"Is something wrong?"

I start to shake my head, but my words contradict that.

"June, just fucking get out!"

Her hands fumble with the seat belt and then the door, and in seconds she's out of my truck, her medical papers clutched to her chest. The second her door shuts I turn around and speed away with my lights off until I reach the end of the road. I turn the corner and punch the steering wheel.

"Fuck!"

I punch it three more times after I pull to the side of the road. I push my hand through my hair, knocking the hoodie to the back of my neck. I'm hot, so I tug the sweatshirt from my body, getting tangled with the seat belt. The fiasco frustrates me and I growl until I'm basically left raging with a sweatshirt on the side of the road. I throw it at the passenger side once I'm free and stare at it while panting.

I just made June walk home after nearly knocking herself out and getting a concussion diagnosis. All because I'm scared.

My phone buzzes and I pull it from my back pocket, rubbing my palm over my face in an attempt to right my vision. It's my mom calling, and all I can manage to think is how June is probably a hundred feet from crossing her path. I feel sick, and I'm certain I'm an asshole. I'm only trying to be a good son, though, and somehow those two personas have become entwined.

I press ANSWER.

"Hey, Mom." I do my best to sound relaxed, to sound . . . far away.

"Hey, honey. Is everything all right? I just got home and the house looks empty. I was . . . worried."

I suck in my lips. She's lying. She's not worried, she's suspicious. As she should be. Because where is my dad?

"No, everything's fine. I had to run over to the field for something and got caught up talking to Coach. I'll head out soon."

My mom never speaks to my coach. And the odds of her and my father talking football without me being there is near zero.

"Oh, all right. Well, I picked up your favorite sub from the deli. I'll pop it in the fridge."

I smile at her thoughtfulness. I wish I were hungry.

"Thanks. Be home in a few," I say before ending the call. I toss my phone on top of my hoodie and stare at the seat June occupied only a few minutes ago. She probably passed behind my mom's vehicle while we were on the phone. My mom probably followed her movement in the mirror, waiting for her to enter her house. I wonder if June's mom is home by now.

To keep up with my lie, and maybe make myself feel a little less like a jerk, I shift into drive and navigate my way to the football field. Coach's car is in the lot, so I park next to it and head inside to sit with him while he combs through game film for our next opponent. It's not how I want to spend my Saturday, and I'm inundated with his thoughts about my performance—thoughts that are eerily reminiscent of my dad's notes—while I'm there.

I head home after about an hour, and June's house is quiet when I pull into my driveway. I force myself not to stare for long at their window, and I bury the urge to jog over there and check on her. Instead, I close the garage door, head inside, and eat my stale sandwich.

CHAPTER ELEVEN

Our kitchen usually smells of bacon and pancakes and fresh-brewed coffee on Mondays. It's part of the "routine" my mom is so hell-bent on keeping up. I can only think of two or three Mondays that have been bacon-less over the last two years. Which makes the lack of those things this morning a bit of a red flag.

I drop my backpack on the counter and glance around the house. It's quiet, and a quick peek in the garage lets me know my dad isn't home. My pulse ticks up as I piece together clues. *Did he come home last night?*

"I'm so sorry, Lucas. I have a meeting this morning and I got up late." My mom is fumbling with the coffee pot, her hands trembling at the sink. I step in and take the pot from her, filling it with water.

"It's fine. I'm not that hungry. I'll just grab a protein bar."

She nods and quickly turns her back while I take over coffee duty. My eyes narrow as I stare at her back. She's dressed for a meeting, and her hair is nice. It's a sad thing to admit to myself, but I need to get close to her to know for certain whether she spent the night drinking.

"I'll be home late tonight, but I left some cash by the fridge. You and Dad can order a pizza or something maybe?" She glances over her shoulder and I force a quick smile.

"Sure," I say, my hand still gripping the handle of the coffee pot as it begins to drip.

My mom busies herself sifting through a packet of papers before stuffing it in her satchel.

"You look nice, Mom," I say, noting how rattled she seems.

She flattens her hands on top of her bag and lets out a heavy breath before turning to face me and running her palms down the front of her blouse to smooth out any wrinkles. She smiles with closed lips. Her lipstick is subtle and applied perfectly. There aren't any signs of manic behavior or a night spent in tears.

"Thanks, Lucas. I have to talk in front of some really important people today. I'm a little—"

"You'll be amazing," I say, stepping close enough to kiss her cheek. I wish I could say it was to be a good son, but I breathe in deeply while I'm near as a test. The air is fresh and her body smells of her floral perfume and dry cleaning. No hint of alcohol.

I meet her eyes, and she widens them slightly, almost as if she's offering me a good look as proof. No redness. No puffiness or dark circles.

"Well, you'll knock them dead," I say.

"It's . . . it's a mortuary business presentation," she says, laughing lightly from one side of her mouth.

"Oh, wow. I did not see that coming," I say, rubbing my cheek and chuckling at my faux pas.

The coffee finishes its final drip and my mom steps

around me to pour some in her thermos. She leans back and kisses my cheek this time and our eyes meet once more for a silent pact. *No, your father did not come home. And yes, I'm angry. But I am fine.*

"I'll see you later," she says, dragging her bag up her shoulder and jetting through the back door to the garage.

I pour myself the leftover coffee and grab a peanut-butter-flavored bar before grabbing my things and heading to the back yard. I left my cleats out there to air out, so I grab them and tuck them in my backpack before rounding the house and heading to the driveway. I rip open my energy bar and bite a third of it before I'm faced with June standing between our two driveways. I slow my chewing but the rest of me freezes in place. My eyes shift to the right, relieved the garage is shut and my mom is gone.

"I need a ride," June says.

I choke a little on my food.

"Why?" My chest hurts from the instant drum of panic. *Shit, shit, shit. What did I do? I got too close. I opened a dialogue. I . . . I fucking missed her.*

"My car is still at work and my mom had a job," she says. She gulps, and the movement in her throat is almost violent. She hates having to ask me for a favor and it makes me so goddamn sad.

I look toward my truck and then to the closed garage.

"Your mom just left," she says. She's reading my mind now. I wonder if she knows exactly how bad things are?

I chew at my lip while I think through my options. I could tell her it's not my problem, but that would be a dick thing to do. Besides, I don't want to. I *want* to help her. My mom is gone, and my dad is God knows where. The fact she's asking me for help after I kicked her to the curb and made her walk home with a concussion says a lot about her situation. She needs my help, emphasis *needs*.

"You fucking owe me," she pipes up.

I turn to face her as her finger jets out in an accusatory point. I swallow the last crumbs of my recent bite, my mouth suddenly going dry. *Wow! This is a ballsy side of June.* I tongue my cheek, a little impressed, and finally exhale as I look down at my feet and nod.

She tugs open the door the second I press my key fob to unlock my truck, and she is buckled and sitting in perfect posture by the time I open my door. I slip my bag behind my seat and pause in the open space between us. Less than twenty-four hours ago, I was holding her hand in this space. I lean in and yank down the folding console to build an armrest—*aka barrier*—between us.

Normally, I pull my letterman jacket off and leave it on the seat June is sitting in, but I'm not about to ask her to hold it. I'm already imagining the rumor mill that'll be kindled when we pull up together. I can't imagine what fuel her holding my letterman jacket would give to gossip. I hop into my side and jerk my door shut, but the second I do, June twists to the side and slams up the console, opening the space between us right-the-fuck back up.

I chuckle as my head falls to the side and my eyes take in the empty bench seat. *Unbelievable.*

I shake my head, laughing quietly, amused at how childish we've become. May as well get all the things off my chest if we're stuck together for two miles.

"You and Tory friends now?" I adjust the mirror while I ask, doing my best to look ambivalent. Inside, my chest is raging. Rather than look at her, I pull my phone out and slide through a few playlists, finding the most angry rap song I can dig up just to drown out her reply. I don't do it because

I don't really care. I do it because I care *way too fucking much.*

She quakes with a small laugh of her own, and turns her attention out her window. I've turned the bass up as high as I can without blowing out my subs, and my truck vibrates with the beat. I zip us down the driveway, jerking the wheel and peeling out a little when I shift to drive. The quick move jars both of us, and I remember that June got knocked around pretty good yesterday. I glance to my right to check on her just as she lifts her chin to stare at me. She looks pissed, which means she feels fine. At least, that's what I tell myself.

Instead of giving in to the guilt and turning the music down and coddling her, I race through the few stop signs we hit on our way out of our neighborhood. I'm familiar enough with the cops to not get busted for a little rolling stop, though my last one was barely a tap of the brakes.

I'm literally counting down the seconds I have left in this situation when June hits me with more of her ballsy side. More like blindsides me.

"Why did you make me walk?"

My eyes widen. Maybe if I don't react, don't actually turn to face her, I can pretend I didn't hear. I maintain my focus on the road ahead, scanning for distractions. As we get closer to school and there are things like people crossing streets to snag my attention, I'm able to mask my reaction more easily. June, however, isn't letting this drop. I feel her stare. It's hot, and unwavering, and when we finally pull to a stop, I can't bear it any longer.

"June, just drop it," I say, turning toward her, my jaw tight and my eyes burning, hoping to startle her into submission.

She's breathing hard, and I glance down to see her hands balling into fists. She's not letting this go. Without warning, her hand flies to my stereo and she punches the power button off with her thumb. We're drenched in sudden silence with a mile or so left on our trip. I suck in my lips and reach to turn it back on as we roll forward, but June slaps my hand away, her fingernails grazing my wrist and leaving red marks in their wake.

What the—?

I bunch my face and twist to stare at her, wanting to call her ridiculous, despite how unfair that is since I'm just as bad. Before I say things I'll no doubt regret, a car makes a hard turn in front of us, nearly swiping the side of my truck. I swerve, and my arm flies against June's body, bracing her against the seat. She grabs on hard, her grip tight, as if I'm the only thing keeping her inside this truck. Every bit of the three or four seconds it actually takes stretches on for much longer. By the end of the slow-motion panic attack, June and I are left holding on to each other, and my eyes are strained with worry. I feel how tight my brow is, how drawn in my lids are. I will my face to relax before June draws any conclusions, and she unfurls her hands from my arm.

My heart is jacked up on adrenaline, and I'm nowhere near as careful as I should be as I zip us through the last intersection and pull into the school lot.

"You trying to get into another near accident?" June chides.

I hear her, but I don't let on.

Tory and Hayden are hanging by the front of their car, the spot always reserved for me there and waiting, right in front of everyone. June and I will be on display, ripe for speculation and assumptions. Whispers are probably already percolating on the lips of the few people who saw us pull in, though thankfully I don't see Ava lurking around. Or June's friend, Abby, who I'm sure wouldn't be shy about asking us questions and demanding *I* answer. Rather than make this morning worse, I pass by my usual spot and race toward the far corner, near the football field. *Way* out of sight.

We might end up a few minutes late to class, but I'll smooth that over. It's not as though either of us is a shitty student. We'll be excused.

June looks ready to leap from the truck before I shift to park, her bag clutched to her chest and her hand poised to open the door. It takes her maybe two seconds to exit by the time I fully stop, and she's practically sprinting ahead of me, although there's a nice limp to her gait thanks to her fall yesterday. I take my jacket off and toss it in my truck before grabbing my bag and heading after June. Not that I want to catch up to her; I don't want her to fall, but I can keep watch from back here.

I chuckle at how nuts all of this is, and maybe there's a bit of sadness in my amusement too. No matter how hard I try to lag behind June, my stride seems to double hers. Maybe it's because she's hurt, or maybe I'm unwittingly trying to catch her. Before I can dissect my feelings too much, June whips to her side.

"And yeah, Tory and I are friends now. *For now.* I mean, who knows." Her eyes flit to mine for a second then her gaze shifts back to the path ahead.

My blood is on instant boil. She cuts me off when we reach the doors to our building and again as she jerks open the one to our classroom. She slams her body into her seat, practically huffing, and I slip into mine, a little shell-shocked from the last ten seconds. I'm willing to let it go because she's justified in lashing out. I've been a total asshole. I shift in my seat, bracing my right foot against the leg of her chair because my body doesn't fit the space well. I guess my foot is the last straw for June. She pushes her chair back, clanking it against my desktop with the speed of a machete on track to decapitate someone. Our teacher is standing right in front of June's desk, the attendance sheet in her hand, her eyes screwed up as she probably wonders what the hell we're arguing about.

"Sorry, bag strap caught on something," June apologizes. She tugs on her bag at the side of her chair to embellish her fib, and the entire situation scratches at my immature soul. I shift my body and let my foot slam into the leg of her chair again, the force enough to make her hair sway and her body lurch.

Nice, Fuller. You're literally picking on a concussion patient.

My childish behavior doesn't spur another reaction from her, and when I try again a few minutes later, June seems to have completely moved on from our spat.

She's probably busy thinking about Tory, and how they're friends . . . *for now.*

Fuck.

CHAPTER TWELVE

"Yo, check it," Tory says, nudging my arm with his as he walks up next to me on our way to weights. He hands me his phone and I glance at some post on some app I never want to have.

"Yeah, what about it?"

"Nah, nah, nah . . ." He forces his phone back into my palm, realizing I didn't actually look at what he wanted. I stop walking and glare at him before looking down at his phone.

Some dude with the handle RedTedFred wrote "June and Tory totally dating." I grunt and hand the phone back to him, returning to my stride and pushing through the weight room doors.

"I thought it was funny is all," he says after a few seconds of me not reacting. He didn't think that. He wanted to make sure I saw it so he could use it as a tool to pry me open and make me admit to a whole bunch of feelings I'm not even sure I'm capable of anymore.

"I mean, I guess so. Except, aren't you into her best

friend, Abby?" This is the one little fact I have held on to, something I've always had a feeling about. Tory has been pining after Abby Cortez for *way* too long. It's more than just the fact she rejects him. It's not "the hunt" when it comes to her. He likes her. Immensely.

"Nahhhh, not really," he says, turning his back to me as he flips open his locker to dress out. He stares at his phone for a few seconds, and I lift up on my toes to peek for confirmation. He's staring at that post, I assume not finding it quite as amusing.

Tory puts his phone away and locks up his things, turning and flattening his back on his closed locker door. He folds his arms over his chest.

"That rumor should be about you and June, you know. Don't think I didn't see you give her a ride."

"She's concussed," I respond. I was prepared for that question. I had a feeling Tory saw me pull in.

"Sure, but did *you* have to drive her?"

I sigh and flop down on the bench, lifting my right foot to re-tie my shoelace. I glance up at him while my hands work. "Actually, I did. I found her hovering around my truck this morning with nobody left to call."

I shrug and give my friend a crooked smile, feeling as though I won—for exactly three seconds.

"Okay, but I saw you with her when she was hurt. You can lie to yourself and everyone else in this damn place all you want. Hell, you can lie to June, even though deep down, I bet she knows the truth."

"And what's that?" I breathe out, not at all ready for his answer.

"You're in love with her, and you hate yourself."

He pats my shoulder with a heavy hand and shoots me the same smug smile I just gave him before heading out toward the free weights. I lag behind, caught off-guard by his blunt honesty. Tory didn't even wrap his advice in a joke like he usually does. Probably because he's being completely sincere.

I'm not in love with June. Have I *loved* her, in the sense of cared about her? Yes. Do I still? Honestly? Probably. Does the thought of him dating her make me a little mental?

Yes.

Do I hate myself?

Do I?

I slouch back against the wall and consider his dig. I have had that thought, sure, that I hate myself. I rarely like myself. I find fault in my choices, and I despise my weak will. I put my foot down over this June thing, yet I keep going along as if I'm fine playing college football and kissing a future high-tech career good-bye because it might ruffle my dad's feathers. If it were only feathers—

It will shatter him.

"You're a fucking loser, Lucas," I mutter to myself in the solace of the men's locker room.

I let my fist fall to my side and bang against the brick wall behind me. I'm about to do it again, this time with more force so I can *feel* it, when our coach flings open the door and stops in his tracks.

"There you are. Office just called. You have a call from your mom. Run on up there and just drop in with your group when you're done." He squeezes my shoulder and continues on his way toward his office.

My heart jackhammers. In twelve years of public school, I don't think my mom has called the office once. At least, not to talk to me. I shake my head to wake myself from my pity session and head back outside. After a medium jog, I reach the office in less than a minute, and Maggie holds up a finger, waving me to round the front desk and stand by her.

"I've got your mom on hold. One sec," she says, punching a few buttons and handing me the receiver.

"Mom?" My body tingles with nerves. *Is she . . . sick? Did something happen to Dad?*

"Hey, Lucas. I got a really interesting call just now."

I lean against Maggie's desk, relieved and now unnerved for other reasons.

"Okay?"

"Did you apply to MIT?"

The phone slips from my hold and I catch it somewhere near my stomach, which is about where my heart is.

Shit!

"You all right?" Maggie asks.

I smile and nod and move to lean on the other end of her desk, as if that somehow is more private. I swallow hard and bring the receiver back to my face.

"I did." I roll my shoulders as I speak the words, owning them. It's the first time I'm admitting this to anyone other than Tory and the few people on campus I needed assistance from.

"Lucas!"

I scrunch my eyes closed.

"I know—"

"I'm so proud of you!" My mom's words lead me on a complete one-eighty. I was about to apologize.

"You are?"

"Yes! Honey, I think you got in!"

I stand, no longer needing to sit on the edge of the desk. My hand finds its way to my forehead and I breathe out a laugh that's part disbelief and maybe a little exhaustion. My eyes land on Maggie's and she holds up a thumb. She's one of the few people in on my plan, since she handles transcripts.

I shrug and mouth "Maybe."

"This woman, Candace, called and said she was in town. She wants to sit down with you for the MIT formal interview. I guess it's one of the boxes they need to check."

I start to pace the office.

"Yes, yes!" I'm blinking while I walk and think, my mind riffling through my day, searching out a window to make this possible—without alerting Coach or my dad.

"Okay, did she say when?"

I lick my instantly dry lips.

"I told her to be at the house at three. I know you have practice, but Lucas . . . it's MIT. We'll make it happen. Just blame me and say I need you for something, or tell Coach you left one of your cleats at home."

My mom never condones lying, especially not since my dad cheated on her. But the fact she's willing to indulge in a little fib for me, for this—my dream? It means everything to me.

"Got it, yeah. I can do that. And hey, Mom?"

"Yeah?" Her voice wavers with happiness. It's been a long time since I've heard her like this.

"Thank you," I say.

"Of course."

We hang up and I leave my hand on the receiver on Maggie's desk for a few extra seconds, simply taking it all in. I lift my head and meet Maggie's gaze, her hands cupping her mouth as she holds her breath.

"I have an interview. Today!" I whisper shout.

Maggie leaps from her desk and begins running in place, her hands in the air one second and reaching for me the next. She pulls me into a hug, and I'm not sure if she's possessed with super strength or something, but I swear she lifts me off the ground.

"Lucas! That's amazing!"

My heart is pounding so hard my ribs actually vibrate. I'm sweaty, and my body tingles with so much adrenaline I feel as though I need to sprint and climb buildings and sing from the rooftops.

"I've gotta get to class. I'll let you know tomorrow," I say, holding out a fist for her to bump. She does, tickled by the act as she giggles me out the door.

I'm practically skipping my way across campus, and there's no disguising the aching grin on my face when I meet back up with Tory. It's no use holding my news in, so I pull him to the side, and for the first time in a while, he looks at me as if he actually admires me.

I worm my way out of the start of practice using one of my mom's lies. I even went as far as hiding one of my cleats in my truck before practice so I could act with some authenticity. There's no way I can magically enter my house wearing a suit, but at least I'm not completely baked with sweat.

I tap nervously on my steering wheel as I drive, somehow hitting every stoplight on the way and getting stuck behind two or three cars at every stop sign. No rolling through anything today. I zip into the driveway and find the garage door open with a red car parked inside, my mom's SUV parked just outside. I cruise up slowly, pulling myself as close to both cars as I can, trying to not be seen, and I dash around to the back.

I can't imagine June's mom giving a shit about seeing me

home during practice time, but I can't be too careful. I slip inside and catch voices in the other room.

"That you, Lucas?" my mom calls.

"Yeah, I'll be there in one second."

I don't have time for much, but at least I can wash my hands and maybe make the most of a gray practice shirt and football pants. I dip into the powder room and wash up, taking three deep breaths to settle my nerves, then head to the sitting room where I am instantly *way* underdressed. Focusing on my mom's proud smile instead of my unprofessional attire, I rid myself of any worries about the lack of shirt and tie and turn my attention to our guest.

"Lucas, nice to meet you. I'm Candace. Your mom explained how important your role is with your football team, so thank you for making this time work."

My eyes flutter a little as I take in the prep work my mom laid for me.

I take Candace's hand and give her a solid shake.

"Of course. My team understands. Besides, my absence gives someone else a chance to lead." *What a load of crap I just spilled.* Candace's eyes sparkle. She loved it.

"Great, well, this won't take too long. The university asks us to make formal visits when we're offering a student an opportunity to take part in one of our main trustee programs. I just have a few forms to give you—"

"Wait, I'm sorry. Are you saying—"

Candace leans back in her chair and clasps her hands in front of her body as she laughs. Her red dress vibrates as my eyes start to tunnel. I feel as though I might pass out, so I lean back in my own seat.

"Yes, Lucas. We'd like to welcome you to MIT."

I shift my gaze to my mom, who's covering what I assume is a massive smile.

"It's a full ride," Candace continues.

My heart stops. I don't need a heart anymore. I have a full ride.

"But you aren't formally enrolled until you complete all of this and pay a small deposit that unfortunately we can't gift to you. Something about accreditation or whatever." She waves her right hand while handing me a deep blue and maroon embossed folder with the other. I take it into my hands as if it's an ancient relic that could break at any moment.

"Understood," I say, flipping open the folder in my lap as my mom moves to stand behind me and read over my shoulder.

My mom pulls her glasses on and takes one of the forms in her hands. I'm grateful she's here because right at this moment I'm not sure I wouldn't be willing to sign my life away. I do my best to focus on Candace's mouth, holding on to key words as she explains everything I'm supposed to read and sign and return to the college. My mom's phone rings while I'm entranced in the way Candace's mouth says the word "Boston." It's not until she coughs to get my attention that I break from the trance and realize it's my dad on the phone.

"Oh, no, Todd. I'm not sure where he went." My mom holds up a hand to excuse herself so she can slip into the kitchen and tell her second lie. This one is going to hurt because she's lying to my father, the man she holds in contempt for lying to her. I can't let her live with that. I need to have this conversation with him on my own and let him know what I want out of my life.

"Well, I think that's about it," Candace says. I missed half of her words, but I got the important ones. My mom dashes back into the room to join us just as Candace stands, and we all shake hands.

My mom leads Candace back through the house to her car, and the second she pulls away, I reach for my mom's hand and bring it to my mouth to kiss the back of it. She cups my hand between both of hers and turns to face me with tears in her eyes.

"I'm sorry you had to lie."

Full ride. Full motherfucking ride.

"You're worth it," she says. bringing my hand to her mouth and kissing it. A single tear scales her cheek, it's fall slow then quick as it cascades over her skin. Her smile never wavers, and that tear was made of pride.

CHAPTER THIRTEEN

The first thing Coach says to me when my feet hit the field is "run."

Twenty laps. That's five miles. I miss the rest of practice running, and Darren, my backup quarterback who throws like shit, has to take snaps all day. I couldn't care less.

The one thing that claws at me is the fact Coach is pissed I left something at home. He lectures me about being responsible and being a leader, though I have never, not once, been late or not showed.

No room for leniency when you're Todd Fuller's kid.

I'm sure this subject will come up when my dad meets with Coach. They talk way too often. And it's not as if I can even tell my dad he's making me look bad, because Coach Loma freaking loves hanging out with my father. They stroke each other's egos and relive their glory days through stories.

I push that stress to the side for the rest of the night. I drive home with my radio cranked and Kanye praising me. As confident as I was about getting in to MIT, never in a million years did I think the financial part would be worked out.

There are still expenses, sure, but with tuition covered, I no longer need to depend on my dad's blessing.

I'm barely paying attention to the landscape as I pull into my driveway, and I don't notice Tory's car parked at the end of June's driveway until I shift my truck into park. My mind is catching up to him being bold enough to park there when I realize it's not only his car I'm staring at—it's him and June.

This is how rumors happen. I'm sure someone drove by and saw him sitting out here, at least *parked* here. If he doesn't care, though, why should I?

Because you don't want him to date June, you asshole.

I clear my throat—and my mind—and push open my door. Both feet are barely on the ground before my best friend harasses me.

"Hey, princess!" Tory calls.

I pause and focus on my reflection in my tinted windows. I give him way too much power over me. This doesn't bother me. I'll prove it.

The scent of pepperoni pizza hits my nose as I round the back of my truck, my arms weighed down with my gear and backpack. My stomach rumbles.

"You got your car back," I say, gesturing toward June's ride, which is serving as a lounge chair for her and Tory.

"I did," she says, patting her hand against the trunk. Her head rolls to the side but stops when our eyes meet. That post Tory showed me on social media flashes through my head, and for a millisecond, I think about mentioning it. The singular purpose would be to push her, though, in hopes that she would argue with me. We have to be done with that. *We are done with that, aren't we?*

"That's good." I can tell my answer surprises her. I shuffle forward a few more steps, stopping just short of the property line. Her eyes trail down my legs to my rolled down socks and slides.

"Your feet never grew after that big burst, huh?" She nods toward my feet and I glance down at them, lifting my toes.

I smirk.

"Yeah, well, it took me a few years to grow into my size thirteens," I say, a natural laugh flowing from my chest. It feels good to laugh. My body feels lighter somehow. It's been like this all day.

I'm tempted to step across the thin patch of grass that divides us and join them, but all of the easiness that was brewing in the dusk is erased by the sound of my father's truck pulling in behind me. My head falls on instinct, like a puppy about to be smacked in the nose with a newspaper. I roll my shoulders and tug my bags up higher. I shift my weight back and forth and give in to my fate, turning and heading toward my dad's truck as he stops short of the garage.

"Lucas?" His body is already out of the cab, the sound of the door slamming shut echoing in the garage.

"I was just talking with Tory," I start to explain, trying to erase June from this scene. There's no need to mention her to Mom.

"Mind telling me why Coach called me tonight?"

My mouth tightens. He doesn't care that June's here. I figured he'd at least wait until we were alone or inside.

"Well, I wasn't on that call, you were, so . . ." I'm flirting with danger using this tone, but I'm so fucking sick of my dad and the way he tries to manage my life.

"Tory, do you know why my son skipped out on an hour of practice today?" My dad leans to look at my friend beyond my shoulder. I step up in an attempt to block his view, which irritates the shit out of him.

"Thanks, Tor. You're a real fuckin' help," my dad barks,

his stare sinking back to me. Of course my friend kept his mouth shut. What friend would answer that question? It's ridiculous.

"Let's go inside," I urge, my feet digging at the pavement with every step I take away from my father, from Tory—from June. It's as if I'm dragging a million invisible pounds, immoveable tonnage.

"This a joke to you, Luc?"

Something in my father's tone strikes through the center of my chest, halting my feet and suctioning me to the ground where I stand.

"Maybe Mrs. D'Angelo knows," June utters.

Suddenly, we're all looking at her. Only June is looking up at the stars. Tory snorts out a laugh, amused by her distraction. But there's something maybe only I notice about what she said, the *way* she said it. *Why would Tory's mom be relevant to this conversation?*

June inhales and slides from her perch on the back of her car. Her gaze falls back to the earth, to my father's face. He matches her bravado with his typical grit. He stretches out his arms to show how taut his suit is on his muscles, and his nostrils flare, an affectation he's perfected to put people on edge. The closer June comes, the more his grin stretches, pushing up into his eyes. She stops a few feet short of him and he waves a hand at her, puffing out a laugh as if she's some trivial teenager who's seeking attention.

She's not. She's never been the type.

"Get inside," my dad says, glaring at me as he passes by and climbs into his truck. The garage door opens as his tires begin their slow roll forward. Mom's home, and it strikes me as interesting that my dad wants to have this argument in front of her rather than out here in front of Tory and June.

"Call if you need me, Luc," Tory shouts. I glance over my

shoulder and hold up a half-hearted peace sign. This isn't the first time Tory's been around to see my dad have a conniption over football. This is new to June, though.

I stand in my place, stuck between following my dad's orders and drifting to the other side of the driveway to take up Tory's place and lay back on June's car to look at the sky. As Tory's lights flash on and he backs out of the driveway, I let my focus linger until my eyes adjust to the brightness, and then my gaze lands on June.

Her arms are limp at her sides, and her eyes and mouth are pulled down toward her chin. I recognize the torture of guilt.

"I'm sorry," she says, her voice barely audible.

She means it.

I believe her.

"Don't be," I say, forcing a tight smile in place of the hurt and pain I know I'm wearing. I nod toward the pizza box still resting on her trunk. "Glad you got your car back."

I make my way into the garage, and before I can turn around one last time, my dad makes sure the door is already dropping.

My mom is working through some new recipe at the counter when the two of us lumber through the door. She pauses to wipe flour from her hands and leans in to kiss my dad's cheek. He grumbles in response, his affection practically robotic, and he jerks at his tie on his way to the stairs. I wait until he's entirely out of earshot before saying a word.

"I'm sorry. It's my fault he's like that," I admit. I dump my gear bag by the laundry room and swing my backpack up on the counter to pull out my lit assignment. I need to get some reading done tonight, but my eyes are begging for sleep.

"Lucas, your father is in charge of his own attitude. That has nothing to do with you." She flutters her eyes and shakes her head, giving both him and me a pass. I'm not sure he deserves one.

"He found out I wasn't at practice on time."

"Ohh." She takes a step back and covers her throat with one hand before glancing toward the stairs. "I see."

We knew this would be his reaction.

"He doesn't need to know you covered for me," I say, trying to ease her conscience. I've turned her into a hypocrite with one lie.

She waves a hand and turns her attention back to her recipe, the counter littered with rolled dumplings and slices of bacon. I wash my hands and dry them on the towel before stepping in next to her.

"Put me to work," I offer.

"Yeah?" Her grin lights me up.

I nod. She loves it when we do things like this together. I do, too. It takes me back to when I was a kid and our weekends were filled with Mom and Lucas activities. I never realized how absent my father was back then. My eyes are wide open now. He's never really been a fixture here. If it's not about football and his kid proving some legacy bullshit, he's not interested in this family.

"Take a strip of bacon . . ."

"Okay," I respond, copying her as she folds the bacon up in the thin layer of dough. She pinches the end and dips it into a bowl of oil and seasoning.

"Can we eat this now?" I joke.

She breathes out a slight laugh and moves toward the fridge, opening it with the only clean finger on her hand. Pulling out a plate of what I'm guessing was her first attempt at this recipe, she flashes me a quick grin and winks on her way to the microwave. She pops the plate in and punches two minutes on the timer. My mouth waters in anticipation.

"You rock."

"I know," she answers fast.

We work through a few more wraps and when the cooked ones are hot enough, she tells me to wash my hands and sit down and enjoy. The treats are as delicious as I imagined, and I have half the plate eaten in minutes. The room is quiet, save for the sound of my chewing her occasional rolling out of dough. She hums when she works sometimes, never a complete song. Only fragments.

"So tell me . . ." Her lips pucker as she works, her fingertips kneading the dough. If she weren't my mom, I would simply assume she was concentrating. But I know better. She has something on her mind, one of *those* topics. She always hems and haws her way into the hard things, like the time she brought up contraception when I turned fifteen.

"How has your senior year been? Besides all of that business with him upstairs, I mean." She wipes her hands then folds them and leans forward, giving me her full attention.

I pop a bacon wrap in my mouth and shrug.

"Fine, I guess."

She studies me, reading my face, waiting for me to break and admit that things aren't so great. I won't do that, though. Even if I am struggling with this whole MIT thing and June and . . . *June.* My mom doesn't need to know those details.

"I was worried when you told me she was in your class," she says, working her way closer to the target subject.

June.

Whom I do not want to talk about.

"Yeah, but it's been fine. We don't interact much. And it's mostly pleasantries."

Her eyebrow quirks, and why wouldn't it? What boy my age uses the word *pleasantries*?

"It's fine," I say, busying my stupid mouth with an entire wrap. Chewing is so much easier than talking.

My mom eventually stands tall and cools her stare. I finish my plate and help her clean the mess. She doesn't bring June up again, and I don't give her a window. I head upstairs as soon as we're done and tiptoe my way by their bedroom door where my dad is watching *Sports Center*. I have a feeling he's done talking tonight. And if for some reason he's not and decides to wander toward my room to chat about me missing practice, maybe I'll ask him what June meant when she brought up Mrs. D'Angelo. I have a feeling I know, but I don't want to. Life is better in blissful ignorance. At least, it was last time.

CHAPTER FOURTEEN

Abby's in the driveway this morning. A part of me, a bigger part than I care to admit, was rooting for June to need another ride. I think I'm ready to talk to her. I want to explain why I've been distant. *Apologize for being so mean.* The more we interact, the less I believe she is truly aware of the forces against us. June would be sympathetic when it comes to my mom. That's just how her heart is. And maybe . . . maybe June doesn't know the details about her mom and my dad. I don't relish the role of being the one to tell her, but I would like to be the one who understands how she feels.

I wait for June to hop into the car with Abby, and when enough time has passed I grab my gear, lock up the house, and head to my truck. My parents left early this morning, my dad not interested in sharing more of his critique, I suppose. Or he didn't want me asking about June's D'Angelo comment in front of my mom. My mind keeps going back to that moment. There's something to it.

I ride to school in silence, something I do from time to

time. Not every day feels like a song, and lately, my mornings have not required much of a soundtrack. Instead of pulling to the back and hiding like yesterday, I park next to the twins. It's clear Tory filled Hayden in on my dad's little show last night because they both stare at me with funeral expressions when I get out and join them.

"It's fine," I say, shaking the conversation off before it even gets started.

Hayden nods and pulls out his phone, busying himself and giving me the peace I want on the topic. Tory, however, keeps his gaze on me for a few extra seconds. Eventually, I cock my head to the side and sigh.

"I promise. I'm fine." I literally cross my heart with my finger to make it count.

"Okay." He shuts his mouth tight but keeps his eyes on me. I try to ignore them, pulling my phone out and scrolling through social media. He doesn't relent, though. No matter how hard I try to ignore his stare, it penetrates—like a laser cutting through my skull.

"What?" I huff, clicking my screen off and stuffing my phone back in my pocket. I sink my hands into my letterman jacket pockets, glad it's a little cool out today so I don't look like a douchebag for wearing it. I've been fucking self-conscious about it ever since June made that remark.

"You and June were civil last night. It was weird." He shrugs but I know that's not all he has to say.

"Yeah, well, we're both nearly adults. We can be grown-ups, I guess."

"Nah, you've made progress. Both of you. It was almost as if you enjoyed each other's company. I think that theory needs to be explored," he says, bringing his hand to his chin and scratching.

I give him side-eyes, and thankfully, the school bell saves me from delving into this theory he has. He chuckles and points a finger at me.

"You're lucky," he teases.

"Yeah. Real fuckin' lucky." I roll my eyes, thinking about my dad last night and the MIT offer burning a hole through my soul.

Tory walks with me until he peels away near the middle of campus. My eyes search through everyone ahead of me, looking for June. When I reach the building doors, I chance a look over my shoulder, kind of hoping she's behind me. I pause when I realize nobody is. I'm the last one through the door.

I must have missed her.

When I step into our classroom, the first thing that hits me is her empty seat. Puzzled, I scrunch my brow and dart my eyes around the rest of the room. It's possible she moved her seat, tired of our lame game of chair kicking and shoving. That doesn't seem to be the case, either.

My notion that she's just late for class is dashed by the time there are only fifteen minutes remaining. Worry sets in when the bell rings, because I know I saw her leave this morning. I saw Abby's car, and I know they made it here. The only thing I have yet to see on this campus, is June.

I pull my phone out and thumb through various posts and updates on my apps while I leave the science building and make my way toward the gym. Nobody is gossiping about anything out of the ordinary. Even Ava seems quiet for now. She's been distant ever since our dinner outing to Two-fers. I wasn't very responsive that night. Actually, I'm not sure if I spoke to her directly at all, except about what to order. Maybe she's moved on?

I'm nearly to the gym doors when I make one last pirouette to scan the center of campus. That's when I see June leave the independent study rooms near the office. Two weeks ago, I basically prayed for her to switch classes. And now, seeing it a reality sucks the air out of my chest.

She actually did it.

This is ironic in the Alanis Morissette sense of the word—I'm finally ready to be around June, and she's done being around me. I'm deep in thought over losing June in my first hour when I turn to head into the gym lobby and run into Ava. Or rather run *over* Ava. My size and swift turn add up to the best tackle of my life, the result me completely caging her to the ground with my arms and legs.

"What the fuck, Lucas!"

She pushes up at my chest and I lift myself enough to roll to the side and get off her. Her friends are gathered around giggling, and one of them says, "I bet he's like this in bed."

Ava smirks but I roll my eyes and get to my feet. I offer her a hand, and as she takes it I'm grounded by the thought that I don't think I would offer one to June. Or . . . I wouldn't have at the beginning of the school year.

"Why are you making that face?" Ava snarks.

I shake my head, realizing I was probably wearing my self-awareness shock.

"I . . . remembered something. That's all."

"*Mmm*," she responds. Her friends whisper and huddle behind her, like her coven, and she juts her hip, hooking a thumb in the band of her jeans.

"We need to talk." She lifts her chin, and I can tell she's practiced this confrontation in her mirror. I've seen her rehearse these types of things. Usually, she practices yelling at her mom.

"Sure. Fine. Whenever."

I don't have much to say to her. I probably owe her some sort of closure to whatever we were, but I don't want to drag us on anymore.

"Today. After school."

"I have practice," I respond. She knows this.

"Are you sure? Or are you going to ditch so you can sign your acceptance to"—she glances over her shoulder and leans forward to mouth the rest—"M–I–T?"

My eyes narrow and my brow lowers as the corner of her lip raises in a proud smirk. Sometimes, she's like a champion chess player. I'm not sure there's anyone better at blackmail in this county.

"How—"

I stop before I get into my question. She volunteers in the office. She sits with Maggie. She probably pulled my final transcripts. I exhale, knowing I have to jump through her hoops.

"Okay, but right after class. Walk with me to the locker room so I'm not late again." I cringe at myself having uttered that extra bit of information.

"You've been late?" Her mouth is practically watering. She wants to know the juicy gossip. Ava seems to secretly love when I get into it with my dad. I feel bad because her home life is total shit, and I think she mostly likes not feeling totally alone in her existence. She wants to commiserate. She also takes too much pleasure in my misery.

"Yeah, I had an appointment, and I don't like slacking on my obligations, so if you aren't in the quad a minute after the final bell, you're going to have to reschedule. I look to her friends, still gathered behind her back. "Have your people call mine."

I make the phone gesture and chuckle as I leave her in the lobby and head through the boys' locker room doors.

Tory is changing out by the time I get to my locker, and I can tell by his smug expression that he saw my little negotiation in the lobby.

"Thought you were done with that," he says.

I fling my door open.

"I *am* done with that."

"Well, that ain't done with you."

I look to my right and drop my chin, leveling him with a hard-lined mouth. After a few seconds, he breaks away and holds out his palms, whispering "Okay, fine."

I toss my backpack in and pull my shirt up over my head, and while my locker door blocks the view between us, I hit Tory with my burning question.

"You know why June switched her first hour?"

He's quiet, and after several long seconds pass, I realize he's not going to answer. I breathe out heavily and finish changing out before slamming my locker door shut and leaning against it to deal with his second smug look of the morning.

"Dude, I have no idea why Maybe Mabee"—this is what he has started calling her, and it's irritating—"dropped your ass. I mean class."

I purse my lips and hold up my middle finger. My friend holds his belly as he falls back with a booming laugh. I walk away, leaving him no choice but to catch up on our way to weights.

"Look, my guess is she's trying to do you a favor. She hasn't said anything to me about it, but I can ask in our last hour if you want. Or maybe, and here's a revelation, *you can ask her yourself.*" He covers his mouth and gasps as he walks backward then points at me.

I wait out his gloating session and decide not to bring the topic up with him again. Not because he's wrong, but because his advice is solid, and the last thing I have the guts to do.

CHAPTER FIFTEEN

I know what my dad is thinking. It's the reason he left after the third quarter.

You get the official offer from Tennessee and the next day, you put on this shit fest on the field?

It might not be his thoughts verbatim, but I guarantee it's in the ballpark.

My dad has left in the middle of three of my games, ever. Once was for an emergency appendectomy. The other time was to catch a plane for a meeting, something I now call into question. And tonight, about eighteen minutes ago. He wanted me to see it, too. It's why he stood and stared out on the field with his hands on his hips. He didn't even bother to glance down to signal anything to me on the sidelines. He was too embarrassed.

I was embarrassed for my mom. She had to weave through people she knew to keep up with him so the two of them could leave together in the middle of my game. The quarterback's parents . . . bailing.

I'm not getting in again. Our defense has been shit all

night, almost as useless as my offensive line. I have a feeling that last sack cracked a rib. With two minutes left on the clock, Pinecrest would be dumb not to just run out the clock.

I'm not embarrassed by my game play. I did what I could with what I had. And I made Tory look good, and his dad is here. He doesn't get to make many games, so the fact the one he came to is one in which his son scored the only touchdown makes up for the three times my face was flattened into turf.

We let Pinecrest run the field, eating up downs, five yards at a time. At this point, I'll be happy if they don't score again and we can say we only lost by fourteen. My team gets excited when their quarterback throws a pass and our defense runs down the tight end, wrapping him up after seventeen yards. They scream and shout along the sideline, waving their arms in the air as they jump and turn to hype up what's left of the crowd. I let them go. I'm happier here on the other end, away from the action.

Helmet at my side, my eyes glaze over as I stare at the clock. I like that it counts the fractions of seconds. Feels like more is happening this way. It's like grains of sand spilling through the narrowing of an hourglass. When the buzzer sounds and fans rush the field, I force my legs to carry me toward the team. Instead of leading them, I opt to fall in step at the end of the line. Coach notices and I make up an excuse in my head for when he asks why I wasn't being a leader.

I wanted our hard-working defense to get the credit.

It'll be this private joke for me and me alone, and the best part is he'll wonder if I'm being sincere or mocking their shitty performance.

We shake hands with the other guys and I go through the motions, grabbing my sweat towel and following the dejected line of massive dudes all heading toward our bus. I glance to our stands as I cross the track, and though nearly everyone has cleared out—probably well before time was up—one person stayed.

June stayed.

I dart my eyes back to my path, holding steady on the Eagles jersey in front of me, the double zeros that our best receiver gets to wear. My helmet balanced on my head, I chew on my plastic mouth guard, anticipation building in my chest. I swear I can sense she's close as we get near the field exit, and I time it perfectly, glancing to my right as we pass through the few people who waited to see us off. Our eyes lock for a single beat, probably the first *real* heartbeat I've felt in months, maybe years.

She stayed. When everyone else left, she stayed.

I barely talk to a soul on our way back to the school, and Coach is too disgusted with us to talk when we get to our locker room. Instead of pausing by the white board as we all file in, he beelines straight to his office, slamming the door and dropping the blinds. His clipboard smashes into them a few seconds later, getting caught between a few of the slats and bending the thin metal. He leaves it there, a reminder and a warning to us to leave him the fuck alone or enter at our own risk.

"You up to party in the woods tonight?" Tory elbows me as we stop in front of our lockers. I pull my mouth in tight on one side and glance at him in my periphery before shaking my head.

"Yeah, I figured. For what it's worth, I think you played great tonight, and fuck Coach for thinking we're a better team than we really are." Tory holds out a fist and I drop mine on top. "I'll catch up with you tomorrow."

He takes off for the showers as I plop down on the bench to drag off my jersey and pads. I'm in no rush to be anywhere, and I'd rather let the hot water of the showers burn off my mood alone. I wait until almost everyone is done before heading in, and I think about Tory's words the entire time. He's right. I played well tonight. Yeah, maybe I could have had a little more fire in my throws, and definitely in my attitude. But none of that would have made a difference in the outcome. Our defense was no match for the Pinecrest offensive line. They must feed their boys beef and steroids for every meal. We kept up, and we should hold our heads up high for that.

My dad won't think so. He'll call my performance second rate. Then, he'll blame Coach and curse the program for not letting me shine. I'll have to listen to it all. Sit through every goddamn word and nod when expected. My mom will listen in from the kitchen, deep down wanting to tell my dad to lay off. She won't, though, because she saves her battles for her grudge, for snide remarks about infidelity and loyalty.

They're both letting me down.

I'm not sure when I decided I would look for June the second I got home. Maybe it was during that long shower, or perhaps during the quiet drive, void of music to disrupt my thoughts. I drove ten under the limit to get home, maybe knowing that the second I pulled into my driveway I would cross a line.

It feels foolish not to. All this time I've avoided June for two people who don't give a second thought to what I might need or want. My mom might support me going to MIT, but she sure doesn't seem concerned about me having to endure one more season of football lectures from Dad.

The brush back by the old Buick is thick and the weeds scratch my calves and snag my sweatpants while I cut through the tall grass on my way into the dark corner of June's back yard. I don't know how I knew she would be waiting for me. I didn't even hope for it. It was this understood safety net my gut told me would be here tonight. *June would be here.* And there she is.

I tug open the busted door and slip into the passenger seat. The lines in the dust from the last time I was in here are still there, only a faint sheen of new dirt filling in the lines. I leave the door open but bring my feet in, sitting back and exhaling. June rolls her window down, only a few inches but enough that the dank air clears out, making way for the evening breeze. For long minutes, it's nothing but me and June and the quiet.

It's a peaceful bliss, and exactly what I need. My mind feels calm, all of my stress at ease and the knot in my gut looser than it's been in weeks. Maybe all I need is this, a timeout in a familiar place with company who actually gives a shit, even though I don't deserve it.

My phone's ringtone plays Kanye and I yank it out, muting it the second I see it's Ava, probably wanting a lift to the party. She rings right back so I power my phone off and toss it onto the dusty dashboard before pressing my palms into my eyes. It feels as if I haven't slept in weeks. The bags under my eyes are like tiny pillows. I scratch at my head, feeling my wet hair run through my fingers. With another heavy exhale, I lean forward, resting my weight on my folded hands and the dash.

"I want to go to MIT." I nod at my faint reflection in the windshield, loving the way those words sound out loud. It's freeing to be able to admit what you want in front of someone.

"That's amazing," June answers almost immediately. I drop my head into my hands and roll it side to side while I toe at the rotting floor. I pull my mouth up into a crooked smile and look at her sideways.

"It is, isn't it?"

Her smile stretches wider, and I try to do the same with mine, but it only goes so far. I flatten my palms and lean forward, resting my head on the backs of my hands while I stare at her face, remembering all the things about it that fascinated me. I always loved the way her chin came to a soft point, and how her milky skin was the perfect canvas for her freckles, and the pink blush that took over her body at even the slightest embarrassment.

"I got an offer from Tennessee," I breathe out.

She nods, her expression steady, unchanged.

"That's awesome too," she says, and I shake with a quiet laugh.

"You're right. It is." I sit back and drop my hands into my lap. Leave it to June to boil things down to the truth: I have two great options in front of me.

"What do you want?" she asks.

My faint smile loses its hold and the heaviness creeps back into my chest.

"Does that matter?" I say with a quick shrug.

"It should."

I huff out a short laugh. Again, she's so right.

June fidgets with the marble ball on the Buick's shifter stick, twisting it until it comes off. She passes it between both hands a few times, tossing it, then holds it out toward me, as if presenting me with a ring. I take it, our hands brushing on the exchange. I'm left with the cool weight of the polished stone in my palm. I always loved this thing. When we were kids, I would pretend it was a jewel with magical powers or secretly worth millions. I even tossed it in the pool once to see if June could dive to the bottom to retrieve it.

"Thanks. I always wanted this thing."

"I know," she responds with a breathy laugh. "It's yours now."

My mouth tugs up for a short smile as I roll it around in my palm and stare at it.

"Or you could give it to Ava."

My mouth sours, but I do my best to appear unaffected by her words. I deserved that.

The silence bakes us for several long seconds. The breeze seems to have disappeared, and coupled with the passive-aggressive words June just uttered, my body feels a dozen degrees too warm.

"Why'd you leave physics?" I know why, and I'm sure that comment she just made has a little to do with it.

"Seemed it was for the best." I glance her way and catch an earnest shrug.

"Yeah," I sigh out.

I settle further into the seat, drawing one leg up while I toss the marble ball in my hand. I line it up with the shifter screw after a minute and twist it back into place. It doesn't feel as special as it used to. Or maybe I don't feel as worthy.

"I don't really want it," I say, flitting my eyes to her. "I just liked that it pissed your dad off."

We both spit out a short laugh.

"It did."

I'm suddenly caught looking at her. It's easier this time, so I indulge, not feeling guilty about it, and let my eyes hold hers through several full breaths. She seems to feel the same. The tension that's tethered our chests together, making it hard for me to breathe, has given us slack. Her gaze meanders around my features, and it tugs my lip up on one side. She's looking at the scar above my right eyebrow, the one from my monkey bar accident when we were kids. The faintest smile rests on her closed lips, and I swear I can hear the memories rushing through her mind, like the best story time ever.

"Ava's not my girlfriend, just so you know."

I'm not sure what possesses me to utter those words, but doing so immediately tightens the ropes around my chest. Breathing is no longer easy.

June doesn't blink, instead drawing in a long, steady breath through her nose.

"She seems like your girlfriend."

She probably does seem like it. She probably feels she is. I've led her on, used her to fill a void.

"She's not. She's just . . ."

What is she? She's a terrible person who bullies June. She was there when I was lonely. She put up with my moody bullshit so I stuck around.

"She's just this mistake I make sometimes."

That came out harsh.

June shakes her head.

"She's not a mistake," she corrects.

"Okay."

She's right. She was a choice I made, but now that I'm staring at the one person I always felt was home, every choice up until this point feels empty and gutless.

"I might not like her very much, but no girl deserves to be labeled a mistake. She's a lot of things, but mistake isn't one of them. Your moments with her had purpose, even if they were brief and not love. Your actions can be a mistake, but not the person."

She cries through the final few words. Other than me, Ava is the one person who has purposely hurt June over and over again, and here she is, defending her. More than that, she's putting me in my place. Most people would probably pile on and agree, and she'd have every right to argue I didn't go far enough. But that's not June. How she's managed to hold on to the high road while the rest of us have tunneled into the deep, I don't know. But she has.

"Okay," I say through faint laughter.

"Okay," she repeats. She wipes away another sniffle, and all I want to do is run my thumb across her cheek to dry her skin. It never moves beyond an urge thanks to the abrupt flash of lights from the back of my house. My dad slides open the back door to pace from one end of the patio to the other.

"He's probably looking for me," I say, squinting and glad I'm hidden in this car. He would never look for me here.

"Let him," June says. I glance to her and breathe out a laugh at the sight of her chest puffed up and her fist in her hand.

"I wish I could, but—"

"But he's the reason you can't go to MIT?" Her dose of honesty cuts like poison.

My eyes drop to her neck then flicker back up to meet her gaze, confirming her question.

"He went to Tennessee, and me and football—"

"You're living his dream," she says, her words overlapping with mine. She gets it. Of course she does.

"He'll come around."

My chest shakes with one silent laugh.

"Doubtful," I say, pushing open the door to head to my lecture. I spin and place my palms on the roof of the car, dipping my head into view to look at her one last time. My thoughts are disorganized and the words I'm searching for don't seem ready to come, leaving me with a mouth hung open and a chest squeezed so tight I feel as though I'm drowning.

"Thanks, June," I finally utter. At least those words are nice. Better than I've uttered over the last few weeks.

I rap on the top of the car and back up a step or two, tossing the door shut on my way. My dad's gone back inside and the lights are all off now. I pause at the edge of the deck, one foot perched on the first step. My house has a faint glow from the entry light and that's it, the kitchen void of life. My mom probably escaped to the bedroom, and maybe that's where my dad is for now. He'll wander back down the stairs to search for me after a few minutes, though; he's got too much to say. He's not going to feel settled until he has a chance to impart his wisdom on me.

Almost automatically, my head swivels to my left, toward the Mabee house. The lights there are all off. June probably headed inside. I was just with her but I want to be again. Not in the morning, or tomorrow, but now. *Right now.*

I back away from the deck and take quiet steps through the gravel into the grass, cutting across our yards until I'm staring up at her window, the blue glow of her lamp outlining the slats of her shutters. I glance around my feet for something to throw, gathering up five or six pebbles that won't cause permanent damage if I toss them. I shake them in my closed palm, like dice. I should probably blow on them for good luck, but I don't before launching them toward June's window. They scatter, pinging in all directions.

June opens the window a few seconds later, but her gaze is lost. She's not searching for what made the sound against her window; she's searching for me. Her focus is on my house —on the darkened back deck, my window.

Your actions can be a mistake, but not the person.

My eyes widen as I replay her words from a few minutes ago in my mind. June thinks she was a mistake— that *we* were a mistake. I drop my gaze and scan for more rocks, finding enough to make another attempt to get her attention, and I look up in time to see her pulling her shutters closed. I rear back and launch the stones at the side of her house, spraying the area around her window with the shrapnel. I immediately gather more rocks and bring my hand up to toss them and am unable to stop my motion when she opens the slats again. She flings both sides open and when the stones hit the surface and I realize that in seconds, I need to have the right words ready to say. I'm so terrible at this when it comes to her, and I can't mess this up.

"What are you doing? You can't run away to here. I mean, he'll find you," she says, making a joke about my dad.

"You were never a mistake." My heart is pounding so hard that I feel it in the tips of my fingers. I went with the most important words first, a reaction to my sudden worry that June thinks I classify her as anything other than important. It's my fault that she does, and only I can correct that.

My hands are balled into fists at my sides as I rock back and forth. June's mouth is open and she hasn't moved in five, six . . . now seven seconds.

"Okay," she finally says. Her mouth curves into a grin and she holds up two thumbs. She thinks I'm nuts.

"No, June." Shit, I can't do this from down here. There's too much distance; my words are going to get lost. I hold up a finger and rush toward her house with the same gusto I did when we were kids. The leap to the eave of the house is easier now, but my body is bigger and I sound like a gorilla climbing a playhouse. *God, I hope her mom is asleep.*

My hands find the familiar grip of her window ledge, a place they haven't been in years. I pull myself up as June takes a few steps back into her room. I'm not graceful, but manage to maneuver my body through her window one arm and leg at a time. I didn't think before doing. I simply acted. And now I'm here, in her room, my hands so fucking sweaty and my body pulsing with the rush of blood and beats of my heart. I bite the tip of my tongue and meet her gaze, breathing out a short laugh at my own expense. My God, what she must be thinking. I disappear for a couple of years then climb in through her window.

"When you said those things, about how no girl wants to be a mistake." I swallow hard and shake my head, my eyes never breaking from hers. "You meant you. You weren't talking about Ava."

I take a timid step forward and her hands ball at her sides. She's as nervous as I am, full of the same caution and fear. She looks to her side, to the mirror by her dresser. I follow her gaze and immediately see the pictures of us taped to the surface. My heart cracks wide open. She's never been far. She was here all along. I'm so stupid.

"I'm sorry, June."

Her eyes are still fixed on her mirror—on our memories—as I inch my way forward.

"You are not a mistake," I repeat. I'm close enough to feel the heat of her body.

"Got it. Thanks," she chokes out. She's putting up walls, waiting for me to sucker punch her with words. I've trained her to expect such. Shame on me.

I reach for her chin, squeezing the feeling back into my fist before opening my palm and brushing my fingertips along her chin. I lift her head with gentle pressure, tempting her gaze my way. When I'm able to hold her head between both palms, I tilt it enough to force our eyes to meet. My mouth goes dry, but even still, my words are there. Suddenly, I know what to say. I know everything.

"You are not a mistake," I repeat. No mistaking my message. I look deep into her green eyes, the glint of moonlight reflecting on their glassy surface. I don't mean to make her cry.

She nods her head, sucking in her lips once before uttering "Okay." One deep breath gathers her nerves, and the slight crooked smile fills me with so much happiness. I've missed her. I've missed *out* on her—on us. I'm so stupid.

I run my thumb under her eye, like I wanted to in the car, and stutter out a nervous laugh.

"Thanks," she says, eyes briefly flitting downward.

"Don't mention it," I say, doing the same to her other cheek.

The slight tremble in her lips catches my eye, and as they part, a tiny gasp escapes. I'm sunk.

My thumb roams from the curve of her cheek to the rise of her upper lip. I can feel her quiver under my touch and her eyes close when my thumb moves from her top lip to her bottom. I don't dare close mine—not yet. It feels as though minutes pass as my mouth inches closer to hers, and when our lips finally touch, my body is powered to life like a man about to die but saved by paddles to the chest.

This is what kissing a girl is supposed to feel like.

My nose grazes hers as I shift my position, tilting my head so I can kiss her deeper. I force myself to be gentle at first, starting with her upper lip and holding it between mine with a tender suckle. Her hands gather my shirt against my chest, bunching the cotton into her fists. The feel of her wanting me strips away my caution, and my eyes fall shut as my hands weave along her neck and into her hair, holding her mouth to mine. We suffocate in this kiss, and it's worth giving up air.

My tongue teases hers, my teeth caressing the softness of her lips. Hers hold on to mine, the threat of her bite rushing my bloodstream with her special brand of dopamine. I'm drunk on her, all at once. This kiss changes everything. It's the middle of the story—the one I told her I wish I could erase her from. I am a liar. I've never wanted June out of my story, out of my life. I've just been too afraid. She's worth the fight. I'm a better man with her. I'm stronger, kinder, smarter —braver.

Dizzy and maybe on the verge of passing out, I pull our mouths apart and rest my head on hers. We're both panting, and our mouths are raw and puffy from the force of our kiss. My hands cup her face, my fingers flexed and my muscles locked. I'm suddenly terrified this isn't real, or what we experienced was temporary—a dream, a blissfully indulgent dream. I rock us side to side in a silent dance.

"That was not a mistake," I whisper. My body shudders when her palms slide to my chest, her nails scratching at the cotton of my shirt, grabbing the fabric. Clinging.

"Okay," she whispers back. She rises up on her toes and presses her lips to mine, holding them still. Her kiss is unending, a steadiness to it she must sense I need. I know she feels my lips tremble. She must. Her teeth graze along my skin, dominant and sure. She doesn't slip away until I draw in a full breath, and when she does, she whispers "okay" again. She says it a few more times, each with a soft kiss somewhere on my chest or neck or shoulder. And somewhere along the way, maybe we both start to believe in this moment.

Naturally, I have to ruin it. I ruin everything. Like father, like son.

Our kiss breaks in slow motion as awareness crowds June's room, swirling around me and invading my head with panic. I do a poor job of masking it in my expression. I can tell because of the way June's brow draws in tight as I move toward the window I let myself in through.

"You don't have to go," she begs. I sense it, her desire. I have it, too, and it's the reason I need to go. I'm not quitting on us, but with the barriers in our way, I need to be smart, take it slow.

"My dad will be circling the property every hour on the hour."

We both let out a nervous laugh. I'm only half kidding.

I slide one leg out the window and hold my weight up on the ledge, careful to make eye contact one last time before I crawl my way back down her pitched eave.

"You can't tell anyone."

Her eyes dim, the green gone, nothing left but black. I asked her to be my secret, same as my dad did to her mom. Even sadder, I know she won't say a word.

CHAPTER SIXTEEN

I called Ava the second I got back to my house last night after being at June's. She'd left me a half dozen messages, each one progressively more belligerent, entitled and possessive. I was right that at first she wanted a ride to the party. Eventually, she wanted *me* at the party. Mostly, she didn't like not knowing where I was. When I called, she was her typical buzzed-at-a-party self. I told her I didn't want to do whatever she and I were doing anymore, and when she asked if I wanted more, I wasn't very nice.

I said, "Yes, but not with you."

She hung up.

I texted her an apology and told her she deserves better. She told me to *fuck off*.

When my phone buzzed at a decent hour this morning, I figured she was still hungover and angry-texting or wanting to complete our usual cycle of break-up then get back together. It wasn't Ava, though. It was Tory.

My friend must have taken it easy last night. Over the summer, I could basically set my alarm to noon the day after a party and still have hours on my own before Tory rolled out of bed hungover and hungry. This morning's message didn't even come equipped with a vomiting emoji, his signature post-party icon.

TORY: *Bowling?*

Dare I say, Tory is maturing.

I find myself ensnared in a strange set of obstacles now that my relationship with June has . . . *shifted.* I need to dissect basic questions and normal tasks, constantly asking myself whether June will be present and how I'd behave if I didn't know how her mouth tastes.

That's how I dealt with the *bowling* text. I didn't lie. I wrote back: *I hate bowling.*

I mostly do, though I'm decent at it. But I love pool. And I want to see June, desperately. I played to my strengths and somehow managed to not spark a million needling questions from my best friend on our way to Eight Lanes.

Abby's sitting at the counter when we walk in, and it helps keep my nerves in check seeing Tory get rattled. His crush on June's best friend has elevated. There's something different about the way he is with her and around her. And it's more than him liking the chase or hating her constant rejection. Maybe that's my ticket to getting him off my back about June. Every time he brings her up, I'll counter with a question about Abby.

"Maybe Mabee, what's up?"

June pops up from behind the counter, her eyes wide and darting to take in her new customers. I offer a one-sided smirk in apology for surprising her, but before she can speak, Tory's reaching over the counter and hugging her. My smile drops and I feel that tightness in my gut. It's fucking jealousy. Her eyes find mine over Tory's shoulder, and I swear she's telling me with her gaze to calm down.

"Nice game Friday, Luc," Abby says while she and June exchange glances. She winks at her friend. *Did June tell Abby about us?*

"Fuck off, Abby," I say, knowing she isn't really complimenting my game. We lost. And old Lucas, the one who doesn't kiss June, would call Abby out.

I slide onto the stool at the end of the counter, away from everyone else, mostly because I feel jittery. I'm overthinking things, but I can't help it. There's a newness to everything, despite the fact I've known June for years. I'm nervous and maybe embarrassed, in a good way.

"Can I get a water?" I nod toward the tap. I'm totally doing this to create physical separation between her and Tory. I hope I'm the only one aware of that.

She eyes me while sliding her feet toward the ice machine. She picks up the scoop and points it at me, her tongue pushed into her cheek.

"It's a buck for the cup."

Abby chuckles and when I look at her, she drops her eyes to the counter and takes a long drink through her straw, draining her cup until she's making the slurping sound.

"Ahh," she adds before sliding the cup forward and tapping it a few times on the counter. "Some of us get freebies."

June laughs at her friend's teasing. It's good. The normalcy. I just can't fuck it up.

I stare at Abby for a few hard seconds and chew at the inside of my mouth. She's a worthy opponent, twisting on her stool and crossing her legs as she stares back at me just as hard. I leave my eyes on her while I lean to the side, pull my wallet out and slip my debit card free. I toss it across the counter toward June, who slaps it down under her palm. She plays it up, waiting for me to turn to face her so she can study the front of my card, and then my face.

"Lucas *A.* Fuller." She over-pronounces my name, the way our principal did once in fourth grade when I dug a hole under the play yard fence during recess.

June flattens the card on the counter and flicks it toward me with her index finger. I manage to catch it in my lap before it falls to the floor.

"I'm afraid I can only take cash."

I laugh silently, enough that my shoulders shake. Chewing on my tongue so I don't break character. I peek at her from underneath the brim of my hat as she threatens to pour out the ice water she put in the cup, letting it go so far as to trickle into the sink. There's a part of her that truly enjoys this, and I'm not sure whether that's a good thing or bad thing. It's definitely a sexy thing. My thoughts keep going back to last night, to her mouth and the curves of her body that my hands traced. I close a fist under the counter to relieve the tension.

"Ah ah," I say, holding up my other palm.

I tuck my card back into my wallet while my eyes hold her hostage. It takes me a few tries to find the right card slot, but eventually the folded up dollar bill shows itself and drops on the counter. Of course, so does my fucking condom.

June's eyes zero in on it, and I'm only a millisecond behind her.

Fuck, fuck, fuck, fuck . . .

In a flash, June finishes filling my cup back up and refastens the lid.

"Here," she says, snapping it down on the counter. She tosses a wrapped straw next to it. My gaze moves from the straw to her face. All I want to do is explain, or apologize. I'm not even sure what to say. I mean, it's a responsible thing to have in one's wallet—*in my wallet.*

Shit.

June drags her palm over the counter before I can put my foot in my mouth and collects both the dollar and the condom. I swallow, and I don't even care that everyone saw it.

She drops the buck in the register drawer, then turns to face the twins and Abby while holding the condom packet between her thumb and index finger, as if it's a rare coin for people to *ooh* and *ahh* over. Tory and Hayden are stifling laughter, fists covering their mouths, and Abby just looks excited. She clearly can't wait to see what happens next.

They don't see the details like I do. I guess that's a good thing. It protects our secret. Only, now it breaks my heart a little too. June's hurt. Her cheeks are flushed, and not from being embarrassed, which is what everyone probably thinks. She's upset. Maybe jealous. I'm sure she's thinking about me and Ava.

I'm such a dick.

"Ribbed for her pleasure," she reads. She annunciates the same way she did my name and initial, ending with a click of her tongue. "Well."

She leans to her side, resting her elbow on the counter in front of me. Her eyelashes bat and her focus shifts from our friends to me. They got the performance. I am getting the truth. She pinches the edge of the packet and holds it out for me. I scratch at my neck and laugh nervously before grabbing the other side. June doesn't let go, and my eyes fly up to meet hers. I draw them in, begging her silently not to make this a big deal, or to make it something we talk about in front of everyone. *Please.*

Her lids weigh heavily and the corners of her mouth turn down. She lets go then backs away a step or two.

"I hope she enjoys it."

Our friends can no longer hold it in, and Tory spits out a laugh, reaching toward June to high five her for nailing me. He hates Ava, so of course he's all over this.

I stand, putting the condom back in my wallet then shoving it into my pocket. Abby is laughing pretty hard now too, and even Hayden—quiet, keep-the-peace Hayden—is repeating June's last line.

Lifting the water cup, I hold it out in a toast, and the laughter dies. They're all on the edges of their seats waiting to see what I'll say. I bite at the end of my straw.

"She better," I say, lips wrapping around the straw. I look to June as I suck, and a fire crackles between us. This push-pull isn't how our relationship should be. Maybe we're too far into our habits to break them. Or maybe it's my fault. I'm the one who set the rules, who asked her to keep us a secret.

"Gentlemen?" I tilt my head toward the pool table, and the twins follow me. Tory's eyes meet mine for a beat, and I see his disgust flash in the background. His expression is always easy to decipher, at least it is for me. Probably because I give him so much to judge.

"What do you say, boys? Five bucks a game?" I gather the balls on the table, racking them . . . *and avoiding Tory's glare.*

"I don't know, Luc. Pretty sure you just gave away your last dollar," Hayden says. He's teasing me, but I sense a little bite in his tone. *Ouch! And he's the timid one.*

"You'd have to beat me, and we both know that ain't happening." I flash a crooked grin at him and he flips me off.

"That was a little much, dude," Tory says as he basically body checks me with his bicep.

"She started it," I snap back. I can only look at him in short bursts. *This is normal Lucas behavior.* At least, that's what I keep telling myself.

"Come on. Five bucks a game. Who wants to go first?"

Tory grabs the stick from my hand and points it toward the counter where June is now alone and picking at a sandwich.

"It's me and Hayden this game. You get the winner. And we'll see if we let you place a wager." His mouth is a stern line, and his eyes move again from me to the girl beyond my shoulder. He's being serious, and deep down, I'm glad to see him respect June so much. I'm also fighting the urge to grab the collar of his T-shirt and tell him that taking care of June is my job.

"Fine. I'll go make nice. Maybe get a refill." I grab the cup from the edge of the pool table and let the burn of guilt torch my insides while I walk to the front counter. June is filling a cup with ice and water as I walk up.

"Employees don't have to follow that dollar rule, huh?" I joke. What I should have said was "I'm so sorry." Instead, I made a fucking joke.

Her gaze shifts to the twins then back to me, a smile the furthest thing from her face.

"You just missed it. I donated a condom to the register." Her monotone response is pretty clear. I should have gone with an apology.

She picks at her sandwich, her focus on nothing but the crust on her bread.

"June, don't be like that," I sigh out. That still was not an apology. Maybe I've played the asshole so long I don't know how to be the gentleman anymore.

June rips at her bread, pulling off the corner and popping it into her mouth before finally lifting her gaze to meet mine. Her jaw works slowly, her chew more of a distraction to her hurt and anger than anything. She forces a smirk onto her face while she leans into the counter.

"Be like what? Like your dirty little secret?" She takes a drink and tilts her head, one eye squinting as she hits me with an accusatory face. I deserve every bit of it.

I glance toward the game, which is still going, then run my palm over my face as I slide onto one of the stools.

"It's complicated."

She just keeps eating. The quiet between us is harder to take than the barbs and insults. I've spent enough time *not* talking to her. I don't want to go back to that.

"Excuse me," she says, wrapping up the rest of her sandwich and leaving it under the counter before tossing a towel on the counter and slipping away.

I spin in my seat, the twins' backs to me as they study a shot in their game of nine-ball. Taking my opportunity, I dash around the corner the way June headed, not finding her in the hallway. The only other option is the ladies' room, and this place is empty. I push open the door in time to catch her ducking into the last stall. I reach her before the latch drops, and push against the door. If I have to drop to the floor and crawl in there to get to her, I will. *Thank God, this isn't the men's room.*

"June, don't do this."

Why can't I just say I'm sorry? What is wrong with me?

June laughs at my attempt.

"You need to get out of here," she says in a raspy whisper. She pushes back hard, her feet sliding along the tile. I smile a little at her attempt to move me. I'm twice her size. Suddenly, though, my weight falls forward, through the door, as she gives up completely and steps back. *Well played, June.*

Fine. We'll do this in here. Where I can trap her.

I shut the door and latch it behind me, pretty confident I can defend her attempts to get past me. Not that I'll hold her in here if she asks to leave.

"What, because two pair of legs won't be a giveaway?" Her face contorts to match her snarky tone before she glances down at our feet.

I lean my head back with a heavy sigh and remind myself why this matters. June matters. Even if I think a condom is a trivial thing, to June, it isn't. And it shouldn't be. I hurt her. *For years.*

My gaze drops to her and I lean forward, resting my palm against the wall on one side of her head. I'm blocking her from rushing out, and when her eyes dart to my arm, I drop it a little lower, afraid she's looking for a quick escape.

Great job, Lucas. You have to hold her hostage.

"Where should I begin?" I'm being serious, despite how vague my question sounds. I owe her so much. I want to tell her everything, to ask her what she knows. If I have to give her every detail of my mom's depression, of her addiction and nervous breakdown, here while surrounded by black and white tiles and the smell of industrial toilet cleaner, then that's what I'm going to do. I'm here for it. Let's do this.

"You said I'm not a mistake." Her voice breaks through that last word, and my bravado dissolves in an instant. She's trying so hard not to cry.

Without questioning it, I move my other hand to her face, stroking her cheek with my thumb and urging her to look me in the eyes.

"I did, and I meant it," I say when she finally does.

This is who I want to be. I need to remember what this man feels like. My mouth aches to kiss her, but it's not the right time. Words first. So many words are necessary.

"Out there," she says, dropping her eyes to the tight space between us. A single tear cuts down her cheek, pausing at the curl of her lip. I want to kiss it away. "I felt like a pretty big mistake out there. And every single second that passed just made me feel more and more like I . . . like me and you? We don't belong."

I can't look her in the eye. Her voice, so raw, cuts through me. I'm afraid when I lift my gaze from her chin I'll see more tears. I can't handle more tears. Not when I'm the reason they're there. Instead, I bring my head to rest against hers, pulling my hands in to cup her face so my thumbs can feel the streaks left behind on her cheeks. I won't erase them. I can't.

"June, nobody can know," I say, my mouth inches away from hers. If only I could kiss this all away.

"Is it Ava? So you can still sleep with her?"

My center of gravity sinks to the floor.

"No, June. Fuck Ava." My response is swift and my words come out harsh. I step back so she can see the proof in my expression, shaking my head and daring to meet her gaze. Her eyes are so fucking red, her cheeks puffy and tear-strewn. I did that.

"Exactly," she laughs out.

My instincts to shout and defend myself push against my insides. June isn't hearing me. Then again, why should she?

"I ended things with Ava. Completely." My teeth clench as my jaw tightens. So help me if Ava is telling people another story.

"*Mmm*," June says, more tears spilling from her eyes. Her mouth is a hard line and her nostrils flair with fight. She's not going to make this easy. It shouldn't be. "That what you held on to the condom for?"

I exhale as my head falls to my shoulder. I'm a bit deflated. I want her to trust me. I guess I shouldn't expect to leap right to that kind of bond again.

"I didn't even know that was in there, June." I swallow down my frustration and glance to the side, letting my focus get lost on the bathroom graffiti. I don't know what else I can say to prove I'm a man of my word. All I want is for her to believe me, for her to know she matters—*to me*.

"Your dad is having an affair."

My gaze snaps to hers. Her hands cover her mouth and her eyes are glued to mine, unflinching. For a millisecond, I think I heard her wrong. In the next fraction of a breath, I mentally run through everything I know to be true. My dad had an affair. With her mom. He's been gone lately when he should be home. My family is teetering on a single card, and June just dropped an entire deck.

Now is not the time for this fight. This is not where she gets told everything I know. The women's bathroom of Eight Lanes is not where we swap and compare broken family tales.

I swallow hard, my mind replaying what June said, over and over. Her verbs were present tense. *Is having* is a lot different from *had*.

Before I make things worse, I spin on my heels and leave.

CHAPTER SEVENTEEN

I had to run home. My head was no clearer by the time I got there than when I left Eight Lanes, so I changed into more appropriate running wear and took off down our street, around the corner, and all the way to school.

I run when I'm stressed. I also run when I'm upset. This translates to an eleven-mile jog that lasts most of the afternoon. I take a break, climbing the bleachers to the top of the press box so I can stare at that goddamn football field for a while. All of those hits, hours of passing drills, my literal blood—all to make my old man happy. Turns out, he's big on getting greener grass in other places. Why do I even bother?

June wasn't lying. And she wasn't spreading a rumor or guessing at something she maybe suspected. I still know her well enough to sense when she's telling the truth. I pushed her to a point she wanted to hurt me, so she pulled out the sharpest tool she had. That one pierced me in the gut.

The sun is setting early, and there's a slight breeze in the air as I jog home then climb in the back of my truck. My sweat has mostly dried, leaving my skin cool. My mom's inside, and I can't face her. I don't want to be another man who lies in her house. My dad has that job all sewn up. Speaking of my dad, he isn't home.

Surprise.

The only person I can talk to right now is still at work. I have no idea when she gets off, and no clue if she'll even want to talk to me when she gets here. But when I crawled into the back of my truck and slid down to sit in the bed, I promised myself I'd wait.

Abby's headlights meet the glare of the setting sun at the end of my driveway. Our eyes meet, so I slump down lower, not really hiding but masking that I've been waiting for them to arrive. I hope she doesn't stay. I want June all to myself. She's the only one who can answer my questions and take away this awful feeling.

She swings the passenger door shut and drags her jacket along the ground as she takes micro steps in my direction. I breathe out a short, amused laugh, too quiet for her to hear. She looks like a kid about to get grounded for coloring on the walls. She's almost to me when Abby honks her horn, causing June to leap in the air and grab her chest.

"Shit!" she shouts.

My heart races, too, from being startled.

When she turns back to face me, a bashful smirk on her lips, I feel bad that I can't be light and happy with her. She got spooked by the car horn, and that should be funny, but nothing is funny right now. Nothing might ever be funny again.

"What's up, Maybe Mabee?" I sneer, glad it's dim enough to hide the details of my expression. That was my jealous side coming out. I hate that Tory calls her that.

June pauses at the end of my truck, her eyes dipping

down, heavy with guilt. She didn't do anything wrong. She shouldn't feel this way. I guarantee my father isn't.

"I'm sorry," she utters, lifting her head to meet my gaze. She truly is sorry. I read it all over her face. She's not the one I need to hear it from.

I give her a nod, unsure what to say in response.

"Okay. Thanks." I shrug then twist the cap from the water bottle I've been nursing. I chug down the rest, put the lid back on, then toss the empty container to the middle of the driveway. June starts to move toward it.

"Let my dad pick it up. Maybe I'll throw the rest of his shit out here too." It's only partially a joke.

June pauses and looks back at me over her shoulder, her eyes studying my face. *Come on, Lucas. Smile. Show her you aren't completely broken.*

I must fail the test because she turns back to the bottle, picking it up and tossing it in her family's recycling bin. She drops her hands in her pockets when she turns to face me, her head tilted ever so slightly to the side. Her eyes are so soft, gentle and caring. Why can't I just scoop her up and hold her like I want to?

Because my mom is inside and might step near the window. She might see something that will break her. Me and the enemy's daughter. And then she will have to learn the hard truth. That my dad? He's screwing her over again.

"Can I climb in there with you?" June nods toward the space next to me. I stretch my hand out and flatten it on the metal bed, as if I'm taking that space up.

"Can't," I say. My face is numb, and I doubt I'm coming close to any form of an expression at all. I'm blank. Erased. Empty. "This—" I sweep my hand around, pointing to June then to me—"does not happen in front of people."

June blinks precisely once then steps forward, placing her

palms on the tailgate, ready to hoist herself inside. My heart thumps erratically. I want her here. I want her here so goddamn badly. But it can't be *here*.

I rush to my feet and hold the side of my truck, swinging my legs over and onto the ground.

"Just get in," I grunt, gesturing to the passenger side.

She flips my tailgate up then slips into my cab, her eyes hovering on my every movement. She doesn't let up as I pull out of the driveway and race down our street. By the time we're a comfortable distance from my home, I pull to the side of the road and flip on my hazards. I can't drive any further with this feeling in my chest. It's an insatiable craving for more information. I need to know it all. *She* needs to know it all.

"Tell me how you know," I blurt out. I tighten my grip on the steering wheel, rolling my hands over the ridges. My hold is so tight I could cause a blister if I keep this up.

The only sound in the cab is June's deep breath. It's a thoughtful kind, the sort that comes with mapping out words and finding delicate ways to deliver bad news. She and I are both versed in this skill.

"I hate that I'm the one who knows this, Lucas." Her voice is soft, raspy even. She's struggling with this burden. I wonder how long she's carried it alone.

"I understand." I work to keep my voice calm. As raging as my heart is and as rabid as my temper has become since she first told me, none of this is June's fault. I have to remember that and not react *at* her.

She draws in another long breath and I hold mine.

"There are details that are hard—"

My eyes flutter closed and I hold out a palm.

"It's all hard. I know. Just . . . just tell me." I'm begging now.

"I was dropping something off at Tory's house while you all were at practice. I'd just put my car in park when I saw their garage open and a truck pull out."

No. This is not happening. No, no, no . . .

"Lots of people have trucks." My eyes flicker open but nothing seems in focus. I'm spinning, my thoughts bouncing from my best friend to our parents to my life two years ago to June.

No!

"They do," she says. I know more is coming. "Not ones with license plates framed in gold with *Tennessee Forever* etched on the top and bottom."

Everything in my body drops to my gut. My mouth is dry, and swallowing is impossible. My eyes are too dry to close. The taste on my tongue is sour, and my head thumps with the flood of adrenaline that courses through my body.

June twists in her seat, and I glance sideways, my weight held up on the steering wheel. Without it, I'd crumble to the floor.

"I saw them kiss, Lucas. Your dad and—"

"Don't." I stop her before I actually hear her speak it. I get the details. I've heard them before; I don't need them again. I glance up and hold my gaze on the roadway. It's mostly empty, minus the occasional car that passes. We're out of the glow of streetlights, and the sun has gone down completely. If I try hard enough, I wonder if I could make myself invisible.

"I don't want to know too much," she continues. "Details have a way of becoming nightmares and they poison everything."

I drop my gaze to my lap, letting my hands fall to the bottom curve of the wheel. I have to tell Tory. We'll both need to tell Hayden. This will wreck their senior year—and beyond. I would know.

"Just promise me that you are sure," I ask with a sideways glance. I can't gamble on this. It has to be certain.

"I wouldn't have ever said it if I wasn't one-hundred percent sure, Luc." She edges her palm closer to me, and I feel myself itch for the contact. I trace the form over her hand, the short nails on her fingertips, chewed off from stress biting I'm sure. She's had that habit since we were kids.

Leaning forward, I glare up through the windshield.

"There's supposed to be a meteor shower tonight. They said on the news that the best views are after midnight."

Stay with me, June. Spend the night with me right here and make everything all right. We'll look at the stars and ignore the trouble here on Earth.

"I don't have anywhere to be," she says. My mouth ticks up, a fraction of a smile. There was a tinge of joy in her voice.

"We need full dark." I lean back and roll my head to face her completely. Her lips curve into a faint grin as we hold our stare through the rush of several passing cars. It's the busiest this road has been in minutes. I think maybe the universe wanted to choose now to light up June's eyes.

"We should keep driving, then."

I hold her gaze for a few more seconds, blinking once, then turn my attention back to the road. I shift into drive and kill the hazards, careful to stay just under the limit along the way. The last thing I want to do tonight is get nailed for speeding.

We're off the beaten path. Old memories came to life, bright spots amid some awfully shitty news. June and I spent a summer treading this road and every tiny route around it on our bikes. I wonder when she's going to recognize where I'm taking us.

I veer onto a side road, and the thick trees give way to an open field. The abandoned drive-in theater comes into view, and I hear June exhale. She sees it. I'm sure she knows. I didn't plan this, but the opportunity to bring her here—to be *us* here—is too inviting. The pull of our past is strong. So many threads tether us together I could never cut them all.

June reaches forward and pushes the power button for my stereo, the Wilson Pickett song "Mustang Sally" spilling from my speakers. I need soothing music, and sometimes classic R&B is the only kind that works. I was listening to this during my run and cut it off right before the chorus, which June sings along with right now.

This was us, and here we are again—two kids singing classic tunes off-key while exploring the fringes.

"I heard this song last week with Tory," she says. Maybe it's childish of me, but her mention of him—of enjoying a song that's *ours* with my best friend—kills my desire to sing. June keeps right on going.

"Oh, yeah?" I'm not even hiding my jealousy now.

"He didn't know the words." She laughs. She's being nice. I can tell. I pucker my lips to hold in my embarrassed smile.

We're getting close to the drive-in spots, so I flip my high beams on so we can navigate the ghosts left behind. I hope they never completely tear this place down. If someone invested in it, I'd be willing to drive out here every Saturday night to see a movie. Probably not a solid business plan.

The old screen comes into view first, along with a few of the sound box posts. There's a rotted old couch in the middle of the lot, and the closer we get to it, the more certain I am it's riddled with bullet holes. Despite the spray-paint tags covering what's left of the old snack bar, this place is perfection in my eyes. June's, too.

"They're still here," she says, confirming why.

A lot of the speakers have broken away—or been stolen. But enough remain.

"Stop the car. Let's see if any work," she says, unbuckled and nearly out of the passenger seat before I stop the truck completely. We skid into a dirt patch and both leap onto the parking lot. The first several boxes I come to are busted, most of them missing cords. It takes at least two dozen failed attempts before June finally finds one that lights up when she flips it on.

"Oh, my God!" She celebrates by holding it out in front of her. The faint green glow that signals the speaker is working is the only thing I can clearly see. June's form is a scant outline lit by the moon.

I race toward her to test it out, reinvigorated to keep going when I see its connection is strong.

"Don't let go. I'll find one, too." I scurry in a new direction. I'm right up under the screen with only three or four left to try when my prayers are answered. The light flickers at first, but after a little push and pull on the wire, it lights up brightly. It seems like a trivial thing to pray for, but I need this escape tonight. I need June and our childhood and simple pleasures.

"Breaker niner-niner," I speak into the box. These things aren't supposed to work like this, but Tory showed me a special setting when we were kids. I dragged June out here to try it one night. It's like a rudimentary web of walkie talkies, or a group chat before that term existed. The power is some leftover line the town never dug up or turned off, and this town is too short-staffed to look for energy vampires.

"I cannot believe we found two that work!"

We laugh together, her voice coming through the small

speaker embraced in my palms. It crackles and I hold incredibly still, not wanting to lose her.

"It's so dark, I can barely see you," she says.

I cup the speaker close to my mouth and let out my best evil laugh.

"Don't be a jerk. You know I don't like the dark." She doesn't, but she's always been better with it than me. She never made fun of me when we were kids, though she knew I didn't like the dark either.

"I wish someone would reopen this place," she says.

"Maybe I do that instead of go to MIT or Tennessee. Look, problem solved." I chuckle, but truthfully, the thought is appealing. Places like this are meant for worlds where profit doesn't matter.

"I think you really want to go to MIT," June says, yanking me back to reality.

"Yeah." I sigh after a long pause. She's right. I do. And anytime I think of giving in and going to Tennessee, I hate my dad a little bit more. As if my opinion of him could get any lower.

"Your dad has even less of a right dictating now," June says, practically reading my thoughts. I shift my weight and clear my throat, my head crowded with thoughts of my father, what June told me, and my obligation to do *something*.

"We can talk about other things," she says, and I'm relieved to have the life raft, but when it comes down to it, everything in our lives is knotted together. My dad. Her mom. My college options, her lack of them. The twins' parents.

The time June and I missed. Time that we could have spent out here, talking . . . like this.

"I'm sorry I was a jerk." This is the apology I should have given days ago. Weeks ago.

Months.

"I miss us, Lucas."

I hold the radio in my fist, resting it against my forehead, wishing it would magically become a time machine.

"What happened?" Her sniffles somehow come through crystal clear.

It's easy to say a lot happened. Even easier to blame everyone else. Life happened. Messy relationships got messier. Lies and betrayals interfered with innocence and coming-of-age. But what it all actually boils down to is June and me. We gave up on each other. Maybe *I* gave up first, but so did she. I didn't make it easy to hold on, and the more I pushed, the farther she went, until we were seas apart.

Strangers.

"Do you think you could help me with something?" I hold my breath, knowing what I'm about to ask her is big, the kind of thing I don't have a right to. It would be a gift if she grants it.

"One date," she says. It's not the response I was expecting, but the twist injects life back into my body. I'm smiling alone in the dark.

"With me, I mean," she continues. I love the way she rambles. "I want to go out on a real date, in front of people."

She wants to be seen. She *deserves* to. Why she would want to be with me leaves me clueless, especially after how awful I've been, but she's still here. She's asking. And how could my mom be more hurt by me going on a date with June than the repeat offenses of the man she took back after he cheated the first time. I wonder how many times he's been unfaithful.

"One date." I repeat the terms, and I can tell she's surprised I'm entertaining the idea by the way her breath puffs through the speaker.

"Yes. That's my offer. Take it or leave it."

I smirk at her confident voice. I bet she's forcing herself to stand up tall and rolling her shoulders.

"Deal. And June?"

The connection crackles, so I repeat my answer again.

"June? Can you hear me? I said yes. It's a deal. Did you get that?"

I hold my speaker to my ear, the fuzz growing more even, until soon it's just a soft hush of audio snow.

"Went dead!" she shouts across the lot.

I drop my box since it's useless now, and it bangs around the post where it hangs from the cord. I chuckle to myself and hang my head, scratching at the back of my neck, amused at the irony. June and I finally get our moment, and our chosen method of communication is some century-old hack in the middle of nowhere. Lifting my chin, I wait for my eyes to adjust on her figure. I wonder if she knows she's beautiful. I wonder if I have the guts to tell her.

I cup my mouth to make sure she hears me.

"I get to pick the place!" I shout.

My hands drop to my sides, a tingling sensation running from my neck all the way down to my fingertips.

"So you can pick somewhere nobody will see you with me?" June huffs out a laugh that's purposeful and jaded. She feels like a secret, and I get it.

We're too far apart for this, the details. It's time for real talk. The more we reconnect, the move obvious it becomes that neither of us has the full story. June obviously doesn't understand why I've been so cold and distant, which means she probably doesn't know about her mom's affair with my dad. If she did, her reaction when she discovered my dad's latest discretion would have been vastly different.

The hundred feet or so between us feels like forever

under my feet. I'm not rushing, instead trying to gather the right words. She's sitting on a crate, her shoulders slumped and brow pinched.

"You ashamed of me, Lucas Fuller? Is that what all of this is about?"

What?

To hear her voice her broken feelings, to utter that word—*ashamed*—spears my heart. She lifts her palms, showing an indifferent shrug, as if she's giving up, and everything in me solidifies.

No. We aren't quitting. Not this time. I'm going to have to tell her everything I know, and it's going to affect her the same way her news about my dad struck me. Probably worse. She'll push me away. But I won't go. I'll stay. Just like she did.

I tilt my head to the side.

"It's nothing like that, June." I shake my head.

"What's it like, then, Lucas? Because here's what it's like to me. We're best friends, then we're not. We live a hundred feet apart, and for two years, I see you only in passing, through open shutters and truck windows. I come back to school and we're enemies. I resent you, but only because you resent me, and I have no idea why—none of it. No clue. But then there are these few tiny moments when I see you. When I *really* see you. My Lucas shows up to take care of me, and he talks and he shares for one night. We kiss, then just . . . like . . . that."

She snaps her fingers and my eyes dart to the motion of her hand. I disappeared. Not like magic, though, because magic is wondrous and special. Nothing about the last two years deserves such an adjective.

"You can't tell anyone."

She throws my own words back at me, and I wince. I blink rapidly for a few seconds and draw in air through my nose. My gaze steady on hers, I try to see our world through her eyes. And then I try to predict how she's going to see things after I tell her the reasons behind it all.

"You're right," I say.

Her brow furrows as she blinks once. I don't think she's joking, either. I think she is actually surprised to hear me admit that to her.

She holds up her broken speaker and presses the button, which does nothing at all.

"I'm sorry, could you repeat that please?" she says into it. It makes me smile. June . . . she's funny. She's also honest and real. No pretense to what she wants or needs. What I see is what I get, and I feel lucky that I can have this amazing creature in my life. I'm in awe of her, actually. I find my head falling to the side again as I study her—the slope of her nose, pink lips, slender neck and tousled hair that falls over her shoulders in twisty waves, probably from braids she had in earlier. The girl I grew up with—the one who played in mud and rolled down the driveway, belly on a skateboard—she's still very much here. But so is this woman, a girl on the brink of eighteen.

Green eyes that I thought were cool because they were the color of a pond are now cool for entirely different reasons. They're wicked, and sexy, especially when her long lashes shade them, kissing her cheeks when she blinks. Once bony arms and legs are now lines that beg my eyes to trail up and down them, taking in the light dusting of freckles on her rounded shoulders—skin kissed by the sun. Her breasts would fit perfectly in each of my palms, and I drop my hands into my pockets at that thought, feeling both guilty for having it and hungry to test it.

"You . . . are right," I finally say, repeating the words she insists on hearing again.

She gives me a sideways look that makes me laugh.

"So, is that a yes? To the—"

"It's a yes to the date. And a yes that it won't be in a cave. I will take you somewhere that has actual living, breathing humans nearby. There might be food, and there will probably be a movie because this is Indiana and our options are slim."

Light and airy laughter falls from her lips.

"Come here," I say, extending my arm and calling her to me with a finger. I drop my hands back in my pockets to still my nerves when I realize my palms are sweating. June holds her stare on me, her mouth caught in a skeptical, open-mouthed smile that draws up one side of her lip.

"Please," I say.

She blinks. Lashes kiss cheeks. Fucking adorable.

She gets to her feet, brushing off the back of her jeans, then pushes her hands in her pockets too. I wonder if she's as nervous as I am. We've already kissed, but everything feels new. She twists her feet into the ground, swaying her hips side-to-side, playing coy. All I see are her curves, and the slight peek of skin where her jeans rest on her hips, her sweatshirt pulled up barely enough to give me this glimpse. I lick my bottom lip with the tip of my tongue, my mouth watering as the thought of running it along her taut stomach and navel flashes through my mind.

The second she's close enough, I close the remaining distance, grabbing her wrists and guiding her hands so they're flush against mine. Our fingers weave together, the feeling so natural. Our fit is perfect, palm-to-palm. I indulge in her beauty, my chest fluttering with the off-beat percussion of my heart. If she weren't holding on to my hands, I doubt I could feel them. I want this. And maybe that's what I was protecting myself from all along—from wanting something so fragile, so fraught with risk.

"I don't want—" I stop, closing my mouth and glancing down, my focus on her chin before I close my eyes. I have to get his right. "I don't want my family to fuck it up. I want to keep this ours for a little while."

I don't want to tell you the things I must. Details that will crush you. Don't make me yet. When I open my eyes, I try to simmer the burning resentments very much alive in my belly. I'm doing a poor job of hiding it when her eyes zero in on mine. It's not that she looks afraid, but that her expression is full of worry.

She steps into me so our elbows touch, and I practice measured patience. I'm sure she can feel my hands vibrating with urgency, fighting against their desire to rush around her waist and pull her into me. My heart is thumping against my breast plate with enough force to make it crack, and my lips tingle with expectation and hope.

June rises on her toes, her mouth so close to take, her gaze on mine.

Lashes dust skin. It's hypnotic.

"What's the favor?" I barely hear the words she speaks, drunk instead on the movements of her lips. The way they wrap around each word. The faint smile that follows. I flit my gaze up to her eyes, and I can only take in one at a time. We're so close. Inches. Breaths.

I need to kiss her.

"I'm going to interview for MIT. And Coach and my dad, they can't know." I glance down, to the tip of her nose. This is a difficult favor to ask, and honestly, it has nothing to do with taking her on a date. I needed to ask this of her regardless, and the option of saying no to taking her out disappeared the moment we kissed.

"They won't," she says. Her smirk settles my nerves. When I glance to her eyes, I see the pride she has in me. I can read her, the crinkled corners that are pushed up by her growing smile.

I let go of the breath I'm holding, and her hands squeeze against mine.

"I have a plan. You'll need to take my truck."

Her smile gets really big. I laugh and shake our joined hands.

"I'm gonna want it back in one piece."

She shakes her head.

"No promises."

I squint at her briefly, a crooked smile that teases on my mouth.

"Do you need help getting ready for the interview? Is it at school? Or do you go to an office?" Her questions spill out, almost as if she's been holding on to them, or has a list in her pocket that includes more.

I'm grinning like a fool when her eyes catch my face.

"What?" Her cheeks blush.

I need to kiss her.

Lifting our hands to my shoulders, I coax hers around my neck before drawing faint lines down her arms, tickling her skin enough to make her breathe out a hushed laugh. I rest my palms on her waist and she drops from her toes, standing flat, her height perfectly fitting under my chin. I close the remaining inches as she gazes up at me and runs her fingers through my hair.

"June?" Her eyes flit to mine briefly, mouth pulled into a tight, nervous smile that pierces the corners like arrows. Her gaze is gone as fast as it was on mine, her stare centered on my chest.

I lift my hand to her face, my thumb brushing over her bottom lip. So soft and supple, my mouth craves the feel of it. I want to suck her in, drink her, and devour her. I run the back of my hand along her jaw, then her cheek. I lift her chin so she has no choice but to look into my eyes unless she closes hers. I'm blessed either way—either the wild green or the feather of lashes.

I nod, a slight movement as my focus drops to her mouth for a fraction of a second. A tiny breath escapes and her bottom lip juts out. My muscles grow tense, the sensation of holding on tight as if I'm trying not to fall taking hold of my body. She's trembling. I feel her resistance out of nowhere, so I step back, giving us space. I hold her stare and search for clues, some warning of what's next. Some sign that it isn't what I fear it is.

"What happened?" Merely asking this question sends ripples through her body and she quivers where she stands.

No. Not now. Please not now.

I slowly shake my head.

"Why did you pull away? Lucas . . . I need to know."

My hands feel along her waist, the numbness returning. She's slipping away, and there is nothing I can do to hold on to her. I'm weak.

Useless.

"Please don't make me tell you. Don't make me say it."

I realize the moment the words leave my mouth that I have no choice. It has to be me, and I've now made sure that it happens tonight. I feel the moment slip away, like silk sheets sliding from a bed. My hands want to claw at them, clutch them and keep them here, but I have no power over my body anymore. I have no power over anything.

June looks sick. I shake my head harder, a fruitless effort that is met by her steeled expression. This is the point of no return. Dead man walking and all that.

"June," I plead, squeezing my eyes shut and hoping when

I open them we'll be back in my truck, holding hands . . . *happy.*

My hands fall from her body and I'm not sure whether I did it willingly or simply lost the strength to hold on. I reach into my hair and grip it, tugging lightly, wanting the painful distraction and a reminder that I'm alive and need to get through this. I have to relive this for her.

Lifting my eyes to take in her face, I exhale the last of before and prepare for this painful now.

"This isn't my father's first affair."

She blinks. The connections are forming. I recognize the slight tug on her lips as they open. I'm torn between taking this slow and ripping off the Band-Aid. I honestly don't know which is the better choice, so I do what I would prefer. I will speak until she tells me to stop. Until she's had enough and can't take anymore.

"My dad was seeing your mom."

She blinks again.

"My mom caught them together."

Her eyes drop a tick to my chest.

"He begged my mom not to leave."

Her mouth closes, the places where our worlds intersect coming into view. This is why it had to be me to tell her. Nobody else would understand.

"My mom wanted him to make you and your mom move, but she settled for us never talking to you again."

I wanted to, June. I almost broke so many times. Somehow, it got easier, though. It got easier to avoid you, and I hate myself for that.

"She said she would tell everyone how your mom and my dad met."

I swallow hard. This is the detail I know she isn't expecting. It's the thing I regret most having shared with Ava. It's the biggest stain on my character, not hers.

"He hired her, June. She needed money to get away from your dad and still be able to afford . . . things. And my father paid. He paid over and over. And he said he wasn't the only one."

Her cheeks puff slightly. I think she might get sick.

"I didn't want you to know. I didn't want anyone to ever know. I didn't . . ."

Nothing else I say is going to fix things for her, and I doubt she can hear me now. I've been where she is, slipping away. She's scouring her mind for arguments against this, for other reasons and alternative timelines. This is the one we've lived, unfortunately. This is the path we are on. And I am the bearer of soul-crushing news.

CHAPTER EIGHTEEN

"We haven't seen the meteors yet."

June lies back on the roof of my truck. I should take her home. I've tried. She crawled up there an hour ago, and I don't get the sense she's coming down. Pushing her won't change the confusion swirling in her head.

She said she wanted to know everything, so I told her. Now, I fear I've filled her head too much. June and her mom are so close. They always have been, and from what I could tell from my self-imposed distance, they have only grown closer the last two years. Now, though, June has to be doubting everything.

I told her about the money exchange and the private investigator my mom hired when she suspected my dad was sleeping around. I showed her the screen shots of text messages I saved, proof to remind myself that my father is an utter disappointment. I needed something to shore up my will whenever I felt weak, to keep me from running next door and talking to June those first few months. I rarely look at them now, but I can't seem to delete them.

"The clouds are rolling in." I hook my thumbs in my pockets and glare up at the sky. This is my second attempt to make her concerned about the weather. I'm sure we won't get rain, I just want to snap June out of this state. It's like a switch flipped after I told her everything. She couldn't really run away, so she hopped on top of my truck.

"Sit with me?" She rolls her head lazily to the side, the smile that was flirting with her lips before we nearly kissed nowhere to be found. I'm not sure whether she's in denial or merely processing. I don't know how to navigate this without leading us back down the rocky road we were on before, as near enemies.

It's getting cold out, and June is probably freezing up there. I sigh and push my hands deep into the front pocket of my hoodie, the hood pulled tight around my face. I wish I had joggers on. These shorts were a good idea when I was sprinting around our neighborhood. That was two hours ago, though.

"You can grab my jacket from the floor of your truck. Use it to cover up?" She's being serious, and it's so fucking sweet. After the things I told her, she's still being sweet.

I smirk on one side of my mouth, breathing out a laugh.

"Okay, June." I open the passenger side and grab her jacket, flipping off the truck's headlights to save my battery and give us a better view. It doesn't take much to run my stereo, so I tune in some chill music then climb my way up top with June.

"Here," I say, handing her the jacket. I slide my legs next to hers and she glances from my knees back to my eyes.

"You're in shorts. I thought you could use it to cover up.

I shake my head and laugh. I'm fucking freezing, but what kind of gentleman would I be if I didn't take care of her first?

"I don't get cold." Those words carry double meaning.

"That's not true." So do June's. She winces, probably feeling bad, but she shouldn't.

"I didn't mean it like that," she adds. She's a terrible liar.

I let my head fall to the side but keep my gaze soft and on hers.

"Yes, you did." My voice is a whisper. Guilt has a way of muting me.

"I'm sorry."

Look how easy it is for her to apologize, you asshole.

"Don't be." I glance down her body to where her hands fist the bottom of her shirt. I unzip her jacket and spread it over her upper body like a blanket.

"Your mom is probably worried about you." She's not going to like that I brought her up. I had a hard time even *thinking* about my dad at first. I won't push too hard, but I won't let her fall into darkness.

I lean back on my palms and let my legs dangle down the windshield. I get dizzy if I crane my neck too long, but I give it a go and let my head fall back for a little while. I hope we see a shooting star. June deserves one. For a moment, I think I catch one out of the corner of my eye. I'm about to ask June if she saw it when her body shifts next to me and her head nestles onto my lap. Suddenly, I hope we don't see a meteor for hours. I don't look down, too afraid to jinx this.

"I'm probably not very soft," I joke.

"You're softer than you think," she teases back, her head squishing against my thigh. I think she's basically calling me a mushy pillow.

I can't help myself and look down, hoping to catch her smile. It's there, and it's breathtaking.

"Okay, then." I draw in a quick breath then let my head fall back again. The second my eyes settle on the black sky, a streak of stardust cuts through the center. Sometimes, it's hard not to believe in signs.

"Oh, my God!" June's voice is pure elation.

"Wow," I say, stretching the three letters out far longer than necessary. I'm reacting more to June's reaction than I am to the meteor, but she doesn't need to know that.

It's just June, me, the midnight sky, and the soft chirp of crickets. I don't even think I breathe for a whole minute. Not until her hand travels up my chest and the weight of her head lifts from my lap. I have no choice but to look down at her, and when her warm palm slides along my jawline and under the hood of my sweatshirt, my eyes threaten to close, soothed by her touch. I force them to remain open. June reaches into my hair, her fingers twisting around the strands. My lips part for their first breath in what feels like forever, and a heartbeat later, June's mouth is on mine.

My mouth first reacts in shock. I never pegged June as being bold. I worry she's trying to kiss away her fears, using intimacy to bury pain. That's what I did with Ava. I don't want that kind of relationship with June. Her kiss softens, and I wage a mental war with myself. I should pull away and make sure this is what she truly wants. Or maybe I should let her lead, simply follow. I know what half of my body wants me to do. Hell, ninety-eight percent of my body wants to let her do whatever she wants with and to me.

June's kisses rain along my jawline as her hands push my hood from my head. There's something intoxicating about the way her hands run through my hair, and I give in to the devil on my shoulder and guide her mouth back to mine so I can kiss her like I really want to. The moment our lips connect, I become ravenous. Every pass of my tongue against hers needs to be memorized. The way her teeth grab my bottom lip and tug drives me to do the same. It's as if we're in a silent competition over who needs this kiss more. Maybe we're both desperate for it. Like air.

We cradle each other's faces and June shifts so she's sitting on her knees. I lean back to give her room to straddle my lap and the second she sits on me, I lose myself completely. I'm so fucking hard. She's so soft and smooth and smells like honey and lemon. I'm sure she felt the groan that escaped my lips the second my cock came in contact with her body. All the sweatpants and jeans in the world couldn't deny the sensation I just experienced.

My weight back, I rest on my palms as June runs her fingers down the front of my hoodie. It's dark out, but the moon is bright enough to illuminate her eyes. They're hazed. Hungry. And I'm fighting my worst thoughts not to give in to my most base desires. Her lips are raw where I kissed them so hard a second ago, the bottom one pink and puffed out. Sexy and wanting. Her chin lifts a bit, revealing her slender neck, tempting me to run my mouth along it and taste, nibble. Her breasts sit up high, the tips poking through her cotton shirt. My mind conjures the sensation of flicking my tongue against that hard, pink tip.

June rocks her hips, and my eyes flutter closed briefly. "Fuuuuuuck," I groan, biting my bottom lip. If she does that too many times, I'm going to come in my shorts.

Her hands slip down to the bottom of my hoodie and I help her lift it over my head, tossing it behind me into the back of the truck. Her hands run along my sides, feeling the dips and curves of my muscles. If nothing else, my hard work in the gym has been for this. Her hands dip lower, toying with the hair below my belly button, teasing the band of my shorts. When her hand tugs the string holding them up, I come to long enough to cover her hand with mine and make sure this is something she means to do. I don't want to be her version of running.

To slow her down, I bring her hands to my mouth and kiss the insides of her wrists. Lifting her arms above her head, I let my fingers roam down the length of her arms, my eyes studying hers as my hands travel. When I reach her nipples, I let the pads of my thumbs run over the tips through her shirt, and she gasps. I continue my descent to the bottom of her work shirt, gathering it in my hands and dragging it up the length of her body. When I clear her head, she takes the garment from me and tosses it in the back of the truck with my hoodie.

She steadies herself, arms braced on my shoulders while her fingers play with my hair. I lock onto her gaze, searching for reservations, but all I see is the same hunger coursing through my body. My eyes close as my mouth falls to her neck, kissing along the curve to her shoulder while my hands slowly slide the straps of her bra down. I kiss each newly exposed bit of her, starting at her shoulder then moving to the center of her chest, each kiss lower until her bright pink nipples are right there for me to taste. I don't pause. I don't even think. I just lick, my tongue memorizing the soft tip it holds hostage. My mouth closes over the tip and I suck gently, blowing her cool as I back away.

June reacts, arching back. It takes seconds for me to peel her lacey white bra away completely, tossing it aside. My hand covers her right breast while my mouth finds home again on her left. I suck until a faint cry falls from her lips, and as they fall open, I clamp down on her nipple lightly with my teeth. Her body rolls with desire, and she rocks her hips against my erection.

Fucking hell, this is better than actual sex. And I *want* actual sex. With June. I want to erase everyone else and feel only her. I want to be inside her, to taste her and feel her breath pant heavily at my neck.

At some point tonight, she twisted her hair up into a knot at the back of her head. I want to see it flying wild. I want to wrap it around my hands and see the curls tickle against her breasts. I run my hand up her neck to the hair band and pull it free, tossing it God knows where. I let her mane fly in the breeze for a minute, then gather it into my palm so I can tug her head back enough to cause her to arch perfectly. Her neck is mine. Her breasts—*mine.* I saw my teeth against the hard peak, and she sinks her weight into me. I flick her nipple raw before giving in and biting it once.

Her hands slink around my neck, slipping to my shoulder blades as she pulls herself into me again. I feel my cock flex under her weight. I can't handle many more of those.

I sweep the stray hairs from her face when our eyes meet. Her lips fall open in a silent plea for me to quench their need to be kissed. I feel it, too. As long as I'm touching her, the world is right. Nothing makes sense except us.

This kiss is somehow hungrier than all the others. June literally dominates me, her need somehow outpacing mine, which seems damn near impossible; I feel as though I'm going to explode. Her hips rock and the hot center between her legs grinds against me. Needing to feel more of her, I drop my hands to her hips, guiding her back and forth over my hard-on. I can see her orgasm build in her face, her eyes rolling back and teeth gripping desperately at her lip, trying to hold on. I'm not sure if she knows she's humming, but the sound is fucking sexy as hell.

I'm intent on giving her what she wants, but before I grab her ass hard and pull her into me, she reaches between us and tugs at the string on my shorts. I'm too weak to stop her, and when her hand dips inside and finds the tip of my dick, the only word I can muster is her name.

She sits back enough to pull my pants lower on my hips, her head resting against mine. Our hot breath mingles with her words.

"I want to touch you," she says. I nod, shift so she can pull my cock free. The cold air shocks my system, but the sensation is instantly replaced with the warm touch of June's hand.

"Am I doing this right?" she asks, her fingers wrapped around me, squeezing with slight pressure and roaming up and down. My cock flexes at her touch and I nod.

"Yeah," I pant before grabbing the back of her head and bringing her mouth to mine. I kiss her hard while her hand flows up and down my shaft. She sits up tall on her knees, and the fact she wants to watch while she strokes me is so fucking hot. I slide my hand up the back of her thigh, and as she glides up my dick, my hand trails up her leg. I tease, flirting with her ass, and when I finally grab it her head falls back. She grips me harder, and I slide my hand in her back pocket. Her ass is perfect, round and firm. I sink my hand in as far as it will go so I can feel the place where it curves into her pussy.

June reaches for my other hand, and my breath stops in a panic. I lost myself in her touch, and I recoil my palm from her pocket, afraid I went too far. This is still June. There's an innocence to her that will always be there. It's part of what makes her so sexy. I hope I didn't ruin that.

Before I can even question things, though, she moves my hand to the front of her jeans, stopping at the button. I glance up to meet her hooded eyes. *Oh, fuck, yes.*

I tug the front of her jeans open, dropping her zipper with one hand while the other glides along the smooth skin of her lower back to her hip. My thumbs hook inside the band of her panties, and I yank both the cotton undies and jeans down her thighs. We shift so I can guide her to lie on her back, and she kicks her shoes from her feet and works her pants off completely, kicking them to the side.

I maneuver on my knees so I'm between her open legs, lifting my gaze to take in this beautiful creature lying before me, naked and writhing. This is June. *Fuck! June Mabee.* I've never seen a more sexual being. I can smell her desire and it sinks into my veins. My eyes trail from her navel to her breasts until our gazes lock. She nods and whimpers "Yes," and it's all I need for assurance.

I fumble for my wallet and pull out the condom, a new one. I hold it up to prove it to June, and she giggles, cupping her mouth. Her cheeks blush, such a pretty fucking sight on the roof of my truck under the moonlight.

She slides her hands under her hips while I slide the condom on, and I can tell she's both nervous and excited. Lowering myself so I'm on top of her, I leave enough room between us for her to arch and breathe. My weight on my forearms, I lean my head down to run my nose against hers then brush a soft kiss on her lips. I take my time, kissing her with teasing nibbles that I hope set her at ease. When our kiss deepens, I move to grab my cock and guide it inside of her. She sucks in a harsh breath when I push the tip in, so I pause.

"Okay?" My lips dance across hers with the question.

She nods, and utters, "Yes."

I take it slow, pushing into her until I feel her surround me completely. My mouth hangs open, my body rippling with tremors because she feels so fucking good. I let her get used to my size before pulling out and gliding in again. My movements are measured, steady and smooth. I don't want to hurt her, and it's almost painful taking it this slow. My mind is drunk on thoughts of me pounding into her, my dick slick with her wetness. The thought alone makes me flex and threaten to come.

I kiss along her neck to distract her as my rocking picks up speed. I suck a tiny hickey into the skin at the nape of her neck and blow on it when I'm done.

"I left a tiny bruise there so you'll see it in the morning and know this was real." I rock out of her and our eyes meet. The pain that was creasing them seems to have eased. She's approaching pleasure.

"Ready?" I ask. She nods again.

Lining my body up with hers, I push in deeper this time, my thumbs running along her cheeks to draw her eyes open. I lift my body enough to meet her eyes and share the smile she's etched on my face. I'm present for this, feeling every new moment right along with her. I may not be a virgin, but June is still my first in many ways. This isn't completely about sex. This night—our connection—is about love.

Love.

I draw back and rock into her again. She whimpers against my mouth, her teeth gripping my bottom lip. The sounds she makes drive me harder, and I sink into her completely. Groaning with every stretch of her body around mine, I slide in and out. We both get lost to the rhythm, and minutes pass of nothing but our moans and my body falling into hers. And then her legs wrap around my waist.

Oh, fuck.

I'm right on the edge. I'm going to come way too soon, and I don't want to ruin her first time, but I'm not sure I'm in control of anything anymore. I try to focus on nothing but her breathing, the light pant that leaves her mouth and hits my neck, the soft hum with every pump. When her teeth clamp down on my shoulder, I know I can give in to my own needs, and let myself feel it all—her pulsing around me, the sheen of sweat covering her skin, the embrace of her hands as she holds my hips tight, tugging them into her as she rolls with pleasure. One last whimper in my ear pushes me to climax, and my dick swells one last time, emptying inside of her.

We roll to the side and I pull off the condom, tying it up and tossing it into the dirt lot. If that was June's first time, I cannot wait to be her second, third . . . hundredth. She's insatiable, already tempting me to touch her again. I'm completely spent, but my cock is still rock hard, so she uses me and I let her.

I hold her hips while she climbs on top of me again, flattening my hard on against my body while she pleasures herself against it. This time, I get to see her body move, and if I were able to stop her and slip on another condom just so I could come inside her again, I would. But I'm out of condoms. And my muscles are still weak from seconds ago. But June—June is hot and young and ripe and breaking apart on top of me for my eyes alone, and she is fucking beautiful.

CHAPTER NINETEEN

The sun is up by the time I get June home. Her mom called and texted all night, but she kept sending her to voicemail. Eventually, she turned off her phone. I worried, but I was also, *well,* distracted. Now that we're in my driveway, and she's seen just how many times her mom messaged, and how many times her friend Abby did as well, I think we're both coming to our senses.

People were worried. I don't like that. Especially when I'm trying to earn trust again. No matter what June's mom was a part of, she's still June's parent. I want her to be all right with the two of us being together. It's going to be enough of a challenge to prepare my mom for this news.

"Tell me this will be okay," she says, sliding out of the passenger seat of my truck. I hold her hand in mine and kiss her wrist. I love this piece of her. It's both strong, full of life, yet delicate and fragile all at once.

"It will be, eventually. Don't be afraid of time."

I wish I could go back two years and tell myself this.

She steps up and crawls across the seat again, placing both palms on either side of my face, staring me in the eyes.

"And people say football players are idiots." I catch a glimpse of her smirk a millisecond before she leans in and kisses me.

"Who says that?" I play the part, laughing as she moves back to her seat.

She isn't ready to head inside. Not yet. I'll sit here as long as she needs, though I fear if we wait too long her mom may come yank me out of the truck and kick my teeth in. I've never doubted her loyalty and love for her daughter. It's her choice in men and marriage wrecking I take issue with.

We sit in silence for several minutes. I can tell by the way June's eyes flicker that she's trying to argue her way through the next several minutes, her lids twitching as her focus moves from one thing to another, never fully settling in. There isn't a plan for the conversations she's about to have. I suppose I could write one, but everyone's journey might be different.

"How come boys have it so easy? It's so hypocritical." She breathes out a smug but light-hearted laugh. "You're rolling in at the crack of dawn, too, but I don't see your mother out in the driveway waiting to rip your head off after she finishes hugging you."

She shifts her gaze to me, blinking over a wry smile, then turns her attention back to her house, the kitchen light glowing through the door's glass.

"I guess it's a matter of conditioning. My parents are kind of used to me not coming home on weekends," I say. I reach across the seat and roll my palm over for her to take again, an offer of strength. She's welcome to whatever she can drain from me. She moves her palm over mine and curls her fingers around my hand, squeezing tight.

"I don't want to do this," she says.

I can feel her pulse. Or maybe it's mine on her behalf.

"That's why I never said anything before." Guilt rushes up my esophagus, burning. I feel sick that I brought this to her forefront. It's my fault she has to deal with it now, in the pale light of morning.

The door to June's house opens while we're both staring at it, and her mom stops at the threshold, arms folded over her chest.

Shit.

I'm not sure whether June says it or I simply think it.

Her mom steps onto the driveway, marching toward us with angry steps, her arms still wrapped around her body. She stops abruptly about a dozen feet from June's side of the truck. The squiggled wrinkle in her forehead is more pronounced than when we were kids and in trouble. I don't think it's a matter of age this time, but rather severity of the crime.

"Wish me luck," June says. I give her one final kiss and watch as she heads into one of the hardest days of her life.

I'm content to sit here in my truck all day. I want to be here for her if things get sour, and I have a feeling they might. From experience.

My tiny bubble of peace and quiet bursts with a flicker of movement to my left, and even before I look to confirm it, I sense my mother's eyes on June. I'm not sure how long she's been standing there staring, but I can tell by the soured expression on her face that she's seen more than enough.

I draw in a full breath and ready myself for the conversation to come. June is worth it, and my mom will understand. She loved June, and I know in her heart, she still does. She's simply blinded by the past, one painted by my father's broad, cruel brush strokes.

Rolling my eyes is probably not the best way to greet her as I climb out of my truck, but it's what happens to my face.

"Oh, am I inconveniencing you? I'm sorry, do you want to go back next door and spend time with the family you prefer? Maybe sign up to be a pimp?"

I pass by her and avoid making eye contact on my way. I hope June and her mom didn't hear any of that. I think they're far enough away by now, maybe even inside their house. I can't look to see because that would require turning around, and my mom is still hovering behind me. I pause at the door leading inside and look down at my feet, trying to catch enough in my periphery to know when my mom has cleared the garage door line. The second she's inside, I slap the button to lower the door and head into the house.

I've never been one to run from my mom when she's like this—manic and paranoid. I have massive empathy for her. I don't believe most of her behavior is entirely her fault. But I wish she would work on getting better. She stopped going to therapy on her own a year ago. I think maybe if she still went she'd have the courage to leave my dad. Maybe this time she will, when she finds out that he's having an affair again, with another parent of one of my friends. I should probably keep him away from Cannon, the new guy, and his family.

"Lucas, I'd like you to look at me." Her voice is stable, so I don't think she's going to ramble out more insults about June and her mom. I give in after pulling a Coke from the fridge, turning and opening it with my back resting on the counter.

"Look," she starts, pausing and pinching her brow while her eyes squeeze shut.

I wait patiently while she gathers her thoughts. This is where my parents differ. While my dad's style is more full steam ahead and scream, scream, scream, my mother is thoughtful and delicate. It doesn't mean she can't be a bit passive-aggressive, and I'm starting to realize she has a manipulative streak.

"I know you've been going through a lot," she says.

"*Mmm*, yeah. I have." My words come out snarky and her eyes snap to mine. I hold up a palm. "Sorry. Continue."

Now isn't the time to ask her where she was while dad was reaming me over football the other night. She probably doesn't even remember it. She avoids those conflicts. They aren't hers.

"Lucas, I get that you maybe miss June. You guys are seniors, and you're going to be heading in different directions soon. Who knows where she'll end up."

Junior college down the street. I don't say it out loud because I'm afraid it might make my mom happy to hear. She'll take pleasure in June's goals getting cut short, and that will make me mad. All of it will be built on my dad's bad deed, and *where is he?*

"She needed to talk, and I was literally the only person who could help." I'm not technically lying. If my mom doesn't dig for details, I won't have to either.

I take a sip of my drink and meet my mom's stare over the lip of the can. My belly is nervous, my stomach rolling with stress and nervous energy. I don't want to fuck this up. This is why I want to keep things secret. As soon as people find out about us, they'll find a way to ruin us.

"I'm glad you could listen. You were . . . late, is all." She's trying to be the bigger person. I can read behind her pursed lips and red-tinged eyes, though. She hates that she walked out and found me with June.

"I've been late before," I egg on. I don't know why I'm pushing. I shouldn't. The more I do, the likelier it is she'll break down, and that would be on me. It's only that I've placated everyone in this house for so long and frankly, I'm tired.

My mom shifts her weight, her arms folded much like June's mom's were.

"You have, yes. And maybe I'm being unfairly upset since it was June—" She stops abruptly, her mouth snapping shut but the words she almost said aren't far from the surface.

I suck in my lips to keep my words in, too. Knowing about my dad's new affair is this tempting card to play. I'm not that person, though—the kind who orchestrates chaos and sets others up. I won't let my mom live in the dark, but I also won't blurt the facts at her without some consideration first. Right now, it would be me lashing out. When I tell her about Dad, I need her ready to make a change. I need her strong enough to leave him, for good.

My mom's motivation has shriveled. I can tell she no longer wants to be angry with me. She's slipped more into the hurt category, but really, that's of her own making. She's the one who stayed after my father cheated. She didn't have to. I wish she hadn't. It's amazing what two years of maturing can do. The younger me was afraid of a world where his parents split up. I knew together they were a bad match. They have been for years. But divorce scared me. It came with unknowns, like who would I live with more often and when? Now that I consider it this way, my mom probably kept the peace and put up with the disrespect for my sake.

Looking at her through this new lens, I see how she struggles, even now. She's trying so hard to keep this elusive peace. She doesn't even realize that we're in the midst of war.

I set my soda down and move toward her. She flinches at first, which makes me sad and worried that my dad's bursts of anger make her that way.

"I want to dance," I offer, holding out a palm.

Her wide eyes jet to my hand then to my face, followed by a timid smile.

"Are you trying to make things better by bribing me? You know I love to dance with my son."

Her hand in mine, I spin her once and form the perfect frame for a little two-step.

"Mayyyybeeee," I tease. Her eyes are already clearer. I don't fool myself into believing she's not still thinking about where I was all night and who I was with, but the smile inching upward on her face is real.

I pause after a few steps and hold up a finger then reach into my pocket for my phone. I skim through a few songs on the latest playlist Tory put together for me, and I find the one song by Florida-Georgia Line that he forced me into halfway liking. I know it's the right choice when my mom's eyes light up.

"Oh, I love this one," she says.

"Of course you do." I chuckle. "Shall we?"

I hold my hand out again and my mom takes it, letting me spin her with a little more flourish this go round. I took a class with her a year ago because my dad never seemed to have the time, and we fall easily into our two-step pattern. For the next hour, we dance and laugh as if nothing in the world is wrong. That sense of impending doom remains in my gut, though. I think it's in hers too. Dancing can only cover up so much.

It's been years since I've messaged this number. I've wanted to for weeks. I'm pretty sure sleeping with someone is a major leap over the level of texting, so I push my anxiety to the side and pull up a new message for June.

I took a nap, and I'm sure she did, too. Her house has

been still most of the day, or it was before I fell asleep. I want to make sure things with her mom went okay. I'm worried about her. And there's a slightly insecure part of me that hopes she doesn't think we made a mistake.

Of all the words in the English language to choose from, I decide to send her one of the shortest ones.

ME: *Hi.*

I pace my room, moving to my window to catch a glimpse of her inside her house. It's past four, and unless she plans on sleeping until tomorrow morning, she needs to wake up.

A minute, maybe two, passes with no response, and I start to wish there was a way to take back a text. When my phone buzzes, I freeze and clutch it in my palm.

JUNE: *Hi back.*

I haven't smiled this often in months, twenty-four of them, at least. I flop back on my bed, body still smelling of June. I haven't showered since we rolled in at the crack of dawn, and my hair is a crazy mess. When I woke, it formed a scarecrow-like shadow on my wall from the sun pouring through the window.

ME: *Don't suppose you can sneak over here to take a shower with me?*

Three dots show up, showing June is responding, then promptly disappear. I laugh out once and rub my tired eyes. Hard to think I can embarrass her now, after everything. I pull the neck of my sweatshirt up to my mouth so I can chew at it while I picture June in my shower, my hands on her soap-drenched body. I bet her hair feels like silk. I'd love to flow it over her tits and drink from them.

Fuck, I'm hard.

JUNE: *I'm not really in good standing at home right now. Rain check?*

ME: *Yes!*

I'm seriously going to *need* to shower after this. *Focus, Lucas. She's had a tough day.*

ME: *Was your mom upset?*

It takes her a few minutes to type, and I spend the time waiting by digging out our freshman yearbook from under my bed. I hang over the edge as I flip through the pages until I get to her picture. Her braids make me chuckle. She's matured a lot since she was fourteen and wearing braces. I flip a few pages back and study my own face, this time spitting out my laugh. Looking at our images through a totally unbiased lens I have to admit. June? She's way out of my league. There's a cuteness to her—both now and then—that I definitely lack. There's a gap in my teeth in my freshman picture, and the one I took before school this year is marred by a deep scowl. I haven't aged gracefully, but June aged into a goddess.

When my phone buzzes under my chest, I roll to my side to read.

JUNE: *We aren't exactly talking. I didn't know what to say and she was angry that I worried her. I feel bad because I don't like making her worry, but I'm also so mad that anything I say right now will be mean and nasty. I'm really sorry you had to go through this on your own. Maybe if I knew back then, we could have helped each other through it.*

I roll the phone in my palm and pull in my bottom lip. This is the dilemma I've had for the last two years—protect June and spare my mom's fragile emotions, or bring her into this web with me so we can suffocate together.

ME: *There have been many times when I almost called you. I thought you knew everything, though. And maybe I blamed you a little. I know. Not fair. And I'm ashamed and sorry.*

I let out a huge breath as I push send, and keep my gaze glued to the screen waiting for her return message. I've been wanting to say those words to her for a long time. Typing them was almost cathartic. Only now, I'm terrified to see her reaction. After five minutes of no response, I sit up on the end of my bed and shove my feet in my shoes. I'm torn between wanting to run to her house and pound on her door or run the other direction and punish myself for being so hateful to her for way too long. If she never writes me back again, I get what I deserve.

JUNE: *I understand . . .*

I fall back in my bed but leave my shoes on. She's still writing.

JUNE: *I'm sorry that took so long. I'm talking to Abby right now too. She requires a lot of attention LOL.*

My palm covers my face and my lips flap with a relieved exhale.

ME: *Tell Abby it's my turn.*

JUNE: *Have you met Abby?*

I laugh.

ME: *Good point.*

I hate that I can't see her right now. I'd propose a swap where Abby gets her on text and I get the phone or video call. I'm sure Abby would drive over here to interrupt, though, so I'm going to give myself the next best thing.

Kicking up to my feet, I head out of my room and creep downstairs, not wanting to get into any conversations with my parents. Although, my dad is gone—*shocker*—and my mom is sitting in her office with soft music playing. It's cover enough for me to slip out the back door and head to the Buick. Out of habit, I move to the passenger door, but I pause right before I answer her text. I'm *always* in that seat—even when we were kids. I round the back of the car through some incredibly sketchy weeds and take a seat behind the wheel. June can see my window from here, but I can also see hers. I sink down so I'm not totally obvious, just in case, and smile when I see her standing in front of a mirror on her wall.

ME: *You're beautiful.*

I can tell when she gets my message because she looks down at her hands, where I assume her phone is, and her body starts to twist side-to-side. I bet she's blushing. She glances back at her reflection, and I hope she sees what I do, all the things I've been blind to as well. That cute girl in braces is underneath it all but the exterior is an incredibly sexy woman.

JUNE: *Thank you. That . . . means a lot.*

ME: *It's the truth.*

Her body shakes and her shoulders lift to her ears. She's embarrassed, in a good way. It pleases me.

JUNE: *Will you do me a favor?*

ME: *I already said yes to the date.*

It's fun to watch her reactions. Her body shifts and I can almost hear the sigh she must let out. She pulls her palms up near her chest and types. She's so damn cute when she's frustrated.

JUNE: *This is different.*

ME: *I was kidding. Ask away. Anything.*

It strikes me while I wait for her to type and probably navigate talking to Abby at the same time that I meant that word—*anything*. It feels like a pretty fast leap to be willing to do anything for June. But also, this was such a long time coming. We've been waiting to get here for years. We detoured.

JUNE: *Will you help me practice talking to my mom? I don't know how to bring this up.*

My chest sinks into my body, my body heavy in the seat. I don't know that I ever had this conversation the right way with my parents. I feel unqualified to help her, but I also know I'm the only one who can.

ME: *I will try. I'm not very good at communication, I'm sure you know.*

JUNE: *You're better than you think.*

My mouth tugs up slightly.

ME: *So are you.*

My eyes widen when I read my own words.

ME: *I totally did not mean it like that.*

JUNE:

June's room is dim, the sun behind her house. Her lamp is on, and she must be sitting on her bed. I can see the curve of her shoulder where she's rolled up her sleeve. She's working a comb through her hair and braiding it. I want her to teach me how so I could do it for her. I never wanted to when we were kids. Well, I tried to weave Red Vines through her hair once but that doesn't count. I'm suddenly obsessed with the way her hair feels, and I want to touch it all the time.

ME: *Are you sure you want to get me started on the things I think you are REALLY good at? ;-)*

It takes about ten seconds for her to put Abby on hold to read my text. When her head falls forward into her palm, I let my laughter fill the Buick. I'm having so much fun out here spying on her.

JUNE: *Oh, my God, you are as bad as Abby. I'm not even going to tell you what she just asked me.*

I sit up, shifting my weight, my cock suddenly rock solid again. Damn, I'm in trouble.

ME: *I'm pretty sure you're going to tell me.*

My gaze moves to the window, to the tiny sliver of June's arm that I can see and the rope of braid that runs over her shoulder. She disappears in seconds, probably laying back, and even though my view is gone, I stay here, staring at that window. Maybe I'll climb up again.

She's talking to Abby about me, and that means our secret is not so secret anymore. It's weird, but I really don't care. There's a weight lifted from my shoulders, and I'm suddenly taking the deepest breaths I have in days . . . months. I want everyone to know she's mine. I don't even care that people will talk about us, warning her that I'm a player. Let them talk their shit. I have this strange faith in us. I mean, look what we came through already. Two years of hell and somehow we meet at the end? What are the odds?

JUNE: *She's asking about . . . uh . . . size.*

"Ha ha!" I laugh so loud that I immediately duck lower than the steering wheel. If anyone is outside, they surely heard me. I'm shocked June didn't hear me from inside.

ME: *And you said . . .*

I'm not sure whether she's dragging out her response this long on purpose to torture me, or she's simply mortified. I amuse myself by flipping through social media for a while, but eventually I'm left tapping my thumb nervously on the side of my phone, waiting for her to, *oh!*

JUNE: *Let's just say from what we have pieced together, you are way above average. OMG I can't believe I told you that.*

I lean on the old center console, resting my palm on the knob June tried to give me. I unscrew it to give my nervous hand something to do and type back: *Well, duh!*

She calls me *cocky* in response, which only solidifies my infatuation with my old best friend, all grown up. She's perfect. Funny, beautiful, smart—*mine*. That weight creeps back in, and this time it's not because of my fear of what my mom will think but rather a new fear, that this won't last.

That I'll lose her.

ME: *Hey*

Before I can send my message off, or even finish my pitiful insecurity memoir, my phone buzzes with a message from someone else. I don't recognize the number, and I'm relieved it isn't Ava. She's not going to be very nice about what's developed between June and me, but like the opinions of so many others, I don't give a shit.

I open the strange message.

PRIVATE LINE: *Hey asshole. It's Abby. I want you to know that if you fuck this up and break her heart, they won't find your body.*

I smirk but also hold my breath. She's joking, but she's also not. I actually like the threat, though. I appreciate it, that June has Abby in her life. I want her surrounded with people there to guard her heart and protect her from "assholes" like me.

ME: *Hi. You have my permission to leave zero evidence behind if I fuck this up. Abby, I'm serious about June. I'm realizing just how long I've felt this way.*

ABBY: *Ok. Good.*

ABBY: *You're still an asshole. Give it time ;-)*

I chuckle and switch screens back to June and our conversation. That *hey* I wrote is still there, a lonely word waiting for me to have the guts to say the rest. These words aren't meant for a text, though. I'll save them so I can speak them. She deserves to hear how special I think she is.

Instead of getting into my feelings, I decide to retrace our past—all of the good times. We spend the next four hours, until my battery is nearly drained, swapping stories about trouble we got in as kids, our favorite holidays, water fights and Halloween costumes. We debate favorite songs and she takes me down a tangent about the Buick I'm sitting in, how she wishes it ran so she could drive it. In the middle of it all, I send out a few feelers to friends who know things about cars, and I've already got plans in the works to restore this sucker. From what I can tell, it will take months.

Months.

I'm planning a life with June that exists in the months ahead. Dare I let myself think in years?

CHAPTER TWENTY

I'm nervous. I actually think my pits are sweating. *This is crazy!*

I woke up excited for my day, and I know it's because I want to see June. I probably could have waited around for her this morning, but I'm still navigating stuff with my mom and how to tell her, well, everything.

Tory keeps motioning for me to get out of my truck but I have no interest. If I go out there and stand with him and Hayden, the other guys are going to crowd around, and June might not be up for coming to see me. Besides, I need to get her my truck key. And I need to kiss her. I don't want Tory involved in that.

Abby pulls up with June in her passenger seat, and neither of them sees me at first. I slink down, resting on my console, cheek on my fist as I watch the two of them. Abby scares the shit out of me, but I like their friendship. She's good for June. I can't take credit for the strong girl she's become. June gets full credit, but Abby probably is due some influence points.

June flashes her eyes my direction and I lift my head from my hand long enough to hold out an open-palmed wave. Abby leans forward and glares at me, and I feel her threat. She made her point and I will abide by her rules. I can make that promise.

The two of them leave her car and stroll toward me, Abby peeling off when she reaches the twins. Tory leaps to his feet and brushes off the concrete bench he was just resting his feet on and Abby sticks up her nose. June gets in while I watch this strange scene unfold, and she's laughing.

"What's funny? I ask.

"Tory thinks being a gentleman is going to win Abby over," June says.

Win Abby over?

"Huh."

With my wrists balanced on the steering wheel, I lean back and observe my friend with this new layer of information. *He's finally actually going to admit to some feelings.*

"So, the key?" June brings my attention back to her and her open palm. She's awfully eager for this. *Hmm.*

"Oh, yeah. Here," I say, killing the engine and pulling the key free. She makes a grabby motion with her palm right before I drop the key in.

"I see that twinkle in your eyes. Don't get crazy." I cover her hand and wrap her palm around the key. She thinks I'm teasing her, but honestly? I'm a little nervous about giving her free rein to the only good thing to come out of my broken family situation. I fucking love this truck. June's more important, though. June and my future.

Does that mean I—

"Let me go over things one more time, just to make sure I have it down. At lunch, we both slip out the gate and you get in the car with MIT lady while I go to your truck and drive it to Two-fers."

All of this so I have an alibi. There are enough people to see my truck at Two-fers to explain why I'm not around for lunch or why I may be late getting back for class. Sadly, I won't be in trouble for being late; I'll be in trouble for skipping lunch to interview for MIT. Ridiculous.

I nod to June, but the second her mouth slips into a smile, my head rushes back to my last thought. *I'm fucking in love with June Mabee.*

"You'll do great," she says. I snap out of my daze and laugh. I'm unfazed by the pending interview. It's a formality. It's sweet that she is bolstering my confidence, though.

I turn my head to the side, rest it on my headrest and drink her in. I blink a few times, waiting for the moment to feel awkward or uncomfortable, but those feelings never come. All I feel is peace and comfort and fortune.

"I'm not really worried about the interview."

I'm worried about you changing your mind.

June twists in her seat to face me, tucking my keys in her bag before leaning forward and taking my hand in both of hers. She runs her delicate fingers over the rough edges of my skin—war wounds from the gridiron. My hands will never be the same. I turn my palm so our fingers weave together then run my thumb over the top of her hand. I smirk at it, but my head is lowered enough that she can't really see how happy this tiny touch makes me.

"Lucas, there is no way your dad can't be proud of his son getting into MIT," she says.

I nod and let out a breathy laugh. My dad will only see the betrayal. Pathetic. I've gotten to the point that I no longer remember a time when I idolized the man. I have doubts that I ever did. I know there were happy moments, like playing catch with him in the front yard, having him celebrate me by hoisting me on his shoulders and running in circles. Those memories are tainted now, my mind quick to rationalize his happiness as nothing more than opportunism. I've always been his second chance. He nudged me down his path, and because I was a boy, I followed, eating up the attention he showered me with when I was good at something he liked.

He never once pinned one of my report cards on the wall. My tests on the refrigerator were put there by Mom. And he called my near perfect SAT score "irrelevant." I'd love to tell him what's irrelevant to me.

The bell sounds, and June pulls her hands away after giving mine a gentle squeeze. We're on full display, and I'd told her—and myself—that we would ease our way into public. But now she's leaving, and I don't want to let her go without knowing how much I am in this with her.

She has her bag. Her hand is on the door handle. Move now, Lucas, or you get what you deserve.

Before she can crack the door more than an inch, I cross the center console and run my hand up her jaw, along her cheek and into her hair. Pulling her to me, our mouths collide as my eyes close so I can shut out the noise and enjoy *us.* I kiss her as if we're all alone, my tongue deep in her mouth, tasting her. My hand curls at her scalp, fingers tangled in her hair. I want more but this will have to do. June moans and it's enough to prod me to kiss her a few seconds longer. I'm sure we're putting on a show, but I couldn't care less.

I hold on to that thought as our lips part. The only thing that could burst this perfect bubble we've created is standing a dozen feet away from my truck. Ava's glare doesn't just penetrate, it cuts like a laser beam.

"Fuuuuuck," I groan, sinking my gaze to my lap. This is going to make today challenging. Ava will be spreading rumors the second her back is to us. She'll be dreaming of ways to attack June by the time her ass hits her chair in first hour. And she will be watching me like a hawk, which normally wouldn't bother me at all, but today . . . *today,* I don't want to be noticed. I have things to do. The last thing I need is Ava pointing out that I'm heading off campus again, especially when she's pieced together why. *Thank you, shitty front desk privacy practices.*

"She'd find out eventually," June says. Her fingertips slide from my arm where she was still clinging to me. I glance her way, and one peek at her expression tells me she's scared. Ava is not going to be nice.

"Yeah," I sigh. I hold on to her gaze, more worried for her than my own selfish reasons.

"Does she know about MIT?"

My nostrils flare at her question. I don't want her to think I shared things with Ava. There's a difference between her nosy ass finding out shit and me confiding in her.

"She doesn't know shit!" My anger gets the best of me, and my response comes out more of a bark.

We both turn to check on Ava's progress. She's almost around the far corner to her first hour building. It's obvious by the way she's practically marching that she's full-on lit. I bet there are a dozen passive-aggressive social media posts aimed at me and June by now. It only takes her seconds to fire off those missiles.

June pushes her door open all the way and slides out, glancing to me over her shoulder.

"I'll see you at lunch," she says.

"I wish you were still in my first hour," I manage to squeak out before she closes the door behind her. Her eyes linger on mine as she walks backward a few steps, an impish smile playing at her lips. She lifts a shoulder, I guess shrugging to apologize that she's not there anymore. Or maybe she's telling me that it's too bad, I took too long.

I did. *Way* too long. I draw in a full breath and remind myself how much I have to lose. I'm thankful that the only casualty to my stubbornness is losing an hour with June every week day.

I thought I could wait out Tory, but I should know better. Dude would be fine getting detention for being late in order to box me in and force me to talk about June. He's standing at the front of my truck, nobody out in the parking lot but the two of us, so I give in and get out of the solace of my truck cab.

"I feel like I missed the middle of the movie. Bro, what am I missing? June hasn't said a word either."

I shrug him off but he punches my shoulder, kind of hard.

"Damn," I say, rubbing the spot he hit. "We've gotten past shit. That's all."

My friend laughs loud enough that the sound reverberates off of the corridor we walk through on our way into school.

"Lucas Fuller, finally coming to terms with the fact he's in love with June Mabee. What's it been, ten years?" I can feel his eyes boring into my cheek as we walk.

"*Pshh*, not that long. I didn't really know her that well until we were ten."

Tory stops in his tracks and I don't realize until I'm holding the door open for him. That's when my admission hits me, too. I turn to see his mouth agape, a tinge of a boastful grin touching the corners.

Shit.

I pinch the bridge of my nose and wince, looking down at my feet.

"Oh, no. You don't get to pass up on this. I heard you. Or

rather . . . you heard me. And you were fine with those words. Lucas Fuller is in love with June Mabee." Tory doesn't have a quiet button. I'm not even sure my best friend knows how to whisper.

I bob my head up in time to catch Ava passing behind him on her way to the office and my stomach sinks.

"Could we take this outside?" I push the door open wider, and my friend finally moves his feet.

He pats my chest with a fat, open palm as he passes and utters a quick "Atta boy."

If I had more time to walk with him, I would turn the tables and question him about Abby. I'll have time for that later. For now, I'm glad he has to peel off to the left for class while I barrel straight ahead. Ava was heading to the office and it's filled my head with all sorts of mistrust. Somehow, she's going to make life miserable for June today. I feel it.

I pull my phone out while I walk, and hover over my text string with June. I want to warn her. I type out the whole scene for her, letting her know that Tory couldn't keep his volume down and Ava heard him say something, but then I stop and immediately delete. I can't tell her *what* Ava heard—that I love her. Or at least in Tory's mind I do.

No, I won't do that anymore. I'm not going to pretend I don't. That's the rule the old Lucas put in place. It's not only in Tory's mind. It's in my mind, too. In my heart. I love her. I love June. I don't want her spending her day worrying about Ava, which is all any warning text would do to her. And I sure as hell don't want to tell her I love her by text. I'm not sure I'm ready to let that thought move from inside my body to out of it. Of course, I blew that with Tory.

I'm the last one to slide into my seat in physics, right before the final bell sounds. We have a test today. I'm holding steady at a ninety-five in the class so blowing one test won't be the end of the world. I didn't study. I didn't even try. There was literally nothing in the world that was getting me to give up messaging June last night. I would have typed through a tornado.

My phone buzzes in my pocket so I give it a quick glance before tucking it away in my bag for the test. My heart hoped it was June, but I see Ava's name in the preview. Instead of letting *her* in my head, I drop my phone in my bag and decide to leave it there for the entire morning.

Getting dressed into interview clothes without having anyone notice proves a bit tricky. I didn't want to leave class early before lunch, so I packed the easiest pants and dress shirt I own. I'm pretty sure I wore these pants to my uncle's funeral over the summer. They're a little snug now. My quads have bulked up since I last pulled these suckers on.

I manage to slip out of my jeans and T-shirt and into the more formal wear in under a minute, rolling my regular clothes up and stuffing them in my backpack. The tie proves super problematic, however. I've never been good with them. My mom always has to redo them. I know I'm supposed to make it snug against my neck, but it makes me feel like I'm choking the whole time. After three attempts, I give up and leave the ends dangling at my chest as I jet toward the parking lot to meet June. I'm so relieved to see her at the front of the school, not because I'm nervous about the interview but because I need her help with this damn tie.

"*Psst*," I say, sneaking up behind her. She startles a little, which is cute.

She spots my tie situation right away, smirking and amused at how flummoxed I am by a strip of silk. I lift my chin as she grins.

"These things are tricky." She takes the mangled ends and gets to work fixing my neck situation.

"I fucking hate ties. They choke me." I swallow hard and tug at my collar.

"You're a big man," she responds, her words so matter-of-fact. Our eyes flit to one another and I catch the blush that creeps up her cheeks. My mouth edges up on one side with my devilish thoughts, and June slaps lightly at my chest.

"Shush, or I won't help you."

I lean back with a thick laugh that I do my best to apologize through. Clearing my throat, I stand up tall so she can finish making me look presentable. She tugs at the knotted tie a few times, either because she's making it straight or simply likes to jerk my body around. I think it might be a little of both.

My mom made sure my shirt was ready this morning. I haven't worn it in so long, the wrinkles looked impossible, but through whatever magic she has, she managed to have it looking crisp this morning. I rolled it for my backpack and somehow didn't ruin her work completely.

"There," June says, her hands loosely gripping my tie, almost as if she's afraid to let go. She glances up at me with a faint smile, and I'm hit with every ounce of feeling all at once. *I love this girl.*

"Wish me luck," I say, holding on to my view of her green eyes.

She shakes her head.

"You don't need it. Break a leg."

I laugh out once and roll my eyes before grabbing the gate just opened by one of the late-start seniors. June follows closely behind me and we pause just outside the gate so I can scan the lot.

"Ready?" I draw in a breath through my nose. I wish my heart would stop pounding. It's not the interview that has me wrecked by nerves, it's the fear that my dad or Coach will show up and catch me in the act. At least our principal is on my side for this. I emailed him about the interview late last night and he said he would make sure I was excused. He's not really a football fan.

June holds up my keys and jingles them.

"Let's do this," she says. We're practically jogging through parking lot. I spot the red car, Candace waiting inside, just like she was the first time I had to slip out for a meeting. June's already sprinted across the parking lot. She'll be pulling out soon, hopefully without anyone noticing it's her driving my truck and not me.

When I reach Candace's car, I give one final glance around the campus, and when I don't spot my coach or anyone who might mention they saw me doing this, I dip inside and finally exhale.

"Lucas, great to see you. I hope you like sushi." Candace gives me a nod and smile as I buckle up.

"I think I'm too nervous to taste. We could be going to a cardboard restaurant and I'd think it was five-star," I joke.

She laughs at my humility and tells me to relax, reminding me this is all a formality. I breathe out and flatten my palms on my thighs to play along.

"Right. Got it," I say, my insides still a twisted mess. Again, not nervous about the interview part.

We drive several blocks to the other side of town to a place called Tiny Plates. I've never been here but I know my mom has. I wish I had time to text her and ask what I should order. She knows what I like.

"So tell me, Lucas . . . what drew you to MIT?"

She's making small talk but I know my answers still matter. I don't merely want to be their selection for this schol-arship; I want to be the stand-out.

"I remember hearing one of my mom's old friends talk

about the school when I was younger, and it stuck in my head. As I got older, I found out that me and math? We gel."

She laughs when I bring my hands together as if math and I are puzzle pieces.

"That's not something many people say," she muses.

"I guess not," I say, laughing lightly at myself. I regroup, though, and set my expression to a more serious one. "But the idea of doing something with this weird skill I have, maybe changing the world in some small way for the better? That's what I see at MIT. It enables so many good things."

Our gazes meet briefly, and she gives me a tight-lipped smile. That was a good answer, the kind the trustees will want to hear. I tuck it away and remember to repeat it in the next thirty minutes over my plate of raw fish rolls.

The restaurant is busy, but we find our party waiting at a table when we arrive. Candace introduces me to a tall man with an incredibly expensive-looking suit and an older woman with short-cropped hair dyed a purplish-gray. She's wearing a black suit with perfectly square frame glasses, and in any other situation I would probably observe how very *Men In Black* she appears. But my dad's old boss from the first law firm he worked for just sat down at a table on the other side of the room, and now the only thing running through my head is fear that he'll see me and feel the need to come say hi.

I twist in my chair, doing my best to shield myself from his view. I'm glad to see three other people join him, but it doesn't stop my imagination from conjuring what ifs.

Hey, Todd. Ran into Lucas at Tiny Plates while he was meeting with MIT. Wow! You must be so proud.

Of course, my dad wouldn't be. He'd be furious. And he'd come home ready to lay into me, which would probably be the final straw to get me to open my mouth about his current affair. It wouldn't be the way my mom should find out, and it would only make these final few months at home with my family worse—if I even had a family left.

"Lucas? You were mentioning in the car on the way here why you liked MIT?" Candace brings my thoughts back to the present, and I realize I spaced out a bit. I don't think for long, though, so I go to work covering my daydreaming.

"Yes, I was just thinking about our conversation, actually." Everyone at the table leans forward and I recite, nearly verbatim, what I told Candace in the car. For the next forty minutes, I switch off the part of my brain that seems to only be out to make my stomach sick, and I play the role of perfect MIT candidate. The two trustees insist on taking photos with me, and I don't worry about my reality again until Candace drops me off in front of school and asks if it's all right to post one of those photos on social media.

"Sure," I croak.

The odds of my dad knowing how to use social media are slim, so I rid myself of the extra worry and shake her hand before exiting the car.

"Oh, and hey, Lucas?" She's rolled the window down.

"Yes?"

I'm so close to getting inside. I'll make it to my next class and nobody will know anything. My truck is in its spot. June pulled it off. I can push off having it out with my dad and wrecking my mom for one more day.

"Welcome to MIT." A grin stretches the width of her face just before she drops her sunglasses down and drives away. I utter "Thanks" but I don't think she hears it.

It's official. A few signed documents is all that stands in my way. I laugh to myself, and as I make my way to class, passing through throngs of students, I catch a few of them looking at me oddly. It's probably because I'm still wearing dress clothes, but maybe it's also the enormous smile and skip in my step. I can't help it. I'm happy. There are things *I* want in my life. The school I dreamt of is within reach, a stepping stone to a life doing something I'm passionate about. The only thing left to do is kiss the girl I love to celebrate.

By the time the final bell rings, I've come around to embracing everything good, and not giving a second thought to the shit brewing beneath the surface. I practically skip toward the locker room, where June and I planned to do a quick key exchange. All of the warmth brewing in my chest grows cold, though, the second June turns her head and I spot her swollen black eye.

"What the fuck happened?" I kneel to inspect her skin. June tries to look away but I follow her face, moving to keep a good view. I also shoot a glare at Tory over her shoulder. He better not have been involved in this.

"I'm fine," June insists. She twists, but I reach up and gently coax her chin back in my direction.

"Your ex had a field day with her face," Tory says. I'm glad to hear he's pissed off, too, but his tone seems to indicate this is my fault. I stand and we have a mini stare-off. I glance down to the bag of ice in his hand, and because I'm an immature asshole, all I feel is jealous that *he* was here to get her ice and I wasn't. Which is not the point. And maybe he's right to take the tone he does with me.

"Gentlemen?"

We both shift our focus to Coach Loma as he walks up. My pulse races, excuses flying wildly around my head. He's going to want to know what happened here, and maybe he also knows I went rogue.

"I had an accident, Coach, and they happened to catch me before I fell all the way. I went end-over-end," June lies. I swallow down my guilt. I should cut her off and tell Coach what really happened. Ava deserves a world that knows what type of person she is.

June takes the ice and towel from Tory, pressing it to her eye.

"Lemme see what you've got going here," Coach says. He straight-arms me out of the way and bends to give June's face a closer look. Tory and I make eye contact above the two of them, and my friend's brow furrows. He doesn't understand why June would lie . . . or why I let her.

"You said you got this falling down the stairs?" Coach is asking June, but he glances to Tory and me with skepticism. His lips are pursed and his eyes squint a hint to show his suspicion.

June nods, lifting one shoulder in a shrug as if to say she's just a clumsy girl. *Fuck, I'm an asshole. Tell the truth, Lucas! Make Ava pay.*

"Mind if I get our trainer to come give you a look? Just a little concussion protocol, and since it happened on campus, we'll need to fill out an incident form." Coach takes things like this seriously. He's the father of four daughters.

"Okay," June says, her voice barely above a whisper.

We all stand, except for June, who flashes the inside of her palm to me to how me she has my key. She wants to give it to me now, but it can wait. It *should* wait. Clearly Coach Loma is ready for Tory and me to move along and get our asses to practice.

I meet June's gaze and lift my bag to bring it to my shoulder, but before I get it all the way up my arm, June yanks it back down to the ground. It's ridiculous, and I have to roll my eyes at her covert attempt.

"Oh, dang, sorry. I thought this was mine," she fibs. Her bag is pink. Mine is black. If anything, she just sold Coach on the idea that she's concussed. She manages to slip my key into the side pocket of my bag during the confusion, though.

"It's fine," I say, lifting my bag to my shoulder. I can't help the constant frown that's forced its way over the smile I was wearing most of the afternoon. Tory and I hover for a few more minutes, but Coach Loma conveniently steps into the space between us and June, essentially boxing us out.

"I guess . . . we're done here," Tory chuckles.

I can't laugh, though. I'm too angry. And guilty. And ashamed.

"She's okay. June's a tough one," Tory says, easing up on me as we head into the locker room. I drop my bag on the bench when we make it inside and it lands with a heavy *clunk*.

"What was that? She gave her a black eye, dude! Who does that?" I press my palms into my eyes and rehearse the conversation I need to have with Ava, one that makes it abundantly clear that she needs to back off when it comes to June.

"I mean, dudes in bars punch each other all the time. And I'm pretty sure I punched you in the face over pizza once." I drop my hands to meet Tory's gaze and he shrugs with a half-smile.

"We were ten," I clarify.

"Yeah, but I'd probably still fight you for pizza. I'm not very mature."

I breathe out a quick laugh, his joke releasing some of the tension. Tory swings open the door of his locker, dropping his backpack inside and pulling out his practice jersey and pads. I stare at his back for a few seconds, wishing there was an easy way for me to tell him about his mom and my dad. This whole thing gives me sickening flashbacks to when I struggled with this same question while looking at June.

"You checking out my ass?"

Tory caught me staring, and is now standing on his toes and glancing over his shoulder at his boxer briefs. I huff out a laugh, then rub my hand over my chin and give his rear a good look before shrugging.

"Eh. I've seen better."

Tory's face contorts. He's playing offended—or maybe he actually is—and does a few calf raises to flex his glutes.

"Nah, my ass is *fiiiine.*"

Damn, his confidence. I roll my eyes and we both dress out for practice.

For two hours, my mind shuts off. Coach never asks about my dad or mentions me leaving campus, and I almost forget that I did. It's only when I'm fishing the key out of my bag that my thoughts return to the fact I pulled off a pretty major secret meeting today. I check my phone, worried about June, but the only texts are from my mom, asking how the day went. I send her back a short reply, letting her know that it's official, and when she doesn't write back right away, I tuck my phone in my back pocket.

Zachery, one of the bigger guys on our defensive line, lingers on his way out of the locker room, stopping a few feet from my bench.

"Hey, Fuller? You hooking up with Mabee or what?"

I glance up and quirk a brow. It's none of his fucking business, but also . . . this is what June was talking about. She doesn't want to be kept a secret. She deserves better. And I'm proud she's willing to forgive me after the last two years of silence.

"She's my girlfriend."

The smirk on Zachery's face falls, and the joke he was

probably waiting to make seems to be caught in his throat. I see him swallow it.

"Oh. Cool, man." He pulls his mouth into a tight smile and awkwardly exits the room.

"That was fuckin' weird," Tory says from behind me.

I nod. But now that Ava's involved, who knows what story she spun about me and June. And the fact I maybe told her things I shouldn't have about June's mom doesn't sit well in my gut. I'm an idiot when I'm drunk.

"Hey, you see anything on social?" I ask Tory as we gather our gear and head out to the parking lot. He flips through his phone while we walk, not really looking too deep into anything, which makes his lack of findings not very credible. I'd rather believe he's right, though, so I take his word for it and drive home under the pretense that Ava hasn't started the rumor mill yet.

That bubble bursts the second my headlights flash on the Mabee garage.

WHORE

The word is sprayed in red and it stretches from one end of June's garage to the other. I gnash my teeth and let a growl simmer in my chest, breathing out a "Fuck!" I kill the lights on my truck and let my temper heat to a boil. I'm tempted to peel out of here and race to Ava's house so I can drag her back and make her fix this. I probably would, too, except I know in my heart that June is inside suffering because of this. And taking care of her is priority number one.

My muscles are sore and tired, so my scale up the side of her house and eave isn't as smooth as last time. June's window is open when I get to the crest of the pitch, wrapping my hands around the sill of the window. I step through and find her sitting on the edge of her bed, her face void of emotion. *Drained.*

"June," I say, rushing across her room and dropping to my knees in front of her. I hold her face between my palms while her eyes hover on the cusp of forming tears.

"I'm so sorry," I say, running my thumb over her puffy skin. The bruising is worse now, the swelling down some.

"I'm so sorry," I say again. I repeat those words every time I take in a new piece of her. Her hair is damp, either from showering or crying. And her fingernails are stained pink on the tips, likely from scrubbing the garage door to no avail.

Fuck, Ava!

Her palms fall to my chest, gripping my shirt, and she falls into me, laying her unbruised cheek against my heart. Her body shakes and she finally lets out a sniffle. I slide one arm under her and lift her to me as I stand, cradling her trembling body while I shift to sit on her bed and hold her in my lap. My hand strokes her back, a smooth rhythm meant to bring her peace. Her face finds reprieve under my chin, and she shivers with another sob.

"I know, June. I'm so sorry. I'm so fucking sorry," I whisper at her ear. I rock her gently as tears well in my own eyes. Mine are a mixture of hurt and anger, like hers but different. I can't explain the vengeance swelling in my chest. I want Ava to pay for what she did. This is inexcusable. So was my act, though—sharing secrets that weren't meant for Ava's ears.

"She painted my house," June cries.

"I know," I say, my mouth against the side of her head.

She painted her house.

I squeeze my eyes shut and the moisture falls to my cheeks. June has been hurt so much in all of this. How could I not see what the last two years has done to her?

I hold her for nearly an hour, never once letting my biceps relax. I keep her nestled into me, my fingers drawing gentle lines up and down her bare arms until she seems to be feeling the call of sleep. Her tears have stopped.

"How was the interview?" Her voice is raspy, and it makes me laugh quietly that of everything she's been through, she's focused on me. I lean back, resting on her bed, but keep her tethered to me.

"There are more pressing things," I say, sweeping her hair into my palm. The waves fall through my fingers, but some of them stick, leaving me to gently smooth them out.

"Not really," June sighs. "I mean, if all this happened and you didn't get in, that would suck." I smirk and let out another tiny laugh. She's funny, even when she isn't feeling it.

She wriggles on top of me and holds herself up so our eyes meet. I dip my chin and she morphs her face into what I think is an attempt to wink. I shake my head slowly and laugh, running my thumb along the bruise. This eye is not meant to wink—or do much of anything—for a good two days.

"I'm in," I finally say, giving her something positive to celebrate. It feels selfish, but June doesn't see it that way, of course. She pushes down on my chest, giving my lungs a compression boost that clears them of oxygen, and sits up higher. I wrap my hands around her wrists.

"Shut up!" she whisper-shouts, but damn is it loud. I cover her mouth and suck in my own lips, trying not to laugh. *Wouldn't her mom love walking in on this?*

"*Shhh.* I can't go to MIT if your mom shoots me first," I tease. Sorta.

June and I both roll to our sides, her hands holding my cheeks.

"Lucas, I am so proud of you." Her eyes flash wide then blink as her focus moves around my face. She's waiting for me to be as elated as she is. I want to be. It's just—

"He'll come around," she finally says. She's trying so hard to be an optimist. I simply don't see it, though.

I shake my head and glance down to our legs, her knee between my thighs. I bet we've lain like this before, as kids. Maybe watching a movie, one of the scary ones we weren't supposed to see. I have vague recollections of my younger self wondering if I would ever be into girls and feel differently when lying with a girl like this.

That answer is a clear yes.

"I don't even care. I'm going, and my mom said with the scholarship money I'll get, they can pay the rest." *They, as if my dad will be involved with our family ever again.*

I twirl June's hair around my index finger, winding it then letting the twist fall loose. My chest is tight, and it's because of everything looming just outside this room—the garage, Ava, my parents, Tory's mom, *me and June.*

"My mom knows you helped," I admit. I decided to tell her, my way of inching into breaking the news to her that I'm not giving June up again. She was surprisingly receptive. I wouldn't say warm, but she wasn't angry.

June blinks at me a few times, her eyes darting from mine to my mouth and back. *I want to kiss you, too, June.*

"And she'll still let you go?" she finally says. She's joking, but I hear the tinge of hurt in her tone. She and my mom were close. I never thought about how much June must miss her.

"My mom doesn't hate you, June. She's just—"

"Hurt," she cuts in.

I stare into her pools of green, bathing in the emotion they hold. June's eyes are a witch's brew of poetry, mystery, pain, and joy. If it can be felt, it exists right there, in those eyes.

"Yeah, she's hurt. When she found out about the affair,

she went through a pretty dark time." My throat gets dry and I try to swallow the scratchy feeling down. I don't talk about this time with my mom often. I don't have to. Tory *lived* through it with me, and he's honestly the only person I talk to about these things.

"You haven't told her about the new one, have you? The new affair?" June says.

I shake my head.

"I haven't told her."

I shift so our faces are close, nearly nose to nose. My eyes shut, the weight of what I've been carrying taking its toll. Maybe I'm finally in a place where I feel safe.

"Have you told Tory yet?" she asks.

I shake my head, my nose grazing hers.

"I'm sorry about . . . the word. On the garage." I hate that word, but more than that, I hate that it was Ava who wrote it. She did it with such malice, trying to cut deep. And I gave her the tools to be cruel.

"You told Ava about my mom and your dad," June whispers. It's not a question. She already knows.

All I can do is let out the breath I've been holding.

"I'm sorry. I don't even know why I did, but it slipped out once."

"*Shhh*," June says, tenderly running her nose against mine. I think she is both trying to soothe me and prevent me from telling her more than she wants to hear.

"I'm sorry, June. I'm sorry, I'm sor—"

She stops my pleas for forgiveness with the gentle touch of her lips to mine. I open my mouth to let her own me, and she brushes another pass of her soft mouth against mine. We take our time, never pushing our kiss deeper. And at some point, her lips on mine still, I manage to find sleep.

CHAPTER TWENTY-ONE

M y eyes pop open, my body rested and my mind at ease for the first time in months. June's room is partly illuminated by moonlight, part by the rising sun. It's a soft glow that shines on her skin, lighting up the tiny hairs on her arm. She looks like an angel this way.

It's early enough that I might be able to slip back inside my house without my mom realizing I was gone all night. She worries, and I think she'll probably continue to worry about me even when I'm all the way in Boston. Part of it probably stems from the times when my father doesn't come home. It's filled her with mistrust. Unlike her worries about him, though, for me she visualizes car wrecks or medical emergencies. Her mind runs wild. It's been conditioned to, I suppose.

June is deep asleep, and while I should take advantage of this early hour and get back to my house, I'm caught in the sight of her. Her breathing is a perfect beat, the small push of air that leaves her nose dusting the ends of her hair that have curled up on her pillow next to her face, moving them like a gentle breeze. Her lips pout when she sleeps, the top one curled up to reveal her top teeth. I stare at them for a full minute, considering blowing off my escape in exchange for a kiss. I don't want to break her peace, though. There's a hint of a smile on her lips that makes me believe she's having good dreams.

I slip my arm free from where it's buried under her neck and she stirs from the movement. Holding my breath, I wait until she nestles deeper into the covers and her pillow before I finally get up and make my way toward her window. We left it open all night, and it's made the room cool. She seems comfortable, though.

My body aches from sleeping in a bent position, but it's worth the massive kink in my neck. I held her through the night. I swear I was aware of every minute of it, too.

I make it to the roof mostly in near silence, but my decent from the eave into the driveway is a little clunky. I end up running through the middle rather than gracefully landing, which I suppose is better than falling. I check my truck on my way to my house, pulling my gear bag from the cab and tossing it in the back so it airs out before I have to get in and drive my ass to school. I still can't believe *that* is happening soon.

My mouth contorts into an uncontrollable yawn that strikes me because I *thought* the word sleep, I swear. It pauses me just long enough to catch sight of my letterman jacket. I smirk at the thought of giving it to June. She'll find the gesture both sweet and passive aggressive . . . in a playful way. She love-hates this thing.

I snag it before closing my door and trek back to the rooftop that just sent me dashing off balance down her driveway. I have to put the jacket on to have full use of my hands to climb back up and through her window, and she moves at the sound of my arms slipping free of the sleeves.

I drape the jacket on the back of her desk chair and twist it so the mascot on the back is the first thing she sees. I sneak out through her window, finding sure footing this time and making it down easily.

Proud of my stealthy moves, I take my time walking back to my house. A door slams shut behind me, though, and I jump and dash behind my truck. I doubt June woke and raced downstairs, so the only other option is that her mom came out the door. I duck low, doing my best to watch June's mom through the glass of my back and side windows. The sun is peeking out more, so I can see her profile fairly well. She doesn't look angry. In fact, she almost seems amused.

She pauses in front of her marred garage door for a few seconds, hands on her hips as she takes in the ugly landscape. Patting her hands together, she marches forward, punching in her garage code and heading into the cluttered space. I should help them clean that area out some day. I think there are a lot of things in there that belonged to June's dad, things I'm sure her mom is anxious to get rid of. Maybe a garage sale is in order.

She comes back out with a ladder and a bucket of paint, one of the large five-gallon types. She works at opening it for several minutes, and I struggle between getting caught lingering out here and rushing over to help. I don't want questions, though, and I have the strange feeling that one look into my eyes would reveal that I spent the night with her daughter. I don't think I'm ready to rationalize that with her, given *everything else* we are all dealing with.

Thanks to a swift hammer swing into a screwdriver, she finally pops the lid loose and goes to work. I watch her brush and roll for twenty, maybe thirty minutes, feeling guilty the entire time because it's my fault in part that she has to cover such a word to begin with. Her paint job is patchy, probably a stopgap until she can get a professional to come out. But when she goes into her garage for another bucket of paint and drizzles what looks to be red around the garage, I'm baffled. I want to stick around long enough to see the end result. I'm so curious about what she's up to, but my mom will be up any minute.

Rather than make noise with my own garage, I crouch down and tiptoe to my back yard, slinking inside through the glass door. I make it up to my room without a sound, noting the sound of my dad snoring as I pass my parents' door. He's home this morning, and from the sounds of it, he was here all night. He doesn't snore unless he's had some serious sleep.

My brain suddenly wired, I ditch my clothes and pick out a fresh T-shirt. I'd shower, but me getting up early would set off all sorts of red flags in this house. Instead, I lay back on my bed and hold my phone to my chest, waiting for June to wake and comment on the gift I left behind.

I must have dozed off, because by the time my phone buzzes against my body, it's almost time to leave for school, and the message is from my mom, wanting to know why she saw June getting into her mom's van this morning in my letterman jacket. My thumbs hover to respond, but rather than overthink things, I decide to keep this bit of my life simple.

ME: *Because I gave it to her.*

I leave it at that and gather my wallet and keys so I can make a mad dash to school. I halt at the end of my driveway, noticing the finished work from what June's mom began in the wee hours. Bold, red and somehow perfectly centered, their family home now boasts a vivid middle finger, one that gives everyone a giant F-U as they pass by. I stop and stare for almost a full minute, fighting the urge to take a picture.

Not everything needs to be photographed. Some things are meant to only be remembered. This is one of those things.

I pull in to school after the bell rings and rush through the main office doors to catch up to everyone else. The last thing I need is someone noticing me rolling in late and mentioning it to Coach. Somehow, it would get around to me skipping out yesterday to meet with a college about something other than football.

When I push through the main office doors, I'm greeted by the familiar stare of a bright golden eagle, wings outstretched, claws ready to grip. Its view is quickly dashed by a curtain of dark brown hair, and my grin grows. June is wearing my jacket.

I jog forward in time to reach over top of her and push the second set of doors open wide. She slows her steps, stopping suddenly, causing me to crash into her. I wrap my arm around her midsection and carry her forward with me in the opposite direction of her independent study room. *Why did she have to switch classes?*

"Earl? Is that you?"

I spin her around, my hand caressing her check and sliding into her hair in one swift movement before my mouth covers her. I kiss her long and hard in front of the entire school population.

"This public enough for you?" I touch her lip with my thumb for good measure, and she smiles around it. Her eye looks better, but I can still see the aftermath of Ava's rage.

"It's getting there," she teases.

I keep her hand in mine as I walk backward, still coaxing her to follow me. I know she can't forever, but a few more steps at least.

"This jacket is really fucking hot," she says.

I burst out a heavy laugh.

"You love it," I tease.

"I love you," she says back. The words slip from her mouth with such ease, all in the same breath, and I feel instantly drunk.

June's eyes widen and I think she considers covering her mouth with her hand. No use doing that. There's no stuffing those words back inside. I don't want her to. I'm stunned to hear them, though. I hoped, and my gut tells me we're at the same place with how we feel about each other, but I truly didn't think we would be able to verbalize things for months. After you spend two years avoiding each other, the pendulum gets stuck rather than swings.

I practice the words in my head, wishing I could shed whatever guard June let down. The bell rings before I'm able, though, and I ready myself to watch her sprint away. I wouldn't blame her. Not at all. But I'm not going anywhere, not until I can find the courage to say those words back.

Students run into us, and despite what I expect, June doesn't leave. We're a slow-motion film caught in the middle of high-speed traffic. People whip around us, cutting between us in some cases, and our gazes never break. I will my smile to inch upward, to be more obvious so she knows her words had meaning, that they were received with equal love, that I needed to hear them. I have a feeling on the outside, it's a stupid—and likely crooked—grin on my face.

"I'm really tired," June begins. She's about to ramble. I can feel it. "I meant the jacket. I love your jacket. Oh, God. Um." She's fidgeting with her hands, and her smile is so wide it practically threatens her ears. She's panicking, and it's so damn cute. She squeezes her eyes shut and twists in place before finally shouting "Good-bye" and taking off toward her classroom.

"I love you, too" I whisper to nobody. It's even hard here, in the safe space of being alone. Maybe if I say it every hour on the hour, I'll be able to utter it loud and clear.

I practice three or four more times on my way to class, then tuck the words back inside my chest so I don't accidentally speak them to the wrong person. I doubt my physics teacher would be into it. She's married—to a woman. A female *rocket* scientist. Pretty sure high school jock head is not in her dream fantasy list.

I count down the hours until lunch, and when the bell rings after second hour, I'm ready to sprint toward the cafeteria like I did in first grade when being first in line felt like it meant something. Only this time? I'm running to kiss the girl I used to push on the swing set.

"Lucas. You're wanted at the office," one of the office aids says. The girl looks young, maybe a freshman, and she probably ran to get the notice here before the final bell. If it were Ava delivering it, I might blow it off, but this girl was sent for a genuine reason.

"Thanks," I say, taking the pass.

I scan the throngs of students filing into the cafeteria as I make my way toward the front office. I don't see June in the mix, and I pull my phone out to message her but am halted by the firm hand of my father on my shoulder.

"Luc, glad I caught you. It's a big day!"

I'm sure the shock on my face isn't pretty. My eyes are so wide they dry out.

"Big . . . day?" I haven't seen this man since he nearly disowned me for throwing what he deemed a shitty pass. And now it's a big day?

"Yeah, Tennessee. It's the admissions rep. It's a formality, really, but they like the pomp and circumstance."

I walk alongside him, my mouth still agape and my brow pinched. My dad punches my arm.

"Your acceptance, bozo. You got in. To Tennessee?" My dad seems puzzled that I have not been waiting with bated breath for this acceptance to happen. I have a four-point-seven GPA with honors. Of course I'm getting in. *I got into MIT.*

"Oh. *Oh!*" I force the biggest grin on my face, teeth showing and all. "Yeah. Of course. I guess it's the whole phone-call-during-school-formality-thing that's throwing me."

Why the fuck are we doing this?

It becomes clear as soon as we step inside the main office. It seems I'm not the only person who got into Tennessee. The D'Angelo twins did, too. They've been accepted into lots of schools with early decisions. They have decent grades and are basketball gods. I guess the excitement of three Allensville students getting into a major powerhouse like Tennessee is worthy of a PR photo for the district.

I'll play along. I know for a fact neither of the D'Angelo boys are going to end up in Tennessee. Hayden was only using the offer to play there as a bargaining chip to play some-where on the West Coast, and Tory has no idea where he wants to go. He wants to be famous and that's about as far as he's gone in terms of hoops.

When the twins' mom walks in, my stomach rolls and my veins light on fire. This is why I'm here. Why my dad is here. *Why I'm not sitting next to June.*

"How long will this take?" I check my phone. Lunch is five minutes in already.

"Got a hot date or something?" my dad jokes. Tory snort-laughs and when my dad turns to face him, my friend waves his hand.

"Sorry, sir. Funny joke is all."

I meet Tory's gaze behind my dad's back, and he smirks because he thinks this is all about my secret relationship with June. I feel sick because for me, it's about the enormous secret my dad and his mom are keeping from the three of us.

Maggie waves us back to the principal's office, and we gather around his ornate desk that's littered with paper, crowding around his tiny phone to listen to this call on speaker. I tune nearly everything out and step to the back, hiding my phone in my palm so I can fire a text off to June and Abby that I got stuck in here. It's all too much to explain, so I leave it at that and continue with the formality of ridiculousness.

"Deeply honored, ma'am. Thank you," Tory says when he's told he's been accepted. He's good at bullshit. Me? Not so much. I feel my dad's stare before I turn and see it in person. It startles me, but I pull it together.

"Oh. Yes. Honor. Huge honor."

Tory snickers at my lackluster contribution and my dad sneers.

"So we'll be in touch with you as we get closer to official signing day. Excited to have you recognize the talent we have here at Allensville Public." Our principal's cheeks are cherries, his grin is so tight. He's loving the attention that comes with this. My dad is loving the mid-day excuse to see Tory and Hayden's mom. I love that whatever the fuck this was? It's done.

Unfortunately for me, my dad has taken the rest of the day off. It means that he doesn't only stick around for "lunch" with Mrs. D'Angelo, but he also whiles away the rest of the day in Coach Loma's office.

"Your dad sticking around for practice?" Tory leans into me as he asks.

"Guess so. I'm going to get my ass on the field because at least he can't talk to me out there." I rush dressing out, mad that I won't get to see June before she goes home. Sick that I have this festering secret burning a hole in my intestines. Tory deserves to know.

I sprint to the field and start warmups on my own, waving our trainer over to help me stretch when I see my dad pacing at the top of the hill. I close my eyes and will him to disappear, but when I reopen them, he's no longer alone. June is with him, and she's proudly wearing my jacket.

There was a day when this situation would have driven my anxiety up seventy notches. Now? I simply smirk and put one hand behind my head while I stretch so I can enjoy the show.

CHAPTER TWENTY-TWO

JUNE: *I told my mom. She's talking to your mom. She's going to bust your dad. Warning.*

I blink at the text, the one I've read a dozen times. The first pass freaked me out, but now an odd calmness has oozed its way into my body, like Pepto.

My dad is talking to Coach, his arm slung out of his truck window all casual-like. He's comfortable, living in his bubble where he thinks nobody can outsmart him. My eyes dim at the visual of him as he laughs. I think the reason I never gelled with Coach Loma is because he and my dad are too much alike. They laugh at the same bad jokes, and I don't think either of them truly listens. When one of them is talking, the other speaks right over them, like a layer cake of words that nobody ever hears.

It's maddening to be in the same room with them. They feed off each other, and I seem to be their favorite topic. More directly, *my future* is.

Coach Loma played college ball. They were both quarterbacks the same year. Unlike my dad, Coach played all four years. He went to a smaller division school, though, not the same cache, so to speak. While he never got hurt, I think he harbors a strange grudge about the whole thing. I wonder if he thinks my dad's opportunity was wasted on him, as though he would have been a better fit since he made it through four years injury-free.

My dad's engine fires up so I shift into drive and lead us home. The closer we get, the wilder my imagination runs. I have a vision of June's mom holding my mom down in an Olympic-style half nelson, or vice-versa. It makes my foot heavy on the gas because those are not the two people who should be tearing each other apart. The man deserving of their rage is shining his brights in my rearview mirror. It's rude, and he does it all the time because he's afraid he'll hit a deer. He's afraid a deer will dent his precious truck is more like it.

I pull into the driveway in time to see my mom and June's in a standoff in my garage. Suddenly, all that bravado I felt over getting this over and done with is out the window. I don't want to go through the next several minutes. I can't back away now, though. *Literally.* My dad has pulled in behind me.

I wait in the truck while he rushes out, his lights still on, illuminating the show. I kill mine and roll down my window so I can hear.

"Babe? What's going on here?" My dad is practically staring down June and her mom, almost as if he knows what they're up to. My hand subconsciously forms a fist. Did he threaten June today when I saw them talking? Something is behind that look he's giving her.

Dad turns to face Mom, his body marking the third point of the invisible triangle drawn between them all.

"Our neighbors were just leaving," my mom says.

My stomach tightens and I instantly grow defensive. I don't want my mom thinking any of this is on June.

I fly out of my truck and call her name, and when our eyes meet, I see the resolve in them. June isn't backing down. And neither is her mom.

"We weren't leaving, Todd. We were just getting to the bottom of this big fat fucking lie you've concocted. That's what we're doing." June's mom crosses her arms over her chest, and my body goes numb. She's intimidating, and I think I actually see my father shake in his boots.

"Kristen, you don't know what you're saying." This is my dad's favorite tactic, deflection. He rolls his eyes toward my mom as he talks to June's, as if to say this is just more of Kristen Mabee's usual drama. He'll follow this with some distraction, a little what-aboutism pointing to something my mom should be angry about instead. He'll fluster June's mom until her words come out jumbled and she's so frustrated with everything that she gives up and storms away. I've seen him do this in court.

Seems courtroom rules don't apply to suburban garages.

"Oh, I know what I'm doing. I'm ruining your day, that's what I'm doing," June's mom says, stepping a little closer to my dad, her arms still crossed in front of her. I think maybe . . . she's flexing her biceps.

My eyes rush to my mom, my concern that she won't be able to take everything she's about to learn. She's been broken so badly, and it took every bit of her strength to rebuild herself. I hate my dad for making her go through this again.

"You never helped me with my divorce out of the kindness of your heart. You were setting up an alibi," June's mom says. That was always the crux of my dad's web—that he was helping Mrs. Mabee with her divorce because she couldn't afford a lawyer up to par with her ex-husband's.

The closer June's mom steps, the more my father's feet itch to take a stride back. I can tell by the way he toes at the ground then puts pressure on the heel of his boot.

"Nicolas was going to leave you with pennies, Kristen. Of course I wanted to make sure your ex didn't absolutely ruin your life just because he had a lawyer and you didn't. I'm just sorry that you blurred the lines of my kindness. Babe—" My dad heads toward my mom now, a sense of desperation in his movements. His hands are out at his sides, making it seem as if there's nothing to see behind this curtain. But there's plenty to see. More than he's ready for.

"She's twisting reality. And I'm so sorry you have to hear it. What happened was a mistake, but I guess to her . . . it meant more."

I swallow hard. Of the millions of words and phrases my dad could decide upon, he goes with that one. I see June lurch forward, but before the words can leave her mouth it hits me—this is how I make amends for everything. It has to be me who undoes this.

"Is Mrs. D'Angelo a mistake too?" I step in between everyone. My hands ball at my sides as my eyes zero in on my father's. I stare so hard that his pupils shrink under my glare.

"The twins' mom?" My mom's voice breaks as she speaks. I look to her, expecting to see her crumble, but instead, she barrels toward my dad, shoving his shoulder with enough force that she may have dislocated it. I sure hope so.

"Who told you that? Did she?" My dad points at June as if she's some untrustworthy liar. I laugh at how sick that thought is. The only one fitting that description is wearing boots and a blazer.

"I did," June says proudly. She steps into the center with me, and for a moment, I feel the earth quake. It's in my imagination, clearly, but the effects of anger and panic rush my body to the point that I think a seismic event occurred.

"Baby, she's lying. I mean, come on!" Stripped down, without his lies to bolster him, my dad sounds pathetic. His lies are so blatant now. Looking at how fragile the entire story was, it's amazing it didn't collapse sooner.

"Tell me everything," my mom seethes. I move closer to her, ready to take her hand or hold her up if she needs it. She seems strong for now.

My dad is clearly not going to reveal the details, so instead, June's mom does the heavy lifting, with a little help from the rest of us filling in the gaps. My dad knew my mom was suspicious, so he used the Mabees' divorce as his distraction, volunteering to help June's mom so they would have to spend time together alone. He left clues behind, including some sketchy labels in his phone's contact list that made it seem he was texting June's mom instead of Hayden and Tory's.

Their affair has been going on for three years, starting from a class trip they both chaperoned. These new facts have ruined old memories.

There's a perfectly reasonable explanation for everything, like the money he was seen giving June's mom. It turns out that was her settlement, just enough to cover expenses. Some fucking lawyer he is.

My dad cooled things off for a while when my mom got sick. Her breakdown didn't scare him for the right reasons, though. Nobody says it, but I know in my gut he was afraid the twins' mom would feel guilty and confess. Or would refuse to keep the charade going. He didn't want to lose his cake and candy. Man's a pig.

"Get. Out!" My mom doesn't waste another second when she finishes taking in the missing details.

"Babe, you're not being rational." My dad is grasping at straws, and the fact he decided to attack my mom's mental state—her mental health that she has worked so hard to care for—is pathetic.

"So help me, God, Todd, if you do not run upstairs and grab a bag full of your shit and leave this house right now, I will throw your things out the window and advertise free yard sale goods." I smirk at my mom's words, biting my tongue and staving off the temptation to volunteer we make it a block sale and bring out June's dad's old shit too, along with the dregs of probably a dozen other deadbeat spouses from the block.

I'm so amused by this thought that I don't realize my best friend has joined us.

"Tory," June croaks. I turn slowly and meet his shattered expression.

Everyone was so revved up and ready to shout over one another a second ago, but now that Tory's here, there's a dull hum in the air. I can always tell when my friend is about ready to fight someone. He has a way of rocking back and forth on his feet while his nostrils flare. His jaw flexes, and his fingers twitch with nervous energy. Blood is pumping through him with too much force to form fists. It won't matter. He's so livid he could take a man down with his pinky and nothing more.

Tory lifts his chin enough that our eyes meet, and I try to impart everything I know without using words. His eyes flicker back to my dad as he steps toward me, his sights set on the weak man just beyond my shoulder. When he reaches me, he places his palm on my chest and pats it. My heart readjusts to the new rhythm he sets.

"I got this one," he says.

Tory continues to march up to my dad until they are

standing toe-to-toe. My dad is a tall man, taller than the D'Angelos who are both well over six feet. At this moment, though, my father is tiny.

"Leave my family the fuck alone." There's an eerie calm to Tory's voice that seems to force my dad to listen. He nods. It's a slight movement, but I see it.

"Oh, and your son? He's going to MIT. You? You were a shitty football player." I barely have time to process those loaded words before my best friend punches my dad hard enough to spin his head around and break his jaw. My dad is left holding his mouth together while blood spews through his fingers.

Tory and I exchange glances as he passes by me on his way back to his car. I don't rush after him. He needs time alone—time to drive too fast and yell way too damn loud. He gets to be angry for as long as he'd like. He can even resent me. Whatever he needs to get through this. I'll be waiting for him on the other side.

CHAPTER TWENTY-THREE

Two years of my life ticked by. It feels as if my freshman year happened forever ago. But the last two weeks have passed in a rush. My dad was gone from the house that same night. And rather than a yard sale, my mom gathered most of my father's belongings and took them to Goodwill.

Seven trips and two hundred bucks in fees. She called it an extermination.

I'm not sure where things go from here. I have no desire to see my dad ever again, and since I'll be eighteen soon, I don't have to. June's mom hooked mine up with the guy who represented her dad in their divorce. Seems a little fucked up to me, but if it takes care of my mom's needs and June is all right with it, who am I to question it.

Maybe it's because I've been on this ride before, but I'm not as messed up as I was the first time my family went through this. Maybe it's because that time was a lie, and now it feels more like a dry run. I'm glad I'm holding it together, though, because it means I can be here for my friend.

I've been in June's bed every night for the last two weeks.

I'd prefer to be there again tonight, but Tory asked for a favor. And since he is pretty much the king of the pity hill for the foreseeable future, I'm beholden to indulge him no matter what. I'm not in this alone, either.

"If I have to go stand on the shore of a freezing-cold lake, so do you," I say.

June is hovering at the edge of her window. I'm not sure why she doesn't just go through the front door. I think she's afraid her mom will see her leave and not let her come. Chicago is a far drive, and June wants to be there with me to support Tory.

"Take my hand. I'll show you where to step." I have been propped in this awkward stance on her rooftop for ten minutes. My calves are cramping. If she doesn't scale down with me soon, I'm going to seize up and tumble into her dead bushes.

"I'm really bad at this," she says between maniacal laughs.

"No shit, you are. It's been an hour," I tease.

She flashes her eyes to me and scowls.

"It's been like . . . five minutes."

"Ten," I correct. That doesn't win me many brownie points.

"Do you want me to carry you like a vampire boyfriend?" I tilt my head to the side and she nods. I laugh out and shake my hand again for her to take.

"Well, that's tough shit because I am not a vampire, nor do I possess vampire strength so I can skip up and down rooftops with you on my back. Now, take my damn hand."

Her lips pucker, and as infuriating as she is, she's also beautiful. After a few seconds, we both laugh. Our moment is broken, however, by a few sharp-edged pebbles.

"Hey!" I glance down and catch Abby loading up her

hand for round two. She lets them fall and puts her hands on her hips.

"Get your asses in gear. I have a photoshoot in the morning so we have to make this crazy-ass trip before the sun comes up."

Abby must have some special gift that I lack, because she motivates June to scale down the roof without my help at all. I'm left shaking my head and chuckling as Abby pats her hands together and calls it a day's work.

It's a two-and-a-half-hour drive to Chicago from Allensville. I manage to get us there in two. Tory was virtually silent for the entire ride. Both of the twins are taking their parents' divorce hard. Even though their dad was on the road a lot, he was a big part of their lives. He was heartbroken by the news, though, and from what Hayden tells me, he's searching for an apartment near the city.

As angry as Tory and Hayden are with their mom, they also have this undeniable loyalty to her. It's hard for me to understand. Cutting my dad out of my life was a no-brainer. Maybe that's because he's a cruel-ass son-of-a-bitch. Tory and Hayden's mom has always been there for her boys.

There's an anger brewing in them, though, and for Tory, it's going to burst. He's always been this way, the kind of guy who holds it in rather than inconveniences others with his feelings. Now, *that* is something I can identify with.

It's freezing when we step out of the car. The beach by Lake Michigan is empty, minus a homeless man I'm pretty sure I just watched pee into a bottle then hoist it into the water like a keepsake.

Gross.

I follow Tory as he takes slow steps toward the edge of the pier. If he leaps in, I'm going to have to go in after him. I hate cold water. Plus, it's dark. I'll have to scream and make a scene, and the lighthouse will fire up like a Fourth-of-July spectacle.

"Dude, don't do anything stupid," I finally say. He glances at me over his shoulder, looking at me like I'm stupid.

"Just covering my bases. It's cold." I shrug and attempt to push my hands deeper into my jeans pockets. This hoodie is doing jack squat to hold back the wind. Why do people live in this town? Indiana's cold too, but this wind makes it feel like someone is throwing knives made of ice.

Tory stops a few steps shy of the edge, so I line up with him. He's still within arm's reach. Our friends' voices are a murmur behind us. They've opted to stay near the truck, a smart decision since the truck has a heater. June would have joined me, but I waved her off. Something inside told me this walk is for Tory and me alone.

"Why didn't you say anything?" he finally asks.

I've been waiting for this question, but I didn't want to offer up answers until he was ready. That's how Tory is—he stews and bottles emotions in. It's not healthy, but he wouldn't have heard me if I told him before he was ready to talk about this. He would have erased the conversation from existence. I lick my lips and hope my voice comes out audibly. I'm shivering, but I'm also afraid of this conversation. I've decided the only way through it all is to be honest.

"I'm a chicken shit."

I glance to my friend and he tilts his head back to stare at the stars. I blink, waiting for him to respond, but eventually decide that his silence is his acceptance of my answer.

"I'm so angry," he says, his voice clear and precise. How is he not freezing?

"I know. Me, too, but . . . different." I move my stare from his profile up to the sky. I get dizzy when I look up like this for too long, but I want to see what he sees. Right now, it's a swath of clouds covering the stars like gauze. The moon is bright, along with a few of the stars. It's hard to see much this close to the city.

"I'm going to end up here. Just so you know." He blinks, not once pulling his gaze away from the stars. I've settled on watching his expression instead.

"Yeah? Next Chicago Bull?" I laugh lightly but shut my mouth when I note the serious set of his jaw.

"Who knows? But I'm going to come here for school. I just feel it. I don't know why." He levels his head again, his focus out on the black water that seems to disappear into nothingness along with the sky.

"I believe you. I think you can do anything, Tor. You're twice the athlete I am." I hold a fist out at my side, desperate for him to acknowledge it. Several seconds pass, and I notice that our friends are no longer talking behind us. They're watching the awkward show. I've come this far, so no sense in backing down. My arm burns with lactic acid while I hold my hand out, the knuckles turning blue and cracking from dry skin in the whipping cold wind. Finally, after a truly ridiculous number of minutes, Tory turns his head and dips his gaze to my hand. In a swift motion he drops his fist on top of mine and we both stuff our hands back into our pockets.

We remain side-by-side in silence for another full minute before Tory finally breaks and I get a glimpse of my friend again.

"I was going to see how long you could hold it out like that," he says.

"I know. Also, fuck off," I respond.

We don't make eye contact again, but we both laugh out once in unison. These little things, they are what make us uniquely tied to one another. It's not the tragedy of our parents' poor decisions that binds us, it's the fact there is no place I would rather be than right here, supporting him, in what I swear to God is the coldest place on Earth.

"Ready?" *Please, Tor, be ready. I want a heater so bad.*

"Just a few more minutes," he says.

I nod, my head bobbing continuously as I adjust my hands in my pockets and dip my chin into the neck of my sweatshirt.

"Okay, sure. Few minutes," I mutter.

"I'm fucking with you. We can go." He winks at me when our eyes meet, but he's quiet once again for the trip home.

The quiet is fine. I'll wait him out, because I know my friend is in there. He's hurting, but he isn't unsalvageable. And now he has June in his corner, too.

CHAPTER TWENTY-FOUR

I n the course of a month, I somehow went from a guy afraid to hold June's hand in my driveway to one getting dressed up for a formal dance preceded by a photoshoot directed by both of our moms, recently-sworn-enemies-turned-besties. It's nuts, but more nuts? I still, for the life of me, cannot tie a fucking tie!

"Dude, you're pathetic," Tory says, swatting my hands from my neck so he can take over dressing me.

"I need to learn this."

"Why? So you can be the smarty-pants math nerd who wears ties? Nah. Be suave and sexy, and wear a shirt with the top two buttons open." Tory tugs on my tie and I'm shocked that in the matter of seconds he has it perfect.

"Was no tie seriously an option?" *Because I'll take this off right now.*

Tory drops his gaze to meet mine and the straight line his mouth forms answers my question.

June's mom is taking photos of us. It's a little overboard, but she's a photographer, so I suppose this is her way of showing her love for us all. We got ready in June's room so the girls could walk down my spiral stairs to meet us all at the bottom. June said something about the dreamy railings I have. If this makes everyone happy—*June happy*—then a foyer photoshoot it is.

Tory, Hayden, Cannon, and I give each other one final check then leave June's house to head back to mine. I knock lightly at the front door and my mom lets us in.

"They're just about ready." My mom's smile is real, and it warms me to see it. These are the things she missed because of my father. Things *I* missed. Milestones that moms want to take photos of to keep in boxes in their closets. My mom deserves those photos. And I'm glad to be giving them to her now.

"What do you think?" June's mom asks, waving her hand around the scene she created in my house. I nod and purse my lips, honestly impressed. There are thousands of tiny lights strung through the iron railings of our staircase. It's very fairytale-like. Of course, as my eyes roam up the stairs, my thoughts turn to the deal June and I made before tonight —that she would be naked under her dress. I step forward and test the view, and my dick flexes in my pants.

"I think we're ready," June's mom says to mine.

"I'll get them." My mom is practically glowing as she rushes up the steps. I wonder if there's a part of her that wishes she had more kids—had a daughter. In many ways, June is like one to her. They used to be so close, and I see glimpses of getting that back. It will take time, which is fine by me because I'm invested in the long haul. I don't care if I have to find a way to fly home every other weekend to see her, June and I are making distance work.

Abby's the first to crack open the door upstairs, and in typical Abby fashion, she owns the runway. Every step is a pedestal for her to own. She's done so many commercials by now that this type of thing comes easily to her. What she doesn't see, however, is the pair of eyes next to me drinking her in.

"Just tell her," I whisper, cupping my mouth and leaning to the side to urge Tory to get off his ass and do something about the crush he has.

His eyes slide in my direction but quickly return to Abby.

"I'm good," he says. He's a liar. He's anything but.

Lola and Naomi, two of June and Abby's friends, make their way down the stairs next, opting for those girlfriend poses that are so popular on social media. I'm baffled by how many ways girls can form hearts with their arms and hands. Even more mystifying is how close the four of them are now, especially since Lola and Naomi were Team Ava at the beginning of the year.

I shift my feet the longer they drag their decent on, and when they reach the last step, I consider rushing upstairs to catch June alone before she steps out for everyone to see. I'm selfish, and I know she's going to blow me away. I want to keep her my secret, one more time, just for a moment.

That chance is lost when the door pops open and she steps out onto the landing. She's so goddamn beautiful that I forget altogether about being greedy. I want to show her off instead. She's a work of art meant to be shared. *Not touched!*

"You are beautiful," I mouth to her. Her cheeks blush and her long lashes flutter along with her stretching smile.

Unable to hold myself still, I move toward the stairs, and with every step she takes down, I take two up. The snapping and clicks of June's mother's camera is our soundtrack, the blast of bright light and flashes nearly blinding me before I reach her. I'd find her by memory if I had to. Somehow, my heart would simply know where to meet her.

June's gained six inches in heels, and it transforms her calf muscles in a way that makes them utterly bitable. I cannot wait to run my hand up that leg, all the way from her ankle to her—

"Look who's all grown up," I say once I reach her. June's eyes move over my body, taking in my clothes. I let her pick out everything, and she's stuffed me into this sweater vest and tie that make me feel like a boarding school bad boy. It seems to work for her, though, because her hands are quick to pull on the knot of my tie.

I hold her elbows in my palms and she rests her hands on my hips as we turn to give her mom the shot she wants. The camera whirs, and my eyes catch up to the lack of focus every time she washes the room in major wattage.

June's body is teeming with nerves. I feel her quiver in my palms so I snake my hand around her back and step in close, holding her to me as I lean her back and kiss her lipstick off her face. My fingertips flirt with the sway of fabric that drapes at the arch of her back, and when my hand slides underneath, I'm greeted with the curve of her ass.

"Fuuuuuck," I groan against her mouth, loud enough for only us to hear. I'm so hard right now, it's all I can do to shift my body away from the camera lens. I don't think *these* are the pictures June's mom has in mind.

When I tip her upright, our eyes meet, and every fear I've ever had washes away. Maybe I need June to remind me that love is possible. My examples in life were never stellar. And my choices up until June, less than.

There's a strength behind her eyes now that pulls me in. At night, she always begs me to stay until she falls asleep. She says it makes her feel safe. I stay for me as much as her, though. June . . . she's my home. I bend down to dust her shoulder in kisses, and am instantly overwhelmed.

"I love you, too," I utter against her skin, pressing a final kiss into the nape of her neck.

"I love you," she mouths back.

My mouth raises on the side only she can see.

The last picture her mom takes is of June tenderly wiping her lipstick from my mouth.

After what feels like a million retakes so June's mom can get "just the right light," Abby finally breaks us all free. Basically, she announces we're done, and nobody argues with her.

June clings to me as we enter the gym, the music blaring from inside. I think she's still half expecting a sucker punch from Ava. I don't think that's coming her way, though. Ava's been quiet, for the most part. I try my best to distract her from stressful thoughts with little compliments. It's also practically impossible to forget about what's under her dress, or rather . . . what isn't.

When "Midnight Hour" comes on, we both suspect the other one for having set it up. We both move to the center of the floor and dance like lost children of the sixties, which makes just about every other person in the room gag. One person is happy for us, though. And it solves the mystery when we catch Tory hovering near the speaker by the DJ, proud of his special request.

June and I sing off-key, and a few people try to join us but they can't keep up. Some private, inside jokes are meant to stay that way. Even Tory only gets it from the outside looking in.

The DJ lets the song roll on for longer than anyone other than June and I probably want it to, but when he breaks it off, it's for the one thing I have been truly dreading about tonight —*homecoming royalty.*

Our friend Cannon is the first to take the stage, set up by the twins. When he realizes he's standing up there alone while we all laugh at him, he throws up a middle finger that earns him a "Hey, buddy" over the microphone from our student council liaison, Mr. Simon.

The twins finally take the stage too, along with a few girls, including Ava. I can tell by the way June's body stiffens that Ava is the only thing she sees. Truth is, June's all that Ava is focusing on as well. It's obvious to anyone in this room that her stare is pointed at one person and one person only.

"She could not possibly hate me more," June says.

They begin to recite everyone's names so I clap while bending my head to hear June better.

"Ava?" As if there could be another person in this room who thinks poorly of June. She's the most adored person I know. It's impossible to hate her, unless, of course, your heart is made of ice.

"Yeah. She hasn't really bothered me since the whole spray paint and black eye incidents. What's weird, though, is I don't get why she hated me so much when you were dating her."

I hum out a half-laugh, half admission of guilt before turning my gaze to June.

"Oh, I know why," I say, smirking at the memory of Ava's party, when we were too young to understand what love really was. I swear I did, though. I know it now. I knew it then.

We both clap through the list of queen nominees, but June's eyes remain on my face, a quirk to her brow. She's not letting this go.

"Let's get out of here," I say, leaning into her to kiss the top of her head. Her hair smells so good, and the way it's pinned into these curls that fall down her neck and shoulders has me desperate to touch its softness. I want to run my fingers through it and leave it wild, spread around her body.

"But you're probably gonna win," June says, holding me in place.

I punch out a laugh.

"I don't really give a shit." With a half grin, I manage to persuade her after a brief pause, and soon, we're both on our way out of the gym. We're blessed with the announcement of Ava as queen just before the doors close completely. At least one thing went her way.

We make it all the way to my truck before June comes back to the question I *knew* she would not let go.

Twisting in her seat, her body primed and ready for me to taste from the arch of her foot all the way to the raw tips of her breasts that are so close to popping out of that dress, June manages to hold her desire in for a few more seconds. Long enough for her to repeat her question.

"Tell me, Lucas Fuller. Why does Ava Pryor hate me so much?"

I smirk. It's so simple, and I'm proud to say it.

"Because when she told me she was in love with me at her eighth grade birthday party, I told her I was in love with you. And deep down, she knows I never stopped."

And I haven't.

I've only gotten started.

EPILOGUE

This surprise is more intricate than the one I surprised June with at graduation.

Yeah, getting that Buick up and running, not to mentioned painted and restored to the level it is today, that was a feat. June's mom helped with the lie, pretending she sold it for scrap. I had a crash course in auto body and called in a ton of favors. But seeing June drive that car every day, the smile on her face when she holds her hand out the window, is worth the grease I may never fully get out of my fingernails.

This surprise, however, it requires a major leap of faith. On June's part . . . and her mom's.

June's last-minute acceptance into Boston College made this possible. I can't imagine a life in that city where she and I don't share the same bed at night. Honestly, the thought of sleeping with her without crawling through a window feels like a lottery win.

I have my laptop set up on my bed and I'm pacing when June finally shows up. She spent the day at her dad's house— a promise she made to herself to find room for him in her life.

I think the fact my dad is such an asshole put hers in new light. He's *less* of an asshole. Not quite forgivable, but tolerable. Family.

Maybe one day I'll get there with my dad. I know he hopes for it. I just don't believe his motivations are pure. I've come to realize what a narcissist is, and Todd Fuller is the walking definition. If he wants to mend our relationship, it's because he wants to gain something from it. His efforts aren't driven by love.

My phone buzzes and I quickly read June's text, letting me know she's downstairs. I left the door unlocked when my mom left earlier. I pop my door open and shout "Come on up" before returning to pacing in circles. When she gets to the threshold of my door, I step in front of her and hold my hands to her shoulders, squaring her with me and meeting her eyes.

"Wow, serious gaze you got there, Fuller," she jokes. She lifts one hand to salute me and I shake it off.

"I need us to be serious for a minute."

June's eyes blink rapidly a few times and her smile falters. *Shit, I made her worry.*

"No, *good* serious. Not *bad* serious."

She nods, but she's still concerned. It's hard to be two damaged kids coming of age together and falling in love. Our baggage matches, too, so working through it sometimes feels more like driving in circles.

I exhale a laugh and shake out my arms and legs.

"Let's try this again. I have a surprise. But I'm afraid you won't like it."

June's mouth twists on one side.

"I'm not making this any better, am I?"

She shakes her head no.

I puff out air and look down at my feet. Tapping my toe a

few times to gather my thoughts and refocus my approach to this, I decide things with us are always best if we start with a kiss. I lift my head and move my hands to her jaw, cradling her on either side, giving her a gentle tilt so I can kiss her deep. She walks back a step and I crash into her, sucking her top lip into my mouth and releasing it with a pop. Her lips are raw, and her eyes have trouble focusing. Mission accomplished.

"Right, so you were saying . . . surprise." She shakes off the daze, playing up how affected she is.

I step to the side, revealing my computer. Of course, in the time spent trying to get my opening lines just right, my screen has timed out, so instead June gets to see my fingerprints and the splatter from my iced coffee this morning.

I sigh in frustration and lean forward, running my finger over the track pad to bring the computer back to life. The screen is consumed by a photo of the coolest looking brick building and an apartment window on a neighborhood street in Boston.

"Ohhhh-kayyyy," June says, still not getting it.

"Click around. Tell me what you think," I say, motioning for her to sit. She does, pulling my laptop onto her thighs. I slide around her body, straddling her from behind so I can watch over her shoulder.

Her first click takes her inside the building. The next one shifts to images of the individual rooms. The space is bright and airy with ceilings that seem too tall to fit into that building when you see it from the outside. Exposed duct work and black iron steps set up a modern feel that is met with bright colors accenting the space and art on gallery-style walls.

"This is gorgeous," she says, falling in love a little more with every click.

"I thought so, too."

She gets to the room that I'm going to propose be ours, and stops. Her eyes roam the empty space, a large bed waiting for sheets and blankets, a desk made for this computer in her hands. June closes the laptop and slowly turns her head. I lean forward to save her the trip, kissing the side of her mouth right before our eyes meet.

"What do you say? Roommates?" I quirk a brow and hers slowly creeps up to match.

"I mean . . . yeah! But also, your mom—"

"Is fine with it," I finish.

"And mine—"

"Will be fine with it," I add.

She shakes with hesitant laughter at my second response.

"My mom said she would talk to her with us if we want. And if we room together, it cuts your room and board in half. And I'm not a bad cook, so I can make sure you eat actual food. Plus, you know I'm good at studying. You'll have a live-in tutor."

June shifts between my legs until she's on her knees and facing me. She pushes the center of my chest slightly with two fingers and I scoot back to make room for her but continue talking.

"Our utilities will be less. And the couple who owns the place, Dax and Conner, are super chill." I'm basically saying words right now. I'm not sure I'm even listening to myself. It's June's fault because she's moved her legs to the outside of mine, and she's lifting her T-shirt up and over her head. And my mom is gone for the rest of the day.

"And if we live together," she cuts in, reaching behind her back to unclasp her bra. The black lace falls down her arms and I help her toss it to the side.

"Exactly." I smirk before drawing her body onto mine,

my mouth covering her bare tit to suck it raw and draw a whimper from her lips. She rolls her hips, and I can tell she wants me to do the same thing to her other breast. I hold back, though, just for a moment.

"Lucas, I'm dying," she whines.

"You aren't dying. You're distracting me. And it's working. Fuck, you're hot," I groan. She rocks her hips again, her center sinking onto my hard-on. I push up into her, needing the sensation to hold me over for a few more seconds.

"June," I say, bringing her focus to me. Her eyes flutter open but when we lock gazes, we're in sync. Her lips quiver, not from our touch but from fear. It's a big step asking your parent to bless your desire to try something incredibly adult. But June and I? We've been adulting emotionally for a really long time. What's the big deal about sharing an address?

"You really think she'll go for it?"

I nod. I happen to know she will. That's the surprise part. I already talked to her mom about everything. I made a fucking Power Point.

An impish grin sneaks onto June's mouth and I nod. After a breath she joins me, and soon, laughter spills out.

"Yes, Lucas. I will move in with you."

I hold out a fist and draw it into my body with a hushed "Yes." Then I promptly get to work pleasing her in every possible way. Just wait until I show her the ring I bought her with the money I got for my truck. That can wait a few years, though. Until she's ready.

Me? I'm not going anywhere.

THE END

By Ginger Scott

**READ NOW:
https://amzn.to/2zluA2u**

A bby Cortez is a girl with goals, on the brink of stardom. Falling in love isn't just something she doesn't have time for—it's something she doesn't really believe in.

Tory "Salvatore" D'Angelo loves falling in love. The star basketball player at Public gives his heart away one night at a time then takes it back when he's ready to move on.

But what happens when a jaded heart opens up to a free

one? Is there a place where these two opposites might just be a perfect match?

Tory D'Angelo

I've never really gotten the appeal of flowers. I mean, one, they're super fleeting. Every time my mom's gotten flowers, I swear they're dead within three days. Feels like a major waste of money. Of course, my mom's flowers probably came from the man she was having an affair with, so it's entirely possible my perspective is tainted. Even so, what do flowers say about a person's feelings for someone else?

I like you enough to pop into the grocery store and pick up this pre-arranged bundle of plant clippings wrapped in plastic.

I mean, yeah. Flowers are pretty and shit, but there are a lot of things that are pretty. Cakes are pretty, and you can eat those. A perfect three-pointer drained within seconds, nothing but net . . . that's a thing of beauty. Art, a really hot red dress, or hell, a puppy! All of that is as aesthetically pleasing as a bundle of flowers. Yet here I am, clipping the stems off some weedy-smelling plant shit over my kitchen trash while my best friend June tells me what a good idea this is.

"She's going to love them," June assures me while she reaches toward my bundle, tugging on the stem of something. She pulls it free and dumps it into the trash with the stems I chopped off at an angle because "angles take in the water better" or whatever.

"She won't love that one?" I cock a brow and laugh. I'm still not sold on any of this.

"That one's dead."

I form an O with my mouth and drop my chin to stare at the drooping flower where it lies in the trash.

"Huh." I nod.

June giggles then wraps her hands around the bouquet, holding it steady so I can slip the giant band around the stems again. I never thought my best friend would be a girl, let alone June Mabee. I've pretty much picked on her since she got boobs, probably before that if I'm being honest. I still call her Maybe Mabee. June and I collided in epic fashion a couple months ago. We kicked off our senior year on a strange note, going through some really awful shit together. We're kinda honeymooning at the whole best friend thing, I guess, but she's not sick of me yet and turns out Maybe Mabee doles out some pretty solid advice. Though, I'm not totally sold on the whole flowers thing.

"You sure this isn't stupid? I feel really stupid." I'm sweating, and I've already showered from basketball practice, changed my shirt twice and put on a whole lot of deodorant. This is strange territory for me. To put it succinctly, I have a fucking crush. It's bizarre because hooking up with any girl at Public High—or in our whole town of Allensville, really—has never been an issue for me. June says it's because I'm used to being chased, and maybe that's true. But I also think it's because the girl I'm trying to impress has never, not once, shown an ounce of interest in my presence. In fact, if I had to make a guess, I would bet on her hating me.

"Abby is going to die . . . in a good way!" June's said that a lot, that little add-on of *in a good way*. Feels like a hedged bet to me.

Abby Cortez is June's *other* best friend.

Fine.

She's her *real* best friend, and I'm the new guy June hangs out with sometimes while she waits on her boyfriend,

Lucas. *My* real best friend. Along with my twin brother, Hayden, we've become our own clique. Except for the little part about me being pretty sure Abby hates me. Oh, and me wanting to kiss her candy lips and wrap her legs around my waist just before I lay her back on the hood of my car.

This is complicated. But flowers is the key. June swears by it.

"You look amazing," June says, stepping into me and brushing something from the shoulder of my shirt. I went with a button down, mostly because this shirt is snug on my arms and chest, making me look a little bit beast-mode. I didn't need June to tell me how much Abby likes man candy. She was digging on the new guy, Cannon, for a while, and she noted his arms and chest a few times. Apparently, though, he's moody as fuck. Thank God!

"Where's your brother?" June asks.

"Job interview," I answer, bending down to catch my reflection in the glass front of the oven. I actually have product in my hair. *Who am I?*

"Wow. D'Angelo boys are going to work?" June mocks.

I shrug as I stand and face her.

"It's hard to be around here, and Hayden's had a harder time than I have. I think he wants something to fill the free time." June's eyes soften, but she's careful not to let them dip into pity. We don't do that around here.

My dad moved out a month ago. It's still pretty fresh for all of us. My mom was having an affair with Lucas's dad, and when it all came out, it basically blew up both of our families.

"Have you guys talked to your dad lately?" June asks. Our pops said we could go to Indianapolis with him if we wanted to, but this is our senior year. We're primed to win state this basketball season, and we both decided we couldn't give up on that. Staying here means sticking out the next few months in a house with a parent we pretty much have lost all respect for.

"Our first family therapy session is next week, with *both* of them. It promises fireworks," I say. June grimaces in response.

"You sure it's not weird, me forcing some double-date with you and Luc?" I squint through my question, and a small part of me wants her to let me off the hook. I've never been afraid of rejection, but with Abby, I put it at a solid fifty-fifty that she kicks me in the nuts when I ask her out.

"Stop," June protests, laughing at my nervous behavior. "It's sweet. And it will make you both more comfortable. Plus, it's Eight Lanes. Bowling is the easiest first date ever."

"Says the Eight Lanes employee who bowls a two-hunny," I say, one brow arched.

June's laughter ticks up but stops when we're interrupted by the familiar rumble of Lucas's truck in the driveway. I start to jump in place because he is supposed to bring Abby to the house with him and suddenly I'm full of enough energy to power a lightning bolt.

"It's go time," I say under my breath. June squeezes my arm and offers me a reassuring smile.

Lucas busts through the door first, and I puff out my cheeks to indicate how stressed I am. But something about the look in his eyes freezes me to the floor. My jumping stops, and my heart does too.

"Abort. Mission," Lucas says, pointing at me then staring intently into his girlfriend's eyes.

"What the—" My protest is cut short when Abby follows Lucas through the door in a rush, her hand gripped firmly in my brother's. My eyes see nothing else. I'm blatantly staring at the place where my crush and my twin are fused together.

What the actual fuck?

"I got the job, yo!" my brother says. At least, it sounds like his voice. I couldn't testify he said the words because I'm not looking at his mouth. I'm looking at the way Abby is holding his elbow with her other hand, bouncing with excitement. That's two hands she has on him now. Two. Hands.

"Did you hear me, bro? I got the job!"

I shake my head—*literally* shake my head—and force my gaze to meet Hayden's. We are nearly physically identical, but our personalities are vastly different. Where I'm loud, he's quiet. My confidence is offset by his reservation. I believe I can make any girl fall in love with me. And Hayden . . . he's never had a girlfriend. Ever.

Until—

"You're looking at the new host at Two-fers," my brother says, holding up his new work shirt. It's bright red with two weenies embroidered on the pocket. It's ridiculous, and my natural instinct is to make fun of it, but I can't seem to find a single funny thing to say.

"Wow," I say, over-exaggerating this terribly small word.

"Right?" He pushes at my shoulder, pressing the shirt into me to take. I unfold it and stare at it while I fake laugh. I toss it on the counter and hold my hand up for him to slap, and we grip each other and pull in for a hug. My eyes catch June's over my brother's shoulder, and they are full of pity. *Motherfucking pity!*

"I hope it's cool that I invited Hayden to come with us?" Abby asks from somewhere behind me. I can't bear the thought of turning around and looking at her.

"Of course. Yeah, totally," I croak out. I cough to cover my weak-ass voice.

"I just gotta change, and we can go. What's with the flowers, dude?" my brother asks, pointing to my fisted palm that's nearly choking the bouquet to death with my grip.

"Oh," I say, lifting them and feeling suddenly numb. "I—"

"He lost a bet," June says, coming to my rescue.

Hayden nods, accepting her answer, then dashes up the stairs, leaving the rest of us here in this instantly shrinking space.

"That a new thing there?" June says to her friend in a half-whisper I wish I didn't hear.

"We've been talking a lot, with everything they're going through, and I don't know, it just sorta . . ." Abby's head waggles side-to-side, but it's the blush that colors her cheeks that has me defeated.

Just sorta.

The sudden need to rush from the room hits me, and I march across the kitchen toward June. "Here you go, a bet's a bet," I say, shoving the flowers I knew were a bad idea into her chest. She hugs them and lets out an "*oof.*"

I keep walking, making eyes at Lucas on my way out, knowing he'll follow me to his truck so I can scream obscenities and feel like a fool with only him as my witness.

"Wow, someone's a sore loser," Abby teases from over my shoulder.

I huff out a laugh, not even able to lob one of my normal comebacks because she's so dead-on. I *am* a sore loser. I'm also done catching feelings for some girl.

ON SALE NOW! FREE IN KU!
Abby and Tory's story continues in Varsity Tiebreaker.
Now available here:
https://amzn.to/2zluA2u

The Fuel Series

A New Adult Sports Romance Trilogy

Set in the High Octane World of Racing

Free in Kindle Unlimited

Begin Your Binge with Shift

Dustin Bridges has always had two things he could count on—his fearless instincts behind the wheel and the support of his two best friends, Tommy and Hannah Judge.

Dustin brought the speed.

Tommy, the brains.

And Hannah . . . she was the glue that held everyone together.

Together, they were unstoppable.

From the dirt tracks of their youth to the late-night drag races under a desert moon as teens, the Judge siblings pushed and watched in awe as their friend edged closer to his dream. Always racing, always running. That was Dustin's gift and curse. And while his life at home was unbearable, his world with the Judges always seemed perfect.

Growing up with people makes for a special bond. But sometimes life has a way of testing just how strong a relationship is. And falling in love with one of your best friends, not to mention your other best friend's sister? Well, that can be the toughest test of all.

Heartbreak doesn't know what it's up against, though, because when there is a prize to be won, nobody bets against Dustin Bridges.

BUY NOW ON AMAZON

ACKNOWLEDGMENTS

I swear the Varsity series was done. When I finished book 3, I clapped my hands together and sighed out one of those warm, gooey kind of sounds you make when you're pleased with the way your cake came out. I loved my cake. I baked a damn doozy.

Turns out, I loved Lucas Fuller more. Damn him!

Good thing he kept talking to me, I suppose. I worked on The Fuel Series, and he would pop up randomly in my thoughts: "Remember me? You didn't let me have much of a POV in Heartbreaker. I'm a bit ticked about that."

Truth be told, I go into every book with a gut feeling of how it needs to be told. And Heartbreaker *needed* to be told through June's eyes, her heart and with her words. But that didn't mean Captain wasn't waiting in the wings. I love the way these two books complement each other. They are peanut butter and jelly. So thank you, readers, for bringing Lucas up when given the chance and reminding me that he deserved his day in the sun. I hope you loved reading it.

This world—the Varsity world—has been a blast. High school, sports, young love, coming of age, self-discovery? This is what I live for. Thank you from the bottom of my heart for giving these books your time and holding my Varsity family in your hearts . . . or at least your Kindles and bookshelves.

I must thank my amazing family for their support in writing this book. I spent a lot of hours in various chairs and beds and couches and ballparks with my laptop while writing this book. Thank you, Tim and Carter, for letting my Mac accompany us on summer and college trips. Thank you, Autumn, for . . . *well* . . . basically everything LOL! Seriously, Lucas is here very much because of the support and love I get from you, professionally and otherwise. So grateful, my friend. Jen and Shelley, your time spent beta reading gives me strength. You always guide and champion me to the end. Mom, you *know* I can't do any of this without you. Frankly, the world gets these stories *because* of you. Any courage I have is from my mom. She is the maker of my backbone. And Brenda Letendre, you know I think you're a saint! I've sent you the reddest of hot manuscripts and you always put out the fires and manage to keep me breathing and at my best. Thank you!

Readers, I meant what I said at the beginning. This book is here because of you. I get to do this job . . . because of you. Us writers are mostly fragile little things, but you give us wings. At least, that's what you do for me. Thank you for always believing in my work, for wanting to go on these journeys with me, for trusting me with your time, and more often than not, your hearts. This is the part where I ask—*kinda beg* —for your review, if you feel so moved. But honestly, the fact that you're reading the acknowledgements and (hopefully) smiling is enough. (Though, I'm not going to turn down a review . . . ever.) Right now, cross both arms over your chest and squeeze. Feel it? That's me, giving you a hug. Feel free to use it when you need a good one. You've given me plenty.

ABOUT THE AUTHOR

Ginger Scott is a *USA Today, Wall Street Journal* and Amazon-bestselling author from Peoria, Arizona. She has also been nominated for the Goodreads Choice and RWA Rita Awards. She is the author of several young and new adult romances, including bestsellers Cry Baby, The Hard Count, A Boy Like You, This Is Falling and Wild Reckless.

A sucker for a good romance, Ginger's other passion is sports, and she often blends the two in her stories. When she's not writing, the odds are high that she's somewhere near a baseball diamond, either watching her son swing for the fences or cheering on her favorite baseball team, the Arizona Diamondbacks. Ginger lives in Arizona and is married to her college sweetheart whom she met at ASU (fork 'em, Devils).

FIND GINGER ONLINE: www.littlemisswrite.com

facebook.com/GingerScottAuthor
twitter.com/TheGingerScott
instagram.com/authorgingerscott

ALSO BY GINGER SCOTT

The Fuel Series

Shift

Wreck

Burn

The Varsity Series

Varsity Heartbreaker

Varsity Tiebreaker

Varsity Rule breaker

Varsity Captain

The Waiting Series

Waiting on the Sidelines

Going Long

The Hail Mary

Like Us Duet

A Boy Like You

A Girl Like Me

The Falling Series

This Is Falling

You And Everything After

The Girl I Was Before

In Your Dreams

The Harper Boys

Wild Reckless

Wicked Restless

Standalone Reads

Candy Colored Sky

Cowboy Villain Damsel Duel

Drummer Girl

BRED

Cry Baby

The Hard Count

Memphis

Hold My Breath

Blindness

How We Deal With Gravity